KARINA HALLE

First edition published by
Metal Blonde Books February 2017

ISBN-13: 978-1543212181
ISBN-10: 1543212182

Cover design by Hang Le Designs
Photography by Wander Aguilar
Edited by Kara Malinczak
Formatting by Champagne Formats

For more information about the series and author visit:
authorkarinahalle.com

Also by Karina Halle

The Experiment in Terror Series
Books #1 – 9

Suspenseful, Edgy Romance reads

Contemporary Romance reads

Love, in English
Love, in Spanish
Where Sea Meets Sky (from Atria Books)
Racing the Sun (from Atria Books)
The Pact
The Offer
The Play
Winter Wishes
The Lie
The Debt
Smut
Heat Wave

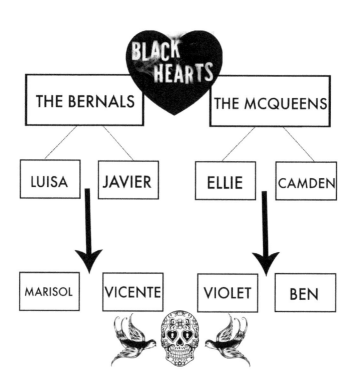

ABOUT THIS BOOK

From *New York Times* bestselling author Karina Halle comes a BRAND NEW standalone duet that will get your pulse racing…

For Vicente Bernal, truth is all he's known. The son of an infamous drug lord, Vicente was born to help run the family business, which means he's been raised on a throne of sordid pasts and dirty laundry, violence and pride. But when Vicente stumbles across someone he's not supposed to know about – a woman from his father's checkered past – he sets out to California to find her behind his father's back.

What Vicente doesn't expect to find in San Francisco is Violet McQueen, the woman's twenty-year old daughter. Beautiful and edgy with a vulnerability he can't resist, Violet tempts Vicente from afar and though he promised himself he'd stay away from her, curiosity and lust are powerful forces. Besides, Vicente has always gotten everything he wants – why shouldn't he have Violet too?

Soon his wants turn into an obsession, one that sweeps Violet into his games as they fall madly, deeply in love with each other, the type of first love that can drive a person mad.

But it's a love with tragic consequences.

Both the truth – and the lies – not only threaten to tear them apart, but threaten their very lives.

Someone has to pay for the sins of the fathers.

And they'll be paying the price with their souls.

Note: Black Hearts is book #1 of the Sins Duet, with book #2, Dirty Souls, releasing March 17th. These books are a spinoff of The Artists Trilogy and Dirty Angels Trilogy – however, you do not need to have read those books in order to enjoy or understand this one!
If you do wish to read those books though, I recommend starting with Sins & Needles.

Also note: This book contains some violence as well as a whole load of naughty sex and bad language. If the word FUCK offends you, please don't read on. Reader discretion is advised.

PREFACE

Once upon a time, a troubled young con artist fell in love with her mark, the drug lord with ties to the man who ruined her life as a child.

It did not end well.

In fact, it didn't really end at all.

Years later, the con artist tried to go straight, live a good and pure life, free of crime and inner torment.

That didn't go well either.

Instead she got hopelessly tangled with her old childhood friend, a friend who never stopped looking for the good in her, never stopped loving her.

Love is a funny thing. It can cause all our demons to go away.

But there was one demon who wouldn't.

The mark.

What followed was a reckless, raw and duplicitous journey for three people who were often more bad than good, people who let love and lust and revenge compete for the same space in their hearts, people who had to fight tooth and nail for their happy ending.

But life doesn't stop at a happily-ever-after.

And as far ahead in the future as you might be, the past is never far behind.

You just have to look over your shoulder.

I was doomed from the start
Doomed to play, the villain's part
"Up Jumped the Devil" – Nick Cave & The Bad Seeds

For the ones who love my black and tender heart

Violet

San Francisco
The not so distant future

EVERYTHING I KNOW IS A LIE.

That's the thought that strikes me at night when the lights are off and my room is dark and my mind keeps tripping over itself, regretting how I wasted the day and worrying about the day to come.

I know it doesn't make a lot of sense. I mean, I know I'm not a lie. But if I was raised in a house of them, by people who aren't who they say they are, what does that make me?

It's ridiculous. I turned twenty a few months ago. I

know my parents love me and my brother loves me, even though we don't always see eye to eye. I know I have a good life and a bright, if not uncertain, future. But that doesn't erase this unease I've had since I was a young girl, that things aren't quite what they seem.

When I was nine, I remember catching my mother outside the house in one hell of an awkward moment. This was back when we lived above the beach in Gualala, just north of San Francisco. I shouldn't say *just* north, like it's a simple hop, skip, and a jump. It's a long, winding, nauseating drive along Highway 1 to get there.

Anyway, I remember this because I thought she had gone down to the beach to take pictures. I wasn't allowed to leave the house on my own (the cliffs were a danger, so they said) and Ben was inside with my dad talking about something in the kitchen. My mom and dad just had a fight an hour before and I was worried about her, the way that daughters are when their mothers sulk off somewhere. The same kind of fear when you see an injured animal slink off to die.

In general, my parents didn't fight all that much, which is something I try not to take for granted. I've heard horror stories from my friends about the ugly divorces and custody battles, or the parents who stayed together for their children, even though their kids would have been happier with them split, rather than being exposed to a hellish home life. Though my parents are pretty odd, I know they're happily married and have a lot of love for each other. Maybe too much at times.

But that didn't mean they didn't fight, and when they did it tended to be about things I wasn't privy to. It was never about me not doing my homework or Ben staying out too late or even that dad forgot to do the dishes. It was always over something whispered in the dark. Something that had my parents checking the corners of every room they entered. Something that sat above them like a dusty cobweb on the ceiling, always there, holding something ugly in its depths, ready to drop.

When I saw my mom go outside that day, I'd never seen her so upset. Usually she kept everything bottled up inside, swallowed it down with a stiff smile. My mom is pretty hardened and cynical, for reasons I don't always understand. But that time she was sitting on the ground by the side of the house, half-hidden by a manzanita tree, her knees up to her chest. Tears were streaming down her face, leaving black trails down her cheeks.

I tried to hug her but she shooed me away, told me to leave her. But I couldn't. I'd always sensed my mother's vulnerability, even at that age, but had never seen it. To be honest, I felt nothing but awe.

So I stood there, watching her crumble inward. I was struck with the thought that I was terrible because I wished that she could be like this more often. I felt like I was finally seeing something real and true, a glimpse at a hidden self.

"I'm a bad mother," she said, and I remember it so clearly because the words sounded painful. "I'm nothing but a fraud." She said this a few times between sobs, shaking her head until finally she began to calm down.

Then she looked at me, warily, like a caged animal. Like she was afraid of me. The whole time I hadn't said a word.

"Why don't you go inside?" she said with a forced smile. "I'm not quite myself right now."

And so I did. My dad asked me where she was and he immediately went outside after me. They talked out there for a long time. I wanted so badly to listen to what they were saying but Ben told me to mind my own business.

A few days later I told my mom she wasn't a bad mother. That she was the best there ever was.

She flinched at that, and when I brought up the part about being a fraud, she said she didn't remember saying that. Then she gave me a hug, smoothed my hair, and told me she loved me. There was such a strange desperation in her eyes that I dropped the subject and never asked her again.

But it didn't mean I never thought about it.

A fraud.

A fake.

A liar.

Then again, I'm starting to personally relate.

It's the end of September and school started a few weeks ago and already I feel over my head, that I'm in a program I don't belong in, that I'm just pretending. It's the second year of my photography degree at the Academy of Art University San Francisco and so far it's a million times harder than I thought it would be. Maybe because the first year of anything is usually the testing period where the weak are weeded out, and I'm starting to think I should have been weeded out in the spring along with the mint in our tiny back garden.

It probably has a lot to do with not measuring up to my mother. She's a well-respected photographer with a small gallery of artsy portraits in the Mission district. Her work is heavy on depth and shadow, always in black and white, and she manages to get the truth out of the subject. She can be a chameleon sometimes, adjusting her personality to suit the person she's talking to. I've seen it work on me, which is why it's no surprise that she's able to get the truth out of her subjects. You can see it in their eyes. She can capture their true selves like no one else can.

And while I think I've majorly improved over the years, especially after starting school (I mean they don't just take anyone), I feel like I'm faking my way through my assignments.

Like this one. My friend Ginny (who is also in my class) and I are supposed to roam the city and take pictures of "absolution." I know, it's like total high school photography class bullshit, but it is what it is.

But Ginny is somewhat of a genius, and she's already snapped a million photos just standing in one spot at Union Square. It's hot, sunny, and busy as hell, filled with tourists and shoppers alike. There's nothing even close to absolution here.

She peers at me out of the corner of her eye, not even taking her face away from the camera, her purple winged eyeliner glittering in the sun. "Vi, stop staring at me and take some goddamn pictures."

I sigh and look around again, the sun making me squint. My over-the-knee boots already feel too hot. I never learn. I live up in the Haight, by Golden Gate Park, and the row house is perpetually shrouded in fog. Every morning I dress like I'm heading out into a frozen cloud, and every afternoon I end up downtown and sweating buckets, hot and itchy. There are a dozen different microclimates in the city and I'm never dressed for the right one.

"Tell me where the absolution is," I challenge her. "It's a city of greed."

Ginny lowers the camera and gives me her driest look. I can feel my soul shrinking away from it. She gives good glare, this one. "And you don't think greed can lead to absolution?" She motions to the department stores. "Many people are finding their salvation right in there, among the shoes and the jewelry and the buy-one-get-one-free underwear." She pauses and her withering look turns to an impish one. "Which reminds me, I should stock up. I've got another date tonight."

I take advantage of the distraction and haul Ginny into the store right away. I hate malls and department stores as a rule but the heat is killing me and I'm feeling all kinds of restless and distracted.

Ginny notices. "Are you even listening to me?" she says, holding up a zebra-printed bra. "I told you that Tamara's favorite print is zebra and you just ignored me like this bra won't make all the difference in the world."

I blink and try to focus. For some reason the hairs at the back of my neck are standing up and I've got chills, but I'll get worse than that if I don't start paying attention to Ginny.

She came out only last year and jokingly refers to herself as the longest closeted queer in San Francisco, even though she's just a few years older than me. She's been going kind of wild in the dating scene but recently fell in love with Tamara, a trans woman who's also a stand-up comic in the Castro. She's hilarious and sweet, though I think Ginny has fallen for her faster than the other way around. Hence why Ginny's putting a lot of thought into a zebra-print bra.

"You know, I'd gladly give *you* advice on what makes your tits look great if only you'd get out there and actually go on a date with someone," Ginny says, throwing the bra over her shoulder and going back to sorting through the messy rack of lingerie.

"And *you* know it's not like I'm not trying. This city sucks for dating," I remind her. "There's no one…eligible in class."

"So then look outside the class."

I open my mouth to say something but she cuts me off. "Just because it's art school and we're in San Francisco doesn't mean every guy there is gay. Trust me." Her attention is quickly captured by a turquoise satin bra that matches the streaks in her shaggy blonde hair. "Oooh, I need this one too."

When I don't say anything, she adjusts her camera bag and lets out a long sigh. "What about Ben? He has to have hot older friends. He's pretty hot himself, you know. I've learned that hot guys tend to have hot friends."

I scrunch up my nose. "He does. But they have girlfriends. And they live in Santa Cruz, so even if one of them were single, and I happened to be attracted to them, and it wasn't weird for Ben, and they happened to be attracted to *me*, it would be long distance. And there's the whole fact that I'd be dating one of my brother's friends and that's bound to be a problem and a half."

"He still overprotective?" she asks. "He knows by now you can defend yourself, right?"

I let out a soft laugh. "Honestly, I think he would be more worried for his friends." I had way too much fun being the teasing, bratty younger sister to Ben while growing up.

Though he's just four years older, Ben has always been overprotective of me, even though our father had us both in martial arts from an early age, who knows why. We were so young when we started karate and judo that it just became our thing. As we got older and were able to make our own decisions about sports and extracurricular activities, we decided to stick with it, albeit in different ways. I did some Capoeira during high school and still do kickboxing. Ben got into MMA when he was a teen and he's still training, even competing in state fights.

I'm grateful for it though. While my friends were all forced to play the piano or football, my brother and I were out there after school, learning to kick ass. My dad's in really good shape but when we press him about whether he did anything like MMA or some kind of fighting when he was younger, he says he was always a lover, not a fighter.

"It's a good skill to have," he would always say. "You never know when you'll need to defend yourself."

And he's been right, unfortunately. It was only last year that I was attacked walking up our street, just around Buena Vista Park. It was some sketchy dude, high as a kite, trying to take my backpack, but I managed to deliver a kick to his face before I ran all the way home. At first I was too terrified to walk anywhere alone after that, but then I threw myself back into kickboxing and even had Ben train me in some MMA stuff. Now I feel ready for a fight, even though I hope the opportunity never arises again. It's just good to feel confident that you can protect yourself.

"Well, maybe we should stop hanging out in the Castro," Ginny muses, now moving on to babydoll lace camisoles and teddies. "You're never gonna meet a straight guy at drag queen bingo."

"Honestly, I'm fine being single," I tell her, wanting to drop the subject. "I'll live vicariously through you and Tamara."

Ginny raises her brows to the heavens. "Like hell you will. Look at you, girl. You're twenty, you're stupidly pretty, you have amazing hair, and your thighs and booty make anyone with a pulse want to give them a good ol' smack. You can have anyone you want. You just have to meet them. And you have to want them."

"Suddenly I have the urge to get back outside and take some pictures," I tell her. This sort of talk makes me uncomfortable.

But after Ginny is done with her shopping, she heads out to her apartment in Emeryville and I get on the bus heading home, my mind flipping back and forth between the idea of absolution and thought of never finding the right guy, two entirely different trains of thought that somehow feel the same.

I get off the bus on Haight, just before Ashbury, and my world is back to damp fog. I take my fringe scarf out of my messenger bag and quickly wrap it around my neck as I make my way toward my father's tattoo parlor.

Sins & Needles is the reason we moved down from Gualala to the city back when I was twelve. My father used to have a successful shop by the same name in Palm Valley in SoCal, before I was born. I imagine he must have sold it for a pretty penny back then and let the stocks grow, because sometimes I wonder how on earth my parents could afford to not only buy a business on upper Haight but a house around the corner. San Francisco housing prices have been the highest in the country for decades now and I know my parents do okay for themselves with their businesses, but they're still artists, not traders or lawyers.

The door chimes above me as I step inside the shop, my nose met with the familiar smells of antiseptic, ink, and incense from the hippie shop next door. Sometimes I can only stay inside the shop for a few minutes because the patchouli and sandalwood scent is too overpowering for me, but today it's mild.

Lloyd is leaning against the glass counter, flipping through an old, faded magazine. He looks up at me, his long hair falling across his eyes, and smiles. Lloyd's been working at the shop since the start and I've seen him go from a gangly and guileless twenty-something to an accomplished artist, taught by my father. What hasn't changed is his awkward affection for me, whether he has a girlfriend or not.

"Hey," I say, eyeing my father in the corner of the room where he's diligently working on a client. My father eyes me briefly, his eyes crinkling warmly before going back to small talk. He's working on a design on a guy's shoulder, probably a new person since I've never seen that crazy green mohawk before.

"Hey yourself, cutie pie," he says. Lloyd has called me cutie pie since I was twelve, and I have to be honest, I'm glad it hasn't evolved into anything sexual, especially with my dad always within earshot. "How's school so far?"

I sigh, plopping my camera bag on the counter. "Shitty. Feeling way over my head and totally overwhelmed." I pause, knowing being overwhelmed is pretty much the status quo for me. "What else is new?"

"Give it some time, you just started a new year. Everyone is a little creaky when they're getting used to something. Camden could tell you exactly how long it took for me to stop fucking up shade work." I hear my dad grumble at that.

"Then it's a good thing I didn't let your needle touch me until you were a pro," I tell him.

"How is your T-rex doing?"

"He's good." I pull up the sleeve of my striped sweater on my right arm and show him his work that's inked into my skin of my forearm. He did it a few weeks ago, a Tyrannosaurus rex with itty bitty fairy wings. It's my second color tattoo and Lloyd does color really well. Every other tattoo I have is black and white, courtesy of my father.

I'm not absolutely covered in them like my father or Lloyd is, but I do have my fair share. No surprise that it was my father who gave me my first one, an old-fashioned skeleton key on the inside of my left forearm. I've been fascinated with collecting keys since I was young and this one is still my favorite. I was fifteen but felt so much older as I sat in that chair and my dad gave me my own key, perfect down to each rusted detail. It didn't even hurt, I was just so happy that I was part of the "circle." My mom, Ben, everyone had them at that point except me.

I also have a bull skull across my back shoulders with a crown of flowers adorning it, a handful of snowflakes to the left and below it, a mermaid on my inner bicep, music notes at my wrist (to match music notes on my mother's arm), the death star on my other wrist with the words *resist* underneath, the symbol of my favorite band at the back of my neck, and a colorful sugar skull on my hip (also courtesy of Lloyd). Okay, sounds like a lot when I list them off like that, but both my dad and Ben are covered in them by comparison.

And now, of course, the dinosaur.

"You know what your next one is going to be?" Lloyd asks, pushing his straggly hair out of his eyes.

I shrug. "I think I'm done for a while. Unless something strikes my fancy."

My dad laughs, his focus intent on the man he's working on. "Violet, you and your fancies are going to get you in trouble one day."

He's kind of right. I have this tendency to get really obsessed about things for a few months, sometimes even for a year, and then suddenly I lose interest and move on to something else. Just like that. I have a feeling that one day my body might be a map, like that guy in the movie *Memento*, except mine will remind me of all the things I stopped caring about.

I don't spend too long at the shop, I just wanted to say hi. My dad will probably work until seven tonight, just before dinner, and it's only three in the afternoon right now.

Still, that restlessness, a strange twinge of unease, is running through my veins. I'm half-tempted to head into the Magnolia bar for a drink—the owners know me and don't care that I'm not twenty-one, even though I have a high-tech fake ID thanks to some of Ben's computer handiwork—or even rifle through the stacks at Amoeba Records, just for something to do, some time to kill.

I go home instead. It's just around the corner, a periwinkle-colored Victorian. Not as big as many others in the area but now seems oversized with Ben living in Santa Cruz for school. I know when I'm done with school I probably should move out, but that means moving out of San Francisco since there's no way I'll be able to afford an apartment here, not unless I have a million roommates, and even then we'll probably be relegated to the Tenderloin.

"Mom?" I call out as I take the key from the lock and step inside the foyer. The house is humming with silence. She must be out.

I look down at my feet as I nearly crunch a stack of envelopes and quickly bend down to pick up the mail. Some fliers and bills. As usual, nothing important or interesting.

Until I spot one addressed to my father, Camden McQueen, with no return address. I flip it over in my hands as I make my way into the kitchen, placing the rest of the mail on the counter. The stamp is domestic, and the postmark is smudged and hard to read.

I don't normally snoop through my parents' mail but there's something about this that has uneasiness creeping through me again. Maybe because my parents rarely get mail like this, maybe because I'm a brat, bored and curious.

I take the letter over to the stove and put on the kettle. While I wait for the water to steam, I examine it further. It's a thin envelope and it seems like there isn't even anything in it. Maybe a slip of paper or a sticky note or something.

Finally, steam begins to rise from the kettle and I hold the back of the envelope over it, just enough for the glue to start to lose its hold. Then I take a knife and carefully slide it under the flap until the envelope is open. I shake out the contents.

I was right about it not being a letter.

It's a newspaper clipping.

I pick it up gingerly, afraid to harm it.

It's a small square with the headline: **<u>Ex-Sheriff George McQueen Laid to Rest on Sunday</u>** above an old photo of a man in his forties. A man that would have looked like family even if I hadn't see his name.

He has my father's eyes.

He has our ears.

My hands start to shake as I read the article.

Palm Valley's ex-Sheriff George McQueen was laid to rest on Sunday afternoon at the First Baptist Church on Main Street. McQueen had been battling cancer for the last year, having been put into the Palm Valley hospice before he started undergoing treatment. Aside from controversial arrests, he was also known for a scandal involving his only son, Camden McQueen, back in 2013. While Camden's name was later cleared by police, his son was never seen or heard from again, and evidence points to his possible death at the hands of a Mexican drug cartel. The investigation has long since closed.

George McQueen served as Sheriff from 1990-2015 and was an advocate for the church and briefly ran for mayor in 2018 before his health started to decline.

He is survived by his second wife Raquel and his step-daughters Kelli and Colleen. Donations may be made to the Baptist church.

The paper slips out of my hands, floating slowly to the counter.

I can hardly breathe, hardly move. My heart is

thumping, slow and loud, until it's all I can hear.

What the fucking fuck did I just read?

I snatch the paper back up, blinking at it, trying to understand the words and what they're saying.

Sheriff George McQueen.

My grandfather I never met.

My grandfather that my own father told me had died when he was a teenager.

I've had a grandfather all this time and never knew about it. I spent my whole life thinking he was dead.

Why would my father lie to me?

Why was my father involved in a "scandal" over twenty years ago, why has he been presumed dead or missing this entire time, and what the fuck does he have to do with drug cartels?

I don't know what to do with this information.

There's nowhere for it to go, no space in my brain.

There's only that zinging feeling at the back of my head, traveling down my spine, the feeling that tells me I was right.

I *was* raised in a house of lies.

The only thing I know is that I can't let my parents know I found this. I have to assume that my mother is in on this truth as well. I have to keep it to myself and carry on until I have a better idea of what's going on.

I have to talk to Ben.

Please, lord, don't let him already be in on it.

I know I'm running out of time, that my mom could come home at any minute and bust me, so I take out my phone and take a picture of the clipping. Then I put my phone away, stick the clipping back in the envelope, take out a small vial of Krazy Glue from the junk drawer, and carefully glue the flap shut.

Footsteps coming up to the front door.

My mom.

I quickly jam the letter back into the stack of mail and leave it on the counter so it looks like I casually threw it there as I often do.

Then I turn and run as quietly as I can up the stairs to my bedroom, going inside just as I hear the front door open.

"Violet?" my mom calls out.

My heart is racing now, galloping around and around in my chest, and I've got a horrible feeling that I'm on the edge of losing control, of losing any sense of understanding who I am, who my family is.

"I'm here!" I manage to cry out, my voice breaking.

"Okay!" she calls back, and I hear her go into the kitchen.

I wait a few moments, staring blankly at some of the city shots I have on my wall. There's a black and white print of the ferry building, swamped in fog, looking like something out of a film noir. I took it when I was still in high school, one of those days where my ex-boyfriend Hayden and I would roam the streets, pretending to live bigger lives than we did. And now, with one letter, I feel my life is growing too large, too fast.

If all of that about my father and grandfather is true...

Who sent that letter? Why wasn't it addressed? They obviously wanted Dad to know that his father had passed away, so why not a phone call?

"Hey, Vi, were you making something?" my mom

shouts up, sounding distracted. "The kettle is on."

Crap. "Uh yeah, was going to make some tea."

"What kind? I'll make it for you."

I take a deep breath and make my way down the stairs, trying to appear as casual and normal as possible.

My mother is standing in the kitchen and rifling through the cupboard where we keep the tea and coffee. I eye the stack of mail. She's already gone through it, and I can see the envelope folded up and sticking out of the back of her jeans.

I quickly avert my eyes and get two mugs out. "You want some too?"

When she turns around to face me, she shakes a box of green tea and jasmine at me, smiling.

"I need the caffeine. This okay?"

But her smile seems forced, on edge, her eyes wary. I wonder if mine look the same.

I don't think she suspects a thing.

And now I suspect everything.

Vicente

Sinaloa, Mexico

"**A**LWAYS KEEP YOUR PROMISES."

It was something my father often said, like it was some bit of personal wisdom of his, a catch-phrase with a copyright. He says it in such a grave way, like this type of honor is more important than any other. He holds being a man of your word above all else.

It doesn't matter that he's killed thousands, wounded thousands more, made billions, ruined millions. He wants you to believe that above all else he is honorable and good.

I can't take it seriously. Especially when I know of more than a few occasions when he gave his word and then did the opposite. But in his twisted, warped logic, he never sees that he's at fault. There's always an excuse.

But tonight there is no excuse.

My father is drunk again.

It doesn't bother me. He doesn't get vicious—no more than he is sober. He doesn't get loose—he's as composed as always. If anything changes, it's his honesty. He starts to spout the truth, and I always make sure I'm around, like a fucking dog, eager for any scraps. Anything at all.

Tonight he's in his office, a bottle of expensive tequila open beside him. He's invited me to have a drink with him. I know it's because of what's been happening this last week.

He's afraid.

I don't drink much, but I smoke like a chimney. I sit down on the leather seat across from him, light up a cigarette, and accept the highball glass half-filled with amber liquid. My mother jokes that I have tequila eyes, like my father, the color of the darkest, most golden reserve.

"I say that a lot, don't I?" he says, his mouth twisting into a crooked smile. He's watching me closely, as he always does. Trying to figure me out, trying to see if I will ever measure up. The thing is, I don't want to.

"About keeping promises?" I say after a sip. The drink is smooth and bracing all at once. I take a drag of the cigarette and blow it toward the ceiling fan which disperses it toward the open window. We're in the jungle, the compound well hidden beneath the thick canopies but close enough to the Pacific that we still get the breeze. It's one of a dozen houses I've grown up in. Drug lords can't stay in one place for too long, and my family is extra diligent.

Or I should say, was. It's been five years since our cartel

lost its footing as top dog. There was a while there, when the wall was being built, that people were panicking. My father was the first to use submarines to send drugs into the US and Canada, and our cartel became more wealthy and powerful than you could ever imagine.

Then the wall was only partially completed. A scar across Texas. The Zetas made deals with the DEA on the other side. We were nearly wiped out. We haven't been able to best them since.

It's not all horrible. It means we haven't moved around so much, from place to place, because not as many people want us dead. That's something. It's an inkling of stability.

But it means that my father and his injured ego have been searching for a way to claw itself back.

It means me.

I'm the prodigal son, the one who is supposed to take over when my father commands me, the one who is supposed to get things rolling again. He says that I'm almost the age when he first started being the right-hand man to one boss. The boss he would eventually kill.

But I would never kill my father, and it certainly wouldn't be for the fucking cartel.

I don't want it.

I've been trained for it, I've grown up in it. I killed my first snitch when I was fourteen. I killed a few more since. I've sat in on deals, I've made decisions, I've gone in place of my father sometimes, much to my mother's dismay. If it wasn't for me flying to Germany and Italy and the UK to meet with buyers, I wouldn't speak so many languages, know how to deal with so many different, dangerous people. Or know how to disappear. That's the most important one.

I've had a taste of the power, the glory, the respect, and the money.

I'm not saying I don't want it.

But I want it my way.

Not his.

And he knows it.

"Yes. Worthless promises," he says, his mouth tightening before he throws back the rest of his drink.

He needs me and I think he hates me for it. He's got a few men who have stuck by him over the years. There was Diego, who was by his side for decades, and then there's Barrera, Parada, Tio, Nacho. They've got my father's respect but not his truest trust. My dad learned a few hard lessons about trust, and it's only in family, in blood, that it exists.

"Vicente," he says slowly, tapping his fingers along the redwood desk, the lamp throwing spidery shadows from his hands. "I've done some thinking. About your plan."

I don't say anything. I know never to interrupt him. Always let him deal the deck first, every last card, before you throw yours down.

"I've talked it over with your mother. Your sister also." He pauses and his fingers do too. He clears his throat, his eyes shadowed and focused on nothing at all. "I can't figure out why you want to leave but your mother thinks it would be good for you to get it out of your system. To see how the other half live so you'll be more grateful than ever to have the life you have here."

His eyes swing to me, squinting softly. "You know that this is what you were born into. That you would be crazy not to want it."

I nod. I never said I was sane.

"That this is in your blood. You've got the brains and the guts for this job, dare I say even more than I did at your age. But there's a lot to learn and you have to be willing to learn that from me." The room seems to grow darker. Outside, a rooster crows. "Time goes by fast. Too fucking fast. It seems just yesterday that you were born, and now you're a man. You know this, yes? You see how each day changes things. We don't have the luxury of time in this business. No one does. We have to act now. We should have acted yesterday. So, while I give you permission to go to California, or wherever it is you wish to go, it is just for two months. Then you must return."

And if I don't? The question is on the tip of my tongue but I don't dare ask it. The truth is, I'm relieved. I didn't think he'd let me go at all, and if I dared to leave Mexico without his permission, I wouldn't get very far.

I may have everything I want, but I don't have freedom.

Not yet.

"Just tell me," he says. "What are you hoping to find out there?"

Pieces of buried truth.

I give him a quick smile. "An American girl."

Not a lie.

I watch him carefully for his reaction, not expecting one. But there is a tic of muscle along his jawline. It's not much but it's enough.

"You better watch out for them," he tells me, and though his tone is light, his words come out slow and deliberate. "They never stick around."

I press my luck. "And do you have experience with

that?"

He raises a brow, gives me a withering look. "Son. Please. You know I was in the states for a long time."

"A long time ago."

He sighs quietly. "Yes. A long time ago. But I'm sure their women haven't changed. Just as duplicitous and naïve as ever." He pauses, taking a sip of his drink. "Where will you go? What will you do?"

I shrug. "I don't know. Head up the coast and figure it out. Maybe end up in Seattle. Experience the rain."

"We get enough rain here," he says, studying me. "You won't be going alone, you know this."

"I can protect myself."

He lets out a caustic laugh, leaning back in his chair. His fingers run along the rim of the tequila glass as he smiles to himself. "Yes. Yes you can. I have no doubt. But the moment you leave this house, you know what happens."

"No one is targeting me anymore. Not when we continue to be second best."

His eyes fly to mine, sharp as knives. The fury of a million suns burns behind them. "You think this is funny? This position we are in? Or the fact that your fucking life is at stake every second moment you continue to live?"

I snap my mouth shut. Arguing won't get me anywhere and where I need to go is far away from here. I'm inches from reaching it and I know that one wrong word will make my father call the whole thing off.

I can't let that happen.

I need to find her.

The proof that my father once had a soul.

The whole thing started by accident. About a week

ago my father was off on business and my mother asked me to find a file in his office, the very one we're sitting in now. She said it would be old, dated before I was born. Information on the Tijuana Cartel before they joined with ours.

I did as I was told. Got to work in the office and spent the whole muggy afternoon going through metal boxes and rubber bins full of folders. I had to wonder why this wasn't all digitalized, but most of the papers were computer print-outs, maybe as a failsafe in case a file got deleted.

For the life of me I couldn't find the specific file she was looking for. I brought every folder on the Tijuana Cartel out to where she was sitting by the pool, but none of them were old enough. She told me to look harder.

Of course I wanted to tell her that she should look for them herself but being disrespectful to your mother gets you a slap in the face, and as the only son, I'm expected to do a lot of shit I shouldn't have to. Besides, my mother has seemed increasingly fragile lately. She's only forty-four years old—she had me pretty young—and yet she's losing weight and is constantly on edge. She's always spooked fairly easily but now it's like you can't even approach her without her jumping out of her skin.

So I went back inside and went through the last cabinets. I pulled out an old wooden box, locked with a small padlock. The chance of me finding a key was pretty small—knives, machetes, handguns, rifles, AKs, even goddamn whips are plentiful but not much else.

I took a hammer from my father's desk drawer (it's in case some business deals go south—not a pretty sight) and brought it over to the box, smashing the lock off with a swift blow.

Given how far back in the cabinet the box was, I doubted anyone would notice that I broke it open, and so far no one has. Besides, she had told me to check anywhere and everywhere. You'd think she would have otherwise mentioned to "keep your hands off the secret box of mystery."

Inside the box were a few file folders and yellowed and cracked newspaper clippings, so faded in places it was hard to read. They weren't about the Tijuana Cartel at all and I probably should have closed the box and put them back.

But I didn't.

Every paper in there was about one woman, a white woman. Sometimes her name was Eden White, sometimes it was Ellie Watt, and the more recent papers had her as Ellie McQueen. There were photos of her taken with a telephoto lens. In them she had long, white blonde hair. There were passport IDs with dark hair, there were candid photos of her on a balcony, laughing into the sunset. These photos were the most common and I found myself sitting there for a long time, flipping through them.

The way these pictures were taken, printed out on cheap 4x6 photo paper like they did in the old days, showed some kind of…I don't know. Love. Adoration. Something that I've never seen much of growing up. Whoever took these photos of Ellie must have loved her dearly.

But who took them?

It took me another twenty minutes, going through old printouts of emails, unsent letters, newspaper clippings, and sheets of info and data before I knew the whole picture.

Ellie was a con artist, apparently my dad's lover here and there, and the one that got away. The unsent letters, written long before he must have met my mother, told me that much and more. A lot more.

Actually, it was hard to even accept that they came from my father, but his name was signed at the bottom and his handwriting never changed. I'd just never seen my father offer up any part of his heart or soul to anyone. Yes, I had loving parents when I was growing up, but their affection never carried any vulnerability. My parents were fighters, business partners, and maybe more behind closed doors, but it was never anything I had been witness to. Love was expected and accepted in the Bernal family but very rarely shown.

It never made a lick of difference to me. It made me harder, smarter. It protected me, freed me from excessive emotions, and I think that was my father's point all along. You couldn't run a cartel if you weren't built with steel bricks. You had to be a fortress, never bending, never breaking.

But his words on that paper showed a side of my father that I never thought existed. Perhaps the side of him before two of his sisters were killed, before he lost this supposed love of his life. Ellie seemed like the hand that slowly pushed his heart closed.

And that's when I knew, I needed to find her.

I want to talk to her. I want to know who she is. What she has that cracked my father open all those years ago. What she knows.

I want to see his weaknesses.

And I want to use those weaknesses against him.

That's what I've been stewing on all week. I never found the papers on the Tijuana Cartel but by then my mother quickly dropped interest in it.

The paper with the latest date, from a few years ago, states that Ellie lives in San Francisco. I don't know why my father has this up-to-date intel on her, but then again I'm not too surprised. The older my father gets, the more personal he takes any slight. He's also obsessive, manic, and bat-shit crazy at times.

A quick Google search showed me that Ellie still works as a photographer, and with some more digging I found out her husband runs a tattoo shop in the city. Further digging brings up a son, age twenty-four, the spitting image of his father right down to the tattoos, who is an MMA fighter. They also have a daughter. I can't get much dirt from her aside from an Instagram account full of art and professional photos, but her bio tells me she's studying photography at the arts school. The picture of her is too far away, shot in black and white, so you can't get a good look at her, but if she is anything like her mother, she is probably stunning.

And now I have permission to go. To just leave and set out on my own for the first time in my life. Maybe this Ellie turns out to be nothing at all. Just some chick who broke my dad's heart. But even if that's the case, it doesn't change the fact that this is my first step out of this prison.

"What the fuck are you smiling for?" my father asks me, pouring himself another glass.

I let the smile turn into a grin. "Just looking forward to the day I leave."

He narrows his eyes at me. "You're coming back, mark my words."

I just nod at him.

We'll see.

A week later and I'm leaving.

I say goodbye to my mother as she gives me a tearful hug. I send my regards to my sister, Marisol, who is staying with my aunt Marguerite in New York for her first year of university.

My father gives me a firm, albeit reluctant handshake. I tower over him by a few inches and yet he seems taller.

"Tio and Nacho will be your eyes when yours fail you," he says to me, voice grave, and jerks his head toward the waiting SUV. Bulletproof glass and carriage, shiny black. Tio and Nacho stand outside of the open back door, hands clasped in front of them, waiting for me.

They're my babysitters.

Armed to the nines.

"And here is everything you need," my father says, pressing a leather pouch into my hands. "Passport, two in case you need them, one American, one Mexican. California Driver's License. A bank card. Credit card. Nine thousand dollars cash. You're Vicente Rodriguez, American citizen, born and raised in Sacramento. You're twenty-five years old, born in two thousand twelve. At least this way you can rent a car, fucking bullshit laws they still have there. Your parents are Mexican immigrants who came over to America before the embargo. They were self-made millionaires."

"Doing what?" I ask.

"Whatever the fuck you want them to. You know how to lie, don't you?"

"I'm your son, aren't I?"

He raises a brow, staring me down for a moment with glittering eyes, and gives me a hard slap on the shoulder. "Behave yourself, Vicente. Starting trouble over there is completely different than starting trouble over here. One gets others killed. The other gets you killed."

I nod.

Get in the car with my two amigos.

And we're off to the Mazatlán airport.

Off to a new land.

Where I am no longer Javier Bernal's son.

Where the prince can become the king.

Violet

THE ENVELOPE HAUNTED ME FOR THE REST OF THE week.

I could barely concentrate on my assignments and I walked through the school and streets of San Francisco like a zombie, seeing everything and taking in nothing at all. As if school wasn't overwhelming enough with the need to get my projects exactly right, now my thoughts were pulled to a puzzle I desperately wanted to solve.

I had to talk to someone, but at the same time I knew I couldn't confide in just anyone. The article had talked about my father in a negative way. And that's putting it mildly. It said he was involved with a drug cartel and presumed dead, and he's clearly not. Dead, that is.

Plus, there's a reason that this has all been kept away from me, the big, dark secret that I always imagined hung above their heads.

Either way, I can't say anything to Ginny about it so I let it fester inside me, a slow simmer of black heat, all week.

Ben comes up from Santa Cruz most weekends. It's Friday evening and he's downstairs right now, talking to Mom about something. Dad is still at work.

I don't want to appear overly anxious—as I've said before, my parents are paranoid as fuck—but I also don't want to hang out in the house much longer.

I go downstairs and play the part of the bored, petulant child, something I do very well. I lean against the kitchen counter and sigh dramatically.

My mom gives me a wry look as she pushes her long dark hair behind her ears. "What?" she asks.

"Nothing," I mumble. "Just bored." I give Ben a hopeful look. "Want to hit the Haight?"

Ben and Mom exchange a wary look. I get along well with my brother, even more so since he went off to Santa Cruz for college, but it's not like we hang out one on one all that often.

Maybe he can pick up on the silently pleading look in my eyes because he shrugs. "Okay, sure. You got your fake ID? I wouldn't mind a beer."

I know in any other household we'd probably get a lecture. But Mom is as lax as possible when it comes to those kind of rules, especially the ones set by the government. She's been a supporter of my fake ID and underage drinking, so long as I'm responsible. And I am. To a fault.

There's a tiny bar at the end of the street, by Amoeba

Records, that serves delicious Asian fusion food with amazing cocktails. It's dark, narrow, and the music isn't obnoxious or overpowering. It's the kind of place that seems perfect for divulging secrets.

As we walk up the street, Ben going on about some MMA fighter that I'm pretending to care about, I feel my phone burning in my pocket, as if the picture I took of the newspaper article is trying to leak out into the world.

"So, what the hell is going on with you?" Ben asks as we sit in a booth, the waitress leaving with our order.

I chew on my lip until I'm sure my Chapstick is completely scraped off. "Ben..." I say slowly. "Do you ever get the feeling that our parents..." I lower my voice and lean in, "aren't who they say they are?"

He rolls his eyes. "This again?" He attempts a smile, like it's a joke, but it looks forced.

"I'm serious. Just answer me."

He sighs, sitting back in his chair and running a hand through his dark hair, the ends still spiky. "They're weird. Okay? That's it. Mom is just...well, she's paranoid. And Dad is probably the same guy he was when he was young. They've always been very...I don't know, cool, I guess. I mean, I know they're Mom and Dad, but they don't act like typical parents. Doesn't mean they're hiding anything or lying about anything."

I pause as the waitress drops off his beer and my lychee martini. "You sure about that?"

He studies me for a moment. It's amazing how much he looks like Dad at times. I got my mother's high cheekbones, dark eyes, and small bone structure from her Estonian ancestry. It would have been nice to have gotten the striking blue eyes like the guys have, or Ben's darker complexion, or their height, but I'm not complaining much.

"Vi, you're not very good at beating around the bush, so just say it."

I exhale slowly as I pull my phone out. I flip to the picture and slide it across the table to him.

"What is this?" he asks, picking it up.

"Just read it and you tell me," I say. My hair is starting to feel too hot on the back of my neck, the ends tickling, so I put it up in a ponytail as I watch him.

He frowns as his eyes scan the photo, zooming in and out as he tries to read the text. His face goes through a gamut of emotions. Confusion, shock, anger.

"I don't…" he finally says, staring down at it with disbelief. He begins to slide the phone back to me and then quickly snatches it back, looking over it again. "What the fuck?"

"I know. I've had all week to think about it."

"You've known for a week? Where did this even come from?"

"Someone sent it in the mail. That's all there was in the envelope, just the clipping. No note. No return address."

"You didn't tell Mom or Dad?"

I shake my head. "No. I slipped it back in. They never noticed I opened it."

He reads the article again. "Fuck. Vi, I don't get it. Why would Dad lie about his father? He told us he was dead."

"Maybe he was ashamed of him. It obviously seems like something big happened if the word scandal was used."

"Yeah, a scandal involving a fucking drug cartel." He sighs. "Even with the internet regulations over the years, I bet if I looked hard enough, I could find something about this."

"You're Ben McQueen. The internet is your bitch."

He gives me a half smile. "Yeah, well, I never thought I'd be looking for information about our father, that's for sure."

"But this explains a lot, doesn't it," I say to him. "Why they act so cagey sometimes. For, like, no reason."

He purses his lips, nodding slowly. "Could be. I can't believe you've kept this a secret."

"I wanted to show you in person. You probably wouldn't have believed me otherwise."

"You're right."

"Thanks."

"You can be like Mom sometimes, you know."

"Paranoid?"

He shrugs and takes a sip of his beer. "I would have said combustible."

He knows the right word to get to me all right, though at least he didn't call me sensitive. He knows that's a sore spot for me.

When he puts his beer back down, he starts to spin it in his hands. "I can't believe we had a grandfather. That he was still alive. A sheriff? And what about his wife? If that's his second wife, what happened to his first one? Did she die early too or was that another lie?"

"Makes you wonder about Grandpa Gus and Grandma Mimi."

Now Ben looks extra alarmed. "What about them?"

"Nothing," I say as I undo my ponytail, my hair feeling too tight now. "I just hope they're actually who we think they are. Gus married Mimi after we were born. Mom never talks about her real birth mother much. The few times she has have been in passing, and when I was younger I used to ask but she said she was raised by Gus and didn't remember much about her mother. That never sounded right to me. I don't know why."

"Because you're paranoid."

"There's that word. Now you see that maybe I have a reason to be?"

He exhales loudly, his eyes following every move of a hot redhead as she walks past.

"Ben," I chide him. "Focus."

He rolls his eyes back to me, unimpressed. Though brilliantly smart, Ben has ADHD, which he keeps under control with medication. That said I think most men are distracted when it comes to women. "I am focused," he says. "It's just a lot to make sense of."

"Yeah, well. It makes me wonder what else they're hiding."

He's silent for a moment, mulling it over while I take a sip of my drink, the delicate aroma of the lychee having a calming effect. Well, the alcohol too.

"I think we should say something," he finally says.

"What? Why?"

"Because they're Mom and Dad, Violet. I want to see what kind of excuse they could possibly have for this. They might just give us the truth. And maybe it's not the truth that we want, and maybe they were protecting us from our real grandfather for a reason, I don't fucking know. But I do know I want to hear it from them." He pauses. "After I finish snooping around. When I find the real truth before their truth."

I exhale slowly, glad for that. I don't know, I hate having to hide something from them. I'm a good liar even though it takes a lot out of me. But I also don't want to have to confront them either. I just hope we can figure this out on our own.

We stay at the bar for another drink before we head back to the house, but our conversation is stunted. We're all furrowed brows and gnawing lips and there isn't much else to talk about. I know he's thinking the same as me.

What does this all mean?

And what's going to change?

Vicente

AMERICA IS SOMEHOW BETTER THAN I IMAGINED IT
would be.

Growing up in Mexico, hearing the tense and
turbulent history between the two countries, I imagined a
hostile place full of greed and corruption. Ironically, a place
a lot like Mexico. I was all ready for it, ready for a fight.

But for what it's worth, at least in the state of California,
it's an open, friendly place. Not without a good dose of fear
of course, but certainly not what I expected, and I've been
to many countries. In some ways, California is no different
than Germany or Italy, except the women here are more…
friendly.

And fucking gorgeous. Can't forget that. It must be the

sand and sunshine, because as I landed in Los Angeles and spent a few days looking around and soaking up the atmosphere and making plans, I nearly lost my mind with all the choices.

The women are forward, mixed with a self-conscious coyness that hits straight to my dick. Luckily I didn't have to go further than the bar of my hotel on Sunset Strip before I was bringing them back to my room.

Even more lucky that Tio and Nacho decided to retire early. I honestly don't know how I'm going to survive having them shadow me everywhere. I'm used to it—I've always had bodyguards, even though I knew well enough how to take care of myself—but this is a whole new country and if I'm going to do what I want to do, what I need to do, I can't have them shadowing my every move.

They may be armed, glorified babysitters, but like most babysitters, they're also snitches. They're already reporting back to my father on my daily activities. Well, I took a dip at Laguna Beach, then fucked two tanned bitches with grating accents and fake lips, followed by a plate of tuna sashimi. Happy your son is living life to the fullest?

The next day I bought a car. Paid cash. My dream car. A Mustang, my coveted American muscle car from the 1960s. Sleek red, like the glossy lips around my dick the night before.

There was no point in trying to lose Tio and Nacho on the interstate heading up to San Francisco. I tried. Couldn't quite get to that speed, not with so many police drones in the area.

Despite that though, the drive felt quick. For a while there it was just me and the car and the empty brown plains stretching out on either side, whirls of dust stirring up what was once farmland. For the first time in my life I felt free.

I'm holding on to that feeling even now, despite Nacho and Tio trailing me as I walk up San Francisco's infamous Haight street, searching for the tattoo shop.

I take a drag of my cigarette and look down at my phone, the GPS signal blinking closer. It should be right here. I've seen tourist shops, bars, restaurants, marijuana stores, and the wrong tattoo shops. None of them have what I'm looking for.

Then it's right in front of me, next to a shop with clouds of patchouli wafting out so thick that it nearly obscures the sign.

Sins & Needles.

This is the place.

A retro, blinking sign with burnished bulbs, shining through the haze of smoke and the darkening sky.

I don't bother looking over my shoulder at Nacho and Tio. I know they're there, twenty feet back, pretending to be tourists. When we checked into the W Hotel I told them I wanted to check out the famed and historical Haight Street. They didn't object. That's not their job.

I flick my cigarette by the wheels of a parked car and step into the shop.

The chime rings above my head, drawing the attention of a tall, gaunt guy behind the counter, leaning across it like his head is too heavy for his neck. Definitely not Camden McQueen.

"Hey, man," the guy says while my eyes quickly take in the room. The lights are bright and the place is clean. There are framed vintage rock posters on the walls as if to give it elegance. Nirvana. Jane's Addiction. Danzig. The shop tries to skirt the lines between young and brash and mature and respectable.

I'm the only customer in here. I have to wonder how much money this place takes in. I'm guessing not enough to pay this fucker's salary.

I look at the fucker and flash him my most winning smile.

"Hi. Heard this was a great place to get a tattoo."

The guy nods, brushing his hair behind his ears, and shoots me a goofy grin.

"You've got the right place then, my man."

What a fucking dork.

My smile is tighter now. I nod, pretending to inspect the shop. "Any openings for next week?"

"How about right now?" he asks, gesturing to the empty room.

"Are you the owner?"

He lets out an obnoxious laugh. "No. I wish. Been working here a long time though. My name's Lloyd. Camden's the owner, but he takes weekends off. You know, being the owner and all."

"I'll wait for him, then," I tell him, wondering if I should add to that. It's a risk. "I go to school with his daughter, Violet. She recommended him."

"And not me?" Lloyd looks like I kicked him in the gut. I'm guessing he's either oversensitive or he has a fucking hard-on for her. He manages to recover. "Well, any friend of Vi's is a friend of mine."

But as he says that, something in his gaze shifts. Not quite the suspicion I would expect. He's sizing me up. A flicker of jealousy. Wondering who I am exactly to Violet McQueen.

Seems like the guy has a hard-on for her after all. For all I know, they could be together, but from the impression I got from her photography on her Instagram account, I'm guessing he's not her type. Her work is too thoughtful, stark, poetic. This guy seems too simple for her taste.

It doesn't matter. Violet isn't any of my business. It's her mother that I'm curious about.

"So, how about it?" I ask, tapping my fingers along the glass counter, binders beneath it full of tattoos, both designs and pictures of inked skin. "Does next Friday work?"

Lloyd stares at me for a bit too long and I'm seconds from mad-dogging him but I manage to refrain myself and force that polite full-of-shit smile again.

Finally he looks at his computer and scrolls down the screen.

"Five p.m. okay? You know what you want?"

I nod, since I'm going to just cancel the appointment anyway. "I do. And that's fine." I pause. Out of the corner of my eye I can see Tio and Nacho loitering outside. "Have you seen Violet today?"

"No," Lloyd says, his voice on edge. "She doesn't come by often and only when the bus drops her off after class on weekdays. It's Saturday." No shit it's Saturday. "What did you say your name was again?"

"I didn't. It's Vicente." I give him my phone number.

"That's an LA area code," Lloyd says, squinting at me. "I thought you said you went to school with Violet."

"I'm from LA. Going back after the semester is over. I haven't changed it yet." Which reminds me, I'm going to need another phone with a SF number really soon. The moment I purchased this one in LA, Tio and Nacho scammed the number off me and no doubt passed it on to my father.

Lloyd seems to buy that, though I have no doubt he'll probably tell Violet about me when he sees her next, probably in some sniveling way. The truth is, I probably won't be around come Friday anyway, and I'm certainly not getting a fucking tattoo. Everything I plan to accomplish will be done before that.

When I leave the shop I look to my right at the two stooges who are pretending to stare through a shop window. I don't even know why they bother.

"Hey," I tell them. "You guys want a tattoo? I could make you an appointment. Get a couple of naked ladies on your arms, closest to a woman you're ever going to get."

They stare at me blankly, completely void of personality. It's their job to watch me and pretend they don't know me.

I roll my eyes and head out into the street, dodging the headlights of passing cars. It's completely dark now but the night is buffered by fog, painting everything charcoal, onyx, and grey.

They're right behind me, wondering where I'm going and if I'm trying to lose them.

I'm not. I need them to follow me.

I don't know what is hidden in my father's past. He's been pretty open about every last gruesome detail of his life, even the less than charming circumstances of how he met my mother. But I know I'm close to figuring something out here. I just don't know what it is.

I also know that Tio and Nacho are reporting every last

detail about what I'm doing and will be doing. Either to my father over the phone and through email, maybe even to my mother. Either way, he'll hear I randomly went to a tattoo shop.

He'll hear the name Sins & Needles.

And I'm sure it will ring a bell.

As will the name Camden McQueen.

My father doesn't believe in coincidences.

If he is informed tonight, I guarantee I'll wake up to-morrow evening in Mexico with a mouth full of cotton balls and sedatives in my veins. If not tonight, the next day.

The point is, everything I want to find out would go straight down the drain. Everything.

Though I don't know San Francisco well, I know the maps I've been studying and the travel guide audio book I listened to on the drive up here. I head down the street, Tio and Nacho hot on my trail, then cut into Buena Vista Park.

The oldest park in the city, I remember that much. It's mostly steep hill, disappearing into the fog, shrouded by darkness. During the day it's a magnet for dog walkers. At night it's a mountain of drug addicts, dealers, vagrants, the homeless, and a whole other range of less than desirables. No sane man would come here after dark.

And though I'm not sane, I am smart.

Maybe smart isn't the right word.

Fastidious.

Thorough.

And maybe, just a bit ruthless.

I'm yelled at in incoherent ramblings by a few shadows as I pass them by but I pay them no mind. I ignore the darkened steps of a path curving up the hill and go straight up over the grass and brush and into the trees. I briefly turn around before disappearing into the forest. Tio and Nacho have attracted the attention of the bums who are shouting ethnic slurs at them, and I wait, breath held in my mouth, for either of them to overreact.

That would be seriously bad luck. For all of us here. Me, them, the bums. But they keep going, keep coming after me, straight up the hill, feet slipping on the fog-damp grass.

The bums won't remember us tomorrow.

I head into the trees. The light from Haight Street below is dispersed into the mist, leaving a world of shadows with just enough to see by. I duck behind a thick eucalyptus, its scaly bark appearing like loose skin in the night, and take my .45 out of my waistband, quickly slipping on the silencer from my pocket.

Tio and Nacho aren't silent as they enter the forest. They're huffing and puffing from the climb, swearing under their breath. Nacho says something to Tio about Javier hearing all about this when they're done. That's a relief. It means he probably knows nothing yet.

They charge past me, two thick shapes in the ghostly trees.

I have to be quick.

I aim the barrel at Tio, who is closest, a straight shot to the back of the head.

The gun fires hot in my hand, as if the silencer is glowing red with having to silence a scream.

There is still a distinct, muffled sound that brings Nacho's attention around to me, his gun drawn and ready, all before Tio even begins to fall.

The second bullet gets Nacho right between the eyes.

He doesn't even look shocked. It's like he knew I'd cause his death, sooner or later.

He falls too, like a tree, leaves scattering as he hits the damp earth right beside Tio.

If I'm supposed to feel something other than relief, I don't.

Or I try not to.

I take in a deep breath, pushing it all down as I unscrew the silencer and put everything back in its place. Then I slip on a pair of micro-thin gloves and hunch down, searching the bodies. Any fingerprints would mean nothing to the cops but it's better to be safe than sorry.

I leave their guns. They're untraceable. Everything about these two men is untraceable. It's always been that way.

So I take their wallets, phones, and the fifty one-thousand-dollar bills they both have spread between them. Emergency money that my father thought I knew nothing about. I feel almost honored that he would part with those bills, a rare currency he's held on to for years, but I'm sure the money is better off in my hands than theirs. With any luck, I'll have a few left when this is all over.

And when will that be? I think.

Then I head out of the forest and back down the hill the way I came. It's better if I keep to the same witnesses. Any other route might put a new set of eyes upon me.

Not that I'm worried.

The bums aren't even there when I reach the bottom. It's like they knew the whole thing was bad news. Even in their drunkenness, they scattered like rats, smelling the poison.

I head out onto Haight, just a man out for a walk, and hail a cab that takes me all the way back to my hotel.

Peace at last.

The next day, after I call Sins & Needles and talk to Lloyd, cancelling the appointment, I take a chance on Ellie's studio, hoping it will be open on a Sunday. When I find out it's closed, I'm not surprised. She's probably with her family. In a way I'm relieved that I don't have to face her yet. I'm not sure what I'd say—for all my planning I haven't thought that far ahead. It's much easier for me to observe what I can from afar.

I switched hotels, moving to a tiny boutique one just outside Chinatown, with vivid art all over the walls and an old-fashioned elevator that only fits one person at a time. I know my father has probably contacted the W, wondering why the hell Tio and Nacho haven't sent their daily report to him. When he finds out I've checked out, he's probably going to contact every swanky hotel in the city trying to find a Vicente Rodriguez. My father couldn't imagine me staying anywhere but the very best. He'll never think to find me here.

Not under the name Vicente Cortez.

One of the girls I fucked in LA put me in touch with another girl who made fake IDs. I put in my order and paid her five grand in cash. She later came to my room, her equipment in her purse. Tio and Nacho never thought anything of it. She took my picture, printed out the IDs.

She didn't quite succumb to my advances, nervously citing a boyfriend, but I got what I needed anyway.

I can imagine the carnage back at home. I feel bad—briefly—for my mother, who must be locking herself in her room to avoid my father's rage. I'm not sure if he'll be worried that something happened to me or livid that something happened to my bodyguards.

But I can't dwell on it. I made my choice a while ago and knew it wouldn't be easy. I spend the day getting my supplies.

When Monday rolls around, I'm restless. The bad kind, where your mind and limbs have their own agenda. It leads to impulsive decisions, running with anything but logic.

I want to see Violet. I know Ellie is number one on my list, but Violet seems safer somehow, and my curiosity over her is killing me, especially over the way Lloyd was acting.

But the first stop is the bank. I open up a savings account under Vicente Cortez, and deposit nine grand in cash, the safe and legal limit.

Afterward, I head back to the hotel to gather my photography bag, then head up the hills to find the daughter, cigarettes a constant fixture in my hand.

The Academy of Art University is spread out among several blocks at the top of Sutter, and through some digging, I manage to find the photography building.

This is where my restlessness will get me in trouble. If I had put any thought into it, I would have checked this place out before I got here. I would have scoped out the classes to see how easy it is to slip in. I would have figured out how to transfer in as a late student.

Now it's too late. The building is small and there's no

place for me to blend in. When I make my way inside, down corridors of studios draped in sheets and surrounded by lights, I see a classroom with only about forty people, all staring at their computers as their teacher stands at the front, demonstrating something. My eyes take in the backs of their heads but there's no time to figure out which one is Violet.

So much for that. I'll have to think of something new.

I quickly leave the building and grab a seat outside at a café across the street. I sit and watch. I wait. I sneak a cigarette until the couple next to me looks ready to tell the management.

Forty minutes later, fog has rolled in like a silver snake and students are starting to leave the building. I observe each one carefully, searching for the elusive Violet.

And then I see her.

She walks out the door talking to a friend with blonde and blue hair. But other than the color of her hair, I pay her no mind. Violet captures all my attention.

She's beautiful in a dramatic, romantic way. Her face could inspire gothic novels from long ago. If Helen of Troy's face could launch a thousand ships, Violet McQueen's face could launch a thousand stories, all filled with lust, heartache, and death.

Her hair is long and dark, shiny like blackbird wings. Her skin is pale, soft, and free of makeup except on her eyes, where her lashes and lids are dark with mystery. She's a little on the short side, slim in a black leather jacket and a tight, stretchy grey dress that drops down to her combat boots. Her thighs are superhero strong, and her ass is large, tight, and fucking unbelievable.

She and her friend head across the street and I start to follow, watching as they head into another café.

I want to see her up close.

I cross the street, moving between students, business-men, and vagrants, until I'm entering the bustling estab-lishment. I immediately head to a table in the corner, grab-bing a seat then scanning the room.

Violet is at the counter, ordering a drink. While her friend is chattering loudly to the barista, seeming to com-mand all the attention to her, Violet stays silent, offering a polite nod and a shy smile now and then. But she's not really listening. She's staring off into space and I can see the wheels turning in her head. Sometimes such a stark ex-pression comes across her brow that I have to wonder what exactly she's thinking of.

They end up sitting at a table by the window, which is perfect—I can observe her without blatantly staring. There's a steady stream of people and traffic on the oth-er side of the glass that's capturing everyone's eyes, Violet included.

You can learn almost anything about a person by watching them. It was one of the first things my father taught me. He is uncannily good at predicting people. For all his explosiveness and temper, there's a feral calm about him, like a giant cat waiting with endless patience for the mouse to appear.

Watching Violet for even ten minutes tells me many things.

For starters, she gets distracted—her attention is every-where except on her friend, and a few times she has lapsed into some deep thinking that has her brow furrowing like she's trying to solve a puzzle.

She fidgets. When she's not picking at the cardboard sleeve of her coffee cup, she's putting her hair back into a braid, then pulling it out a few minutes later.

She gets uncomfortable easily. The café starts to fill up with more people and a loud group of guys sits down at the table next to them, which in turn causes her posture to become stiff, her lip to snarl, her chair to move further away.

It's not a lot but it's enough to go on, enough information to let me adjust how to deal with her.

The thing is, I'm here because I'm curious. Getting closer to Violet was never part of the plan. But now that I'm staring at her, I'm wondering what her skin feels like, if I could be able to hold her wandering attention and calm her agitated heart.

I wonder what my father would say if he knew I was looking at her.

I wonder what he would say if I brought her home and gave her to him.

Would he respect me more?

I push the thoughts out of my head. For now.

When she leaves the café, I should watch her go and let her be. Focus on Ellie, her mother, my father's once lover, the reason I came here.

But when Violet and her friend get up to leave, I wait a few beats and then I get up too. I watch them part ways outside, giving each other quick hugs before they go in opposite directions.

Violet is heading across the street, back to the school.

Without thinking, I trail her through the crowds like

the wake behind a ship, the rapidly moving mist wrapping around her legs like exhaust.

She disappears back inside the photography building.

I stand in the fog and wait.

Violet

PLEASE, PLEASE LET IT BE HERE, I THINK TO MYSELF AS I hurry up the steps to the classroom. Luckily Anderson, my teacher, is still inside and at his desk, staring at his computer.

I quickly knock on the door and gesture through the glass at my seat while he waves me in.

"Sorry, sorry," I tell him as I make my way over to the desk. "I left my scarf."

"No problem," he says. "I was just wrapping stuff up."

I let out a huge sigh of relief when I spot it and quickly wrap it around my neck. It's not like I have a shortage of scarves, but I always feel so horrible when I lose something. It seriously haunts me for days.

"Getting cold out?" he says, squinting through his glasses at the windows. "Haven't seen fog for a few days down here."

"Try living in Haight," I tell him.

"I live in Outer Sunset, so I know what you mean."

I really like my teacher, but this is the first time I've been alone with him and for some reason that makes me nervous. I don't know why—he's super approachable, friendly, and young too, in his early thirties, maybe. I guess it's just kind of awkward and all I really want is to get out of here before I get sucked into small talk. Not that I have anywhere in particular to go.

Fortunately, I'm able to get out of there and leave Anderson in peace. I head back out of the building and into the fog, which is thicker than gravy now, sticking to the tops of the houses.

A shiver runs through me and I tuck the scarf in tighter as I zip up the top of my leather jacket.

"Excuse me?"

I jump slightly and whirl around to see a man leaning against the building, staring at me with a hesitant smile.

Normally I don't give strange men the time of day (maybe another reason why I'm single) but I'd seen this guy before, just earlier when I was in the café with Ginny. I could have sworn he was looking at me then but figured it was in my head.

And what a damn fucking shame that would be, because now that I'm closer to him, he's the type of guy a girl could have endless wet dreams about.

Tall. At least six feet.

Lean but packed with muscle, the kind that looks

effortless, as if he's got good genes and gets his rounded shoulders, wide chest, big biceps and forearms from manual labor. Even in his thermal Henley shirt—mustard yellow, a surprising color—his muscles are taut underneath the material.

Then there's his skin color. A gorgeous tawny gold, the perfect summer bronze that sets off his dark hair and the low set of arched brows that frame his face.

God, I hope all of that took two seconds to observe and I haven't been gawking at him like a fool. I immediately feel my cheeks start to go hot, my palms sweaty.

This is not like me at *all*.

I clear my throat. "Yes?"

"Sorry to bother you. I just had a question. You're in photography, right?" He nods his head to the door of the building. It's then that I notice the sweet photography bag with him. It's a brand I wanted to get, only I didn't have the money. "Do you know if they're still accepting students?"

His shy smile gets wider and he straightens up off the wall.

Those teeth. That face.

I can't place his age but he seems both young and wise at the same time, his eyes shining with years of experience and a strange naivety. They're the color of amber—rich, glowing, and clear all at once. I feel like if I peered at him close enough I might see ancient life preserved inside of them.

I blink a few times, remembering how to speak. "You mean Anderson's class?"

"Yeah," he says. "I'm here scoping out the schools in the area." His accent is American with a Hispanic lilt that makes me think he hasn't lived here all his life. His voice is smooth and rich and seems to fill every part of me. "I know it's late in the semester, but…it would mean everything if I could get in."

I have a million questions for this guy, and yet when my mouth opens, I say, "I saw you earlier. In the coffee shop."

He looks momentarily startled before his brow smooths. "You're very observant."

I shrug. "You have to be if you're a photographer."

"Touché," he says. "So, did you like what you saw?"

My eyes widen. "What?"

"When you were looking at me. Did you like what you saw?"

Okay, a little bit forward. I normally would back off but there's something keeping me in my place, preventing me from walking away, and it's not that he's giving me a smirk that's just innocent enough to let him off the hook.

It reminds me of an old lyric.

Everyone told me love was blind. Then I saw your face and you blew my mind.

Maybe not the deepest lyric but I'm certainly humming it now.

"I'm just joking," he says lightly.

"Oh," I say, wishing I didn't sound so stupid. I fumble for the right words to say. Anything really. "I could introduce you."

He raises a brow, seeming as surprised as I am at this new development. "To your teacher. Are you sure?"

"Why not?" I try and sound breezy but the moment I turn around and open the door to head back into the building, my eyes are wide and I'm mouthing, *Oh my god, what are you doing*? to myself.

Suffice it to say, the climb up the stairs is pretty awkward and I curse myself for wearing my curve-hugging dress, knowing my ass is totally shoved in his face.

I give the guy an anxious smile as I knock on Anderson's door for the second time since class had finished.

"Forget something else?" Anderson asks when I open the door.

"Actually, no. This guy had a question for you about the program. I hope you don't mind."

I step inside the room while the golden god of a guy saunters right over to Anderson, his hand outstretched. "Vicente. Vicente Cortez," he says to him.

I'm struck by how much I love that name. I'm also struck by the feeling that I should probably go on my way now since my job is done—I introduced Vicente to Anderson and that's that. Yet I hover by the row of desks, watching them.

"So sorry to just walk in like this," Vicente continues, "this girl was kind enough to let me introduce myself."

"Not a problem," Anderson says, pushing his glasses up on his nose and crossing his arms. "How can I help you?"

"Well," Vicente says, "I'm in San Francisco for a year or so and have been thinking about getting serious about my photography, and figured now is as great a time as any. Only I realize classes started earlier this month."

"They did." Anderson briefly glances at me. "And I'm teaching second year students like Violet who have already done their first."

"Violet," Vicente repeats, looking at me as he learns my name. The sound of it on his lips sends a cascade of warmth down my spine. I swallow hard, wishing he wasn't having this kind of reaction on me.

"We could maybe get you into the first year, but even so," Anderson says, taking Vicente's attention away from me, "I'm not sure if any students have dropped out to fit you in."

"And what about this year? Anyone drop out?" Vicente is just as bold with Anderson as he was with me.

Anderson gives him a discerning look. "We did. Last week. Do you have any transfer papers from another school or...?"

"Do the papers matter or does money matter?"

Anderson lets out a nervous laugh. "I assure you they both do. This school has very high standards and, Mr. Cortez, though you might be very capable, I'm not sure this is going to work out. You must understand."

For some reason I expect Vicente to make a fuss and demand they take him, maybe toss a wad of cash on the desk, but of course he doesn't. "I understand completely," he says. "Thank you so much for your time. Have a good day."

He heads back toward the door and his eyes meet mine as he passes. "Thank you, Violet," he says, and I have a hard time tearing my gaze from his. It's like he's trying to pass me information in a language I'm dying to read. I can feel the disappointment rolling off of him, which in turn makes me disappointed too.

I watch as he strides past, getting a whiff of his scent, something like mint and rich tobacco, strangely soothing, and then he's out the door.

I look back at Anderson who gives me a shrug.

"Unfortunately, there isn't much I can do. I'll mention it to the head of the department, just in case. There's a lot to be said for planning ahead. You can't throw money at everything and expect doors to open."

I'm barely listening to him. My feet have a mind of their own. Suddenly I'm out the door and flying down the stairs, my boots echoing in the stairwell, and bursting out onto the street.

I look up and down the sidewalk until I spot Vicente already across the road and heading down Taylor. Damn, the guy moves fast.

I run down and across the crosswalk, hitting the light just in time, and then I'm right behind him and slightly out of breath. This makes me realize I need to start kickboxing more regularly.

"Vicente," I call out, even though I'm seconds from slamming into his back.

He turns around and I dig my boots into the sidewalk. His brows are raised, wondering what I'm doing.

What am I doing? He asked me a question, I gave him the best answer I had, and that's all it should have been. Yet I couldn't let that be it.

I barely know this guy and I think he's already making me a bit mental. Well, more so than I already am.

"Sorry about Anderson," I tell him, looping my thumb under the strap of my camera bag. "It was worth a shot, right?"

He nods, looking away, his golden eyes taking in the street. "It was." He brings his gaze back to mine. "Thank you again. That was very kind of you. Some things just aren't meant to be."

"Maybe because other things are waiting around the corner?" I ask lamely.

He grins at me, white teeth against bronzed skin. I feel myself melt.

"Or maybe good things are waiting right in front of me," he says.

Oh god. Forward again. But instead of it scaring me, I embrace it. I hold my ground. I refuse to feel awkward.

"Maybe," I tell him, wishing I had the nerve to say more.

Something in his eyes change. They become more focused, but with fire. Like there's some sort of tiger deep inside, starting to roar.

It scares me. It excites me.

And I'm still not moving.

"Did you want to get a cup of coffee?" he asks. "I know you just had one and might not want another…"

I can't help but grin. He's asking me out. Even if it's just for coffee, that's still something. "I drink decaf so it's never a problem," I admit.

"Unless you want a real drink?" he says, his eyes going to the bar across the street. "Are you twenty-one?"

"No, but my fake ID says I am."

His mouth quirks up into a sly smile. He's got beautiful lips. I wonder what he tastes like.

"I like you already," he says.

A thrill shoots through me, hot and fast, and I try to keep my smile under control.

"Is that a good place?" he asks, gesturing to the bar. "I'm afraid I don't know the city well yet."

I wish I knew most of the bars downtown, but I tend

to stick to my neighborhood. Still, I know this bar is pretty casual.

Considering it's the afternoon, there's a surprising amount of people inside, but then I realize it's part of the hotel above it. I'm not a fan of crowds, but the noise level is pretty low and the music is mellow jazz. We manage to get two seats at the end of the bar, which is both distancing in the fact that you share your conversation with the bartender, plus it's not as easy to look into each other's eyes, and also intimate because you have to sit right beside the person.

I'm not sure what I like better, but Vicente's fresh yet smoky scent is making the distance between us feel even closer. It doesn't help that when I take my seat, my knee rubs against his.

"What will you have?" he asks. "Order one drink, order several. Get the most expensive thing you can think of. It's on me."

Hmmm. Maybe he wasn't joking when he mentioned money to Anderson. I know my program isn't cheap, I'm just really lucky my parents are able to pay for it.

"Are you sure?" I ask.

He nods. "What would you like?"

Well, considering it's two in the afternoon… "A Bloody Mary." I pause. "With Grey Goose." I might be pressing my luck, but hey, he said he was buying. I usually have it with the cheapest vodka there is (Smirnoff, which I hate, but that's student life).

"Do you like Grey Goose or are you just picking that because it's expensive?" he asks thoughtfully. "No offense, of course. I just think there are better vodkas."

Normally I can't help but take offense, but I can tell he's just being honest.

"You pick," I tell him. "I trust you."

He bites his lip at that, as if my trust was what he wanted all along. I don't even know why I said that, it's not like I know a thing about this guy. Other than his name and a yearning for photography, he's a stranger.

Tiny warning bells go off in the back of my head, reminding me of exactly this. He's a stranger. Just because he's got a pretty face and his forearms are laced with muscle doesn't mean I should let my guard down. I mean, the fact that I'm here at a bar with him is already pretty fucked up in the world of Violet McQueen, who never lets her guard down with anyone.

So while Vicente orders us two Bloody Marys with some foreign sounding vodka I've never heard of, I watch the process closely to make sure that the bartender doesn't slip anything in there (I'm not sure how or why, unless this was all carefully orchestrated, but of course that's my paranoia talking) and then keep my drink to myself the moment the bartender slides it into my hand.

"Here's to…" Vicente says, lifting his drink to mine. "The kindness of strangers."

We clink glasses and I take a sip, his amber eyes never leaving mine, seeming to drink me in. He reaches into my very core, colder and stronger than any spirit.

Speaking of which, the drink is hella good.

"You like it," he says.

I nod. "I never thought I'd be able to tell the difference between vodkas."

"Believe me, there's a difference," he says, taking a sip.

His tongue gently licks the salted edge of his glass, the sight causing heat to build between my legs. Jesus, either this drink is going to my head right away or I'm in trouble. "Though price doesn't always mean quality. Grey Goose is fine and all, but the one we're having is five dollars a bottle cheaper."

With his rich tones and that light hint of an accent, I could listen to him talk about alcohol all day. I could also watch that tongue of his all day too.

He seems to smirk a little, as if noticing my attention, and leans back. "A fascinating conversation or what?"

"No," I say quickly, even though he doesn't look all too bothered. "It is interesting. I'm lame, I don't really know much about it."

"My father taught me all of that," he tells me. "He's a big fan of sipping tequila. There's sipping vodka too, you know. I've had this straight over ice before."

I wrinkle my nose. "No, thank you. That would be way too intense."

"But intense can be good. It can be *very* good."

I'm not sure if it's my overactive imagination or not, but his gaze seems to intensify as he says that. The delicate skin at the back of my neck starts to prickle. I'm both nervous and at ease all at once.

"Violet is a beautiful name, by the way," he says, offering me an easy smile. "Are you named after anyone?"

I shrug, managing to break my eyes away from his, and start stirring the ice cubes around in the glass with my straw. "No. I asked my mom once why she named me that and she said she liked the color. Though I've actually never seen her wear it. I guess it's better than being named after

Violet Beauregard."

"From Charlie and the Chocolate Factory?"

"Yup."

"I prefer the Gene Wilder version," he says.

"Me too," I say excitedly. "Depp was too…pretty for the role. Too calculated, you know? Gene's Willy Wonka was like a natural extension of himself."

"So you know film as well as photography."

"Films are just moving pictures," I point out.

"True," he says, running his hand along his sharp jawline, the dark stubble of his beard brushing against his fingers. "I had an aunt named Violetta."

"Sounds so much prettier in Spanish," I comment.

"Yes," he says, looking away. I can almost feel his heart growing heavy. "Too bad I never had a chance to know her. She died before I was born."

"Oh no," I say softly. And, of course, because I'm a dick, the next word out of my mouth is, "How?"

"Car bomb," he says matter-of-factly, not even trying to keep his voice down, which draws a look of concern from the bartender.

My eyebrows lift. "A car bomb?" I manage to keep my voice in a hush.

He nods. "It was a mistake. It wasn't meant for her."

"I'm so sorry," I tell him, even though I know my words aren't enough. I can feel his pain, and my words can't soften it.

"That's okay," he tells me, giving me a small smile. "Life can be rough down south. It's one of the reasons my parents moved to America long before I was born."

"You still have a bit of an accent though," I point out.

He grins at me, letting out a sheepish laugh that I feel deep inside. "I know. I've tried to hide it but why pretend to be someone else other than Vicente Cortez, you know? Actually, my parents opened a business outside of Sacramento and that's where I was born. When I was five, my parents sold part of it and we moved back to Mexico. My mother missed her family. Family, blood, is everything."

I nod, even though the phrase makes me pause. Family, blood, should be everything, but in the case of my family, it's not.

Lately I'm not even sure who my family is.

"Anyway," he says, bringing me back out of my head. "I went to university in Mexico City, took a bullshit degree in business, which, at least got me to invest in a lot of the right stocks. But now I'm following my passion. I wanted to explore the city by the bay, close to where I was born. I don't believe I've ever seen a city so photogenic." I'm about to open my mouth to agree when he adds, "And I've never seen a girl outshine it. Until I saw you today."

My cheeks turn red and the back of my neck is hot. I nervously pull my hair off to the side, trying to cope with the compliment. "Oh, come on," is all I can say.

"I'm serious," he says, and he sounds serious, looks serious. "You must be the subject of everyone in your class."

I let out an awkward laugh. "Yeah right. Are you kidding me?"

"I never joke about beauty," he says solemnly. "You're the most beautiful girl I've ever seen."

Holy shit. I feel that one in my bones. Warm, liquid honey that spreads to my heart.

"You act like you don't hear that all the time," he

continues, his knee brushing against mine as he leans in closer. I stare into his eyes, counting the threads of mahogany and yellow streaking through the golden brown.

I swallow hard and immediately busy myself with the drink, sucking in more than I mean to. The horseradish and hot sauce burn my throat and chest.

Ah shit.

My face grows hotter, redder, until I can't hold it back anymore and I start coughing uncontrollably.

Just fucking great.

He reaches over and pats me lightly on the back, ordering water from the bartender, and I can't even enjoy his touch—both soft and hot—because I'm too busy dying.

Finally, I'm able to get my breathing under control. Thankfully it's only then that he asks me if I'm all right. There's nothing worse than trying to answer when your throat and lungs are on fire.

"I'm fine," I tell him meekly, finishing the rest of the water.

He raises a brow as if to say, *Are you?*

"Really," I tell him, hoping not to make a big deal out of this.

"I'm sorry my words have this reaction with you. I have to say, I kind of like it."

I look at him as if he's nuts. He might be.

He raises his palm as way of explanation. "You almost choking on your drink brought your intimidation factor down just a bit."

"Intimidation factor?"

"You think it's easy talking to the most beautiful girl you've ever seen?"

A slow smile spreads across my face. I shake my head. "I don't know. Something tells me most things are easy for you."

"Is that so?"

I shrug. "Just a hunch."

He watches me intently for a moment. "Maybe you're right. Then again, things worth having often come easily."

That's not really how the saying goes, so my dirty mind wants to turn that last bit into innuendo. And as he's licking the edge of his glass again, a devious glint in his eyes, I realize that's one hundred percent what he meant.

Then, suddenly, he startles on his stool and pulls out his phone, quickly glancing at it. "Well, I hate to love you and leave you, Violet…"

"McQueen," I say softly, strangely bereft and almost hurt that he's going. "It's Violet McQueen."

"Violet McQueen," he says. "Name fit for royalty." He swings his long legs off the stool and stands up, picking up his camera bag from the back of his chair. "I have to run."

I want to ask why. I want to know what he's doing and if I can go too.

But I don't. Because I don't know him other than he's a gorgeous man who bought me a drink. And it sounds like this is where this tale will end.

"Okay," I say softly. "Thank you for the drink. I hope everything works out with your classes." I give him a stiff smile.

Something softens in his eyes, his shoulders relaxing slightly. "The classes? Who knows. But everything will work out now that I know you." I frown at that. "When are you done tomorrow?"

"Uh, I just have a morning class. It's over at eleven." My heart is picking up the pace, running away with the thought that this isn't it.

"Perfect. I'll meet you here tomorrow. We can have a drink, or not. We can have coffee, or not. But I want you ready to work."

"Work?"

He pats his camera bag. "Photos. If I can't learn from the school, I'll learn from you."

Is he kidding me? "But I…I don't know anything, really. I mean—"

"Violet," he says quickly, leaning in so he's whispering in my ear, hot breath that eats me up inside. "You're everything I want, I need, to know."

My eyes flutter closed for that moment, entranced by his voice, his smell, his words.

Then he kisses me lightly, so lightly, on the cheekbone. Butterfly wings of a kiss.

"See you tomorrow," he says.

And then he's gone. His presence is like a warm storm that's passed over the land, leaving quiet and destruction in its wake.

I start to tip on the stool and my eyes open, one hand flying to the counter to steady myself. I look to find Vicente but he's gone out of the bar.

Holy shit. Holy fucking shit.

What the hell just happened?

None of that could have been real. I mean, none of it.

I blink, trying to get my bearings, slowly facing the bar. The bartender is looking at me in amusement.

"First date?" he asks as he grabs Vicente's half-empty

glass. He didn't even finish his drink.

"I don't know what that was," I admit, rubbing my lips together, bewildered.

"He's pretty smooth, gotta give him that. And he knows his vodka," the bartender says. "Can't say it's not a way to my heart, if not yours."

I let out a soft laugh. One minute I was grabbing my scarf and preparing to head home, the next I'm having a drink with some sexy ass Mexican man, the same man I'm supposed to teach photography to tomorrow. I mean, what the fuck is that? No kidding, the guy is fucking smooth. I don't even know how he managed to get me to go along with that.

Because of those eyes, I remind myself, swallowing hard. *And those lips. And that tongue. And because you're a dirty little bird who hasn't gotten laid in a long time.*

I finish up the Bloody Mary, tipping the bartender even though I know Vicente already did, and start heading back home to try and make sense of it all.

I can't keep the smile off my face.

Vicente

I T WAS A RISK.

Everything.

But I was born to make them. Without risks, there is no progress. And I can't forget the reason I'm here.

Ellie McQueen.

But I never thought I'd get to know someone like Violet.

It makes the most sense.

Go through the daughter to get to the mother.

I just have to figure out how to play the daughter just right.

I was able to get a feel for her by observing her in that café. And I was surprised by how close my predictions were.

There's an acute softness about her, hiding underneath

a thin plate of armor. With her dark hair and eyes, her boots, her leather jacket, down to her defensive stare, she only plays the part of being hard and untouchable. The reality, I believe, is much softer. Not just vulnerable, but volatile, too. A contradiction. Underneath the thickest shield runs liquid fine lava, burning hotter than the surface would ever let you believe.

I was half-kidding about joining the school. I do consider myself to be pretty good at photography, though it's no passion of mine, and I would have been able to fake my way in if my money would have bought me late admission. I had to try and I had to let Violet know who she was dealing with.

She had to know I have money.

She had to know I was willing to do it all for the passion.

That money was worth the arts she held so dear.

And then I took another risk, and I left.

I didn't know if she would follow me or not. I could have walked down that street all the way to Market, and I would have left our meeting in the school just like that. A huge risk considering I still wanted to get close to her mother. I'm not sure how accepting the McQueens are of coincidences. The Bernals sure aren't.

Yet she ran after me. She needed to know more. And my leaving showed her I was the real deal, that I was only after the school and I wasn't interested in her. I could tell from the moment she saw me, even though she liked what she saw, that she was on the defensive.

The drink was a nice touch. I honestly didn't think she'd go for it. And I didn't think she'd have a fake ID either, but I guess when your mother is a con artist, that sort of shit runs in the family.

Then again, I have to wonder how much she knows about her family. She could know it all. She could know nothing. She seemed generally surprised to hear that a car bomb had killed my aunt.

The very aunt she's named after.

Violetta and her mother knew each other.

That's something she doesn't know.

Tomorrow I will figure out where she stands among the branches of her family tree.

What I do know is that I have to keep my head on straight for this to work.

I wasn't lying when I told her she's the most beautiful girl I've ever seen.

To stare at her from afar is one thing.

To see her up close is another.

I've never really felt possessive over a woman before. I've had my fun, I've moved on. But after just having a drink with Violet, watching her expressive dark eyes trying to take me in, to make sense of me, opening herself just enough, I was hit with this raw, hot need to make her mine. To have. To hold. To possess.

But possession is a by-product, not an objective.

I have to be smart for now.

I have work to do.

After I pretended I had to go and headed back to my hotel, I go online and book one of the best rooms in the city, a 1,500 square foot suite in the Intercontinental Mark Hopkins Hotel. Not the most lavish hotel to choose from but definitely the one with the nicest views.

At over $2,000 a night I have no choice but to pay for it

with the unlimited credit card that my father gave me. It's a risk to use it—it will signal to him where I am and if he's following closely, I'm sure it will cause him to send someone out to get me—but it's necessary.

Violet seems to impress easily. This is where I've got to play my cards right.

Let's see what kind of hand I have.

The next day I quickly browse the local headlines. Nacho and Tio's bodies were discovered by joggers the morning after I left them and the case still has no witnesses. There's also no information on their identity, not that it would make much difference. As long as I'm not identified—and I won't be—the homicide will disappear. Just a pair of paperless Mexicans swept under the rug.

I check in to the Intercontinental early, with just enough time to do a quick sweep of the room. Hardwood floors, velvet drapes, three rooms, and a fucking huge bathroom. The whole suite takes up a corner of the building and it's right below the Top of the Mark restaurant. The views from the floor-to-ceiling windows are incredible. Even in the persistent fog, the sharp top of the Transamerica building piercing through the mist like a needle, the city beckons like a sorceress, a spell under your skin.

I head out into the grey and down the slope of Powell Street, the cable cars chiming their way up the hill, tourists hanging on with big smiles on their faces. For a moment I'm envious of their joy, so simple and unfounded in nothing but novelty and freedom.

I push it aside, down, out, away, just as I did when I read about Tio and Nacho this morning, and stay on my path. Violet shines in my mind like a prize, a carefully wrapped gift under a tree.

Instead of going into the bar like last time, I hover around outside of it, lazily smoking a cigarette, waiting. The nicotine is an axe to my nerves, cleaving off the rough ends.

She's a few minutes late when I see her and the other students exiting the building. She's talking to one guy, smiling at whatever he's saying, and though the exchange is brief, it causes my blood to pulse hot with jealousy.

Get a fucking grip, I think to myself, flicking the cigarette away.

She spots me just before she crosses the street, her face breaking into a cautious smile. She's nervous, she's shy. It reminds me to treat her with kid gloves, to never assume anything.

She's got her black leather jacket on, a teal scarf, black jeans, and a blue plaid top that hangs down to mid-thigh. *What a damn fucking shame*, I think, because that means it's covering her ass.

"Hi," she says, stopping on the curb a few feet in front of me. A safe distance. But then she smiles again, showing the slightest gap between her two front teeth. Fucking adorable.

Her hair is loose and dark, like blackbirds taking flight as she swings it over her shoulders. Her cheeks are flushed pink. I like to think it's because of the sight of me and not because she wore blush this morning. That said, if she wore blush this morning instead of other mornings, that could be because of me too. Her lips have a subtle red shine to them. Perhaps she's trying to impress me as I am her, of course for very different reasons.

"Violet McQueen," I say with a nod. "I was worried for a moment that you might stand me up."

She laughs nervously, which means she thought about it. I'll have to tread even more carefully.

"So where to?" I add so she doesn't have to defend it. "It's your city."

"Um," she says, toying with a few strands of hair, looking around her. "Well, what have you seen? I don't have a car so I'm not sure how far I can take you."

"I have a car. I'd be happy to drive anywhere, so long as you're there."

Her cheeks flush even more and I have to hide my smile. I love getting this reaction out of her, and it's so easy to do.

"Okay, well, that might make things easier," she says. "I think some of the best shots in the city, you know, to get a real feel for it, are a little harder to get to by public transport. Doesn't mean I don't do it all the time, but I'm not sure if you're up for that."

I nod my head toward the top of Taylor Street, beyond the school. "Come on, let's go to my hotel and get the car. I'll drive, you tell me where to go."

She seems hesitant, maybe because the two of us on public transport would be safer, or at least less awkward, in her eyes. But my smile quickly convinces her otherwise.

"So, what did you learn today?" I ask her.

She sighs, adjusting the camera bag on her shoulder. "Nothing important. I mean, I guess it is but…just something I'm not thinking about yet. Setting up your own business. How to work freelance. That kind of thing."

"That doesn't interest you?"

She shrugs, flipping her hair. "It does. I mean, I want this to be my career, you know? But…it's scary. Because it makes you think about what's after that. I still don't know what I want to be. I know what people expect me to be…"

"What?"

"My mother," she says, pressing her lips together. She catches me staring at her and gives me a quick smile. "It's not a bad thing. My mom is great. It's just, well, she's actually a well-known photographer. In the bay area, anyway."

"Is that so? So it runs in the family."

"Yeah, we're all kind of artists. Except for Ben. He's my brother. He lives in Santa Cruz, is almost done with school there. He's into, like, MMA fighting and computer hacking and all that." Hacking? It reminds me to tread carefully with that too. If someone with any kind of hacking experience wanted to really find out who I was, they could link me to the cartel pretty quickly.

She goes on and I make myself pay attention. "I don't remember him being very artistic but I could be wrong. Maybe he secretly paints or something. Then there's my dad. He's a tattoo artist."

I give her an impressed look. "You mean he was or still is?"

"Still is. I know, he's like almost fifty. But he's not stopping anytime soon."

"And why should he?" I tell her. "My father is at the height of his…career. And he's not stopping either. Sometimes I think he should take a break and sometimes there's too much pressure on me…"

"Oh yeah?" Now she's really intrigued, chewing on that shiny lower lip. "What does he do? What does he want you to do?"

I scratch at my stubble. "He's an importer and exporter of various products. You're pretty and white, so you must like avocados."

"He grows avocados?"

"Doesn't grow them," I tell her. "He just buys them from other countries, sells them to the US, passes them across the border."

I'm not even lying, not really. The inside of fake avocados can hold an awful lot of opioids and fentanyl. If you held one in your hand, you'd swear they were real. They even squeeze the same way, smell the same way. The drugs come in, the avocados go out. Of course my father and I don't have much to do with that process, but we're the ones who orchestrate it, one of the many different ways we get the drugs where they need to go—right into the hands of the American people.

"By the way, I may be white and pretty, but I don't like avocados," she says a few beats later as we turn onto California Street.

"No avocados? You're rebellious, aren't you?" I tease her quietly. "Do you have any tattoos? Or is that not considered rebellious if your father gave them to you?"

"How do you know he gave them to me?"

"Lucky guess."

"Yeah, well, I guess it's not such a bad-ass statement when your father does it. But yeah, I've got them. The only one you can see right now though is this one." She peels back the sleeve of her jacket to reveal a highly-detailed Death Star from Star Wars with the word RESIST underneath.

"Resist, persist," I say, finding myself warming to her. "You're not just rebellious, you're part of the rebellion."

She laughs. "I wish. My parents taught me to question everything and so…that's what I've been doing." At that, her brows pull together, as if an unpleasant thought has slid into her brain. I want nothing more than to erase whatever thoughts she's having that make her look less than happy. I think, no, I know I could make that happen too, if she gives in to me. The thought of her naked on my hotel bed, eyes rolling back in her head while I count her tattoos with my tongue. She'd have no thoughts, no worries, except me.

Vicente will be the only name on her lips.

"That's probably what makes you a great photographer," I tell her. "Questioning everything you see, never taking anything for granted. Plus, you're observant. You noticed me in the café the other day before we even met."

"Yeah, well," she says quietly, tucking her hair behind her ear. "It's impossible not to notice you."

I grin at her, wondering how much I must look like a wolf.

A couple of minutes later and we're at the hotel and waiting in the lobby for the valet to bring the car around.

"Nice place," she says, looking around. "I've never been inside. I hear the restaurant at the top is hella cool though."

"Top of the Mark?" I repeat. "You mean, where I'm taking you for dinner tonight?"

"Dinner?" she repeats. Her eyes open wider.

"Yes. It's only fair. You show me around the city, the

best places to photograph, I'll take you out for dinner."

"Yeah, but we're taking *your* car," she says.

"Let's just say my generosity knows no bounds."

Just then the Mustang swings around in front of the hotel. Fucking driver took the corner a little sharply, absolutely no respect.

I consider cutting him down while he gets out of the car, but instead, while Violet is in awe over the vehicle, I slip the valet a ten dollar tip, holding on to his hand a little longer, my eyes telling him to watch himself.

He's intimidated. He takes the money, thanking me profusely, and backs off.

"I can't believe this is yours," Violet exclaims softly, turning to face me.

I flash her a smile. "Believe it. And get in."

Moments later I'm pulling the cherry-red muscle car out of the hotel's driveway and we're screaming down California Street like a scene from a classic film. Violet's red fingernails grip the dashboard as she squeals in a mix of fear and delight, her cries getting louder as we burn through green lights until we brake to a hard stop near the ferry building.

"Holy shit," she says, looking at me in awe. "I've always wanted to pretend to be Steve McQueen."

She's breathless, her face flushed, eyes bright and shiny. She looks like sex. It takes all my control to keep my hands on the wheel, my attention on the road. That heated urge to possess her is climbing through my veins and I have to take a deep steadying breath to quell it. I'm not used to having my desires kept in check—I've always been brutally upfront about what I want. But with Violet, I have to be careful. I can't scare her off.

And honestly, I don't want to. Every moment I'm spending with her is another layer unwrapped, and another challenge lying in wait.

I love challenges.

San Francisco is a hilly collection of one-way streets, and while I obviously don't know the city well outside of what I learned from the guidebooks, I take the car down the Embarcadero, past the piers and the trams that trundle between Phoenix palms, past yacht clubs, beaches, Crissy field, until Violet is telling me to pull over.

"I thought you were directing me to old Fort Point," I say, gesturing to the decaying old military fortress beneath the pillars of the Golden Gate Bridge.

"Too cliché," she says, getting out of the car. "Come with me."

We stop at a café where I buy her a decaf latte with almond milk, and then head out onto Torpedo Wharf which sticks out into the bay like a broken thumb.

At the end of the pier, we find a spot where no one is fishing and she leans against the wood railing, staring silently at the bridge.

The fog is continuing to roll in, bringing a briny mist that you can taste. Only the tops of the bridge remain visible, the orange red seeming to glow against grey skies, while shadows of the structure come and go as the fog moves in.

Violet stares in quiet fascination, her dark eyes taking it in. I can see the fog reflected in them, giving her an eerie quality. She appears to be listening but whether it's the fog horns, the chatter of the fishermen, the lapping waves, or the dull roar of the bridge traffic, I don't know. Could be something else entirely.

I don't want to break her concentration or bring her back from whatever world she's in. I just stand beside her and let her be. If anything, it says a lot about her comfort level with me if she lets herself drift away.

After a few minutes, she slowly turns to me and blinks. "How long did you say you were going to be in San Francisco for?"

"I don't know," I say carefully. "It depends if I find what I'm looking for."

"And what are you looking for?"

"A reason to stay." I hold her gaze with mine. The sea breeze picks up a few strands of her hair, moving them across her face like a black veil. Without thinking, I reach over and brush them away, tucking them behind her ear.

I could kiss her. I should kiss her. The feel of her skin against my fingers ignites a million torches inside.

Then she looks away, uncomfortable, the silence between us changing.

I steer the subject onto her. "You said your mother is a famous photographer. Does she have a studio?"

She lets out a soft sigh, her eyes back on the bridge. "Yeah. In the Mission District."

"And you don't want the same for yourself?"

She rubs her lips together in thought before looking down at her hands that hang over the side of the railing. "As I said, I don't know what I want. I'm not sure I feel comfortable with the idea of having a studio. My mom does portraits of people. That's not what I like to shoot."

"Not a people person?"

A wry smile cracks her lips. "No. Not really. It's too…

intimate. My mom is great at it because people feel comfortable with her. She can…I don't know, manipulate their feelings."

Interesting. Very interesting.

People like my father.

"So they end up exposing pieces of themselves that they don't see. I guess I have the same intuition as her but the one on one is too much for me. I prefer to work with nature. With this." She gestures to the fog. "No one else really understands how beautiful this is to me."

I look back at the fog, moving faster now. I wouldn't call it beautiful. Moody. Dark, maybe. If anything, her beauty stands out more because of the bleakness around her.

"My goal is to take photos that show how I see the world. All the beauty in it. The world is such an ugly and beautiful place, horrible and hopeful. I want to show the light in all the dark places." She pauses and gives me a sheepish look. "Sorry. I know that must have sounded hella pretentious."

I slowly shake my head because she sounds anything but that. She sounds real. She sounds like something I want to shake loose from her, to let free and run wild.

"You're not pretentious," I tell her, my voice low. "Not even close."

"That's not what I hear."

"What do you hear?" I move in closer to her, the distance between us just a few inches. She doesn't back up. "What does the world tell you you are?"

I watch her swallow, take a moment. "Oh, you know. I'm too self-absorbed. Narcissistic. Pretentious. I live too much in my head, I'm too anti-social, too distant. I feel too much, care too much. My mother has always chided me for being too sensitive and then I was diagnosed with having hyper-sensitivity, so it turns out she was right. I *am* too sensitive. About everything. And there's not a single thing I can do about it except know that when I experience reality, it's not what everyone else experiences. For better or for worse." She sighs. "Mainly for worse."

I feel like this is something she doesn't unload on many people. My instincts about her were right. She's fragile but not weak, too much a part of the world and too much removed from it. A contradiction.

"I'm sorry," she says, shooting me a glance. "I didn't mean to blab away like that. I know you probably think I'm crazy now. Hell, *I* think I'm crazy half the time. I really wish I could just be like everyone else. To just…shut it all off."

"You're not crazy," I tell her. "I'm just understanding you better."

Her mouth quirks up into a dry smile. "I'm surprised you understand me at all. We've only just met."

"True," I tell her as I reach out and run my fingers along her jaw, tipping her chin up. "But I'm sure you of all people would know that sometimes you can connect with someone in ways you didn't think you could. Or should."

She barely nods, her eyes focused on mine, anticipation on her brow. I'm met with the overwhelming desire to protect and shield her which is extremely inconvenient, if not unwelcome, given the circumstances. One minute I need to fuck her, the next I need to protect her, and in the end, what I really need is to do the job I set out to do.

I abruptly drop my hand away from her chin and nod at the bridge. "Okay, so if you're seeing something different, show me what it is."

A flash of rejection moves across her brow but she quickly shakes it off and fishes her camera out of the bag. I ask her mundane questions as she sets up the shot, what's her aperture, speed, things I know little about, and she answers with full confidence, like she's teaching a class.

She spends about ten minutes getting all the photos she needs, her brow furrowed, her lips pursed as she works, completely immersed with no sign of being self-conscious. She's in her zone. I'm not even there. I can watch her intensely, every little move and mannerism, and she doesn't even notice.

When she's done, she tells me to do the same, but I tell her I'm here to learn from her and that's all. So we head back to the car and we snake up toward the bridge, parking at one of the lots.

"I've never walked across the bridge before," she says as we sit in the car.

"Really?"

She shakes her head. "I've been too afraid."

"Fear of heights? Vertigo?"

"No…more like, I'll fling myself off if given the chance." She tries to look reassuring. "Don't worry, I'm not suicidal. And I know I won't do it. It's just…I fear that I might."

"Fear of losing control."

"I guess. Fear of dying. Fear of those ten seconds as you fall, feeling everything too much for the last time. But you'll hold on to me if anything happens…won't you?"

I can only stare at her for a moment. So far she hasn't ceased to fascinate me. "Of course I'll hold you. The whole way."

And even though I can't remember the last time I held

a girl's hand—maybe my sister's when we were young—when we get out of the car, I hold on to hers. Small, cold and slowly warming in my grasp.

It feels natural. Disturbingly so.

Heights don't bother me in the slightest, but even then, the walk across the bridge is disorienting. Maybe it's the amount of people who are walking, the long span of the bridge which is more up and down than you realize, the cars whizzing past, the fog that twists shapes and throws you off balance. Nevertheless, I stay between her and the tall fence that separates us from certain death.

We don't say much to each other but her hand squeezes mine on and off. I can feel the waves of worry flow in and out of her, and at one point when a pedestrian bumps into her, my arm shoots around her waist, holding her tight. I don't loosen, I don't let go.

By the time we get to the other side and back, we're both tired, her face ruddy from the cold mist, and I'm chilled to the bone. I'm not used to this weather. The steam of the tropics is much more preferable to the cold and damp.

"Where to next?" I ask her as we get in the car. Neither of us took a single picture on the bridge. We were too alive.

Her face seems to crumple before me. "I'm so sorry. I just realized that I should probably go home for dinner." She pauses. "I'm just exhausted. I think I need to stay home and rest."

To be honest, I wasn't expecting her to agree to dinner anyway. It's not like I even asked, I just demanded, and that doesn't work out for me all the time.

Still, I ask, "Are you sure?"

She nods. "Yes, but how about tomorrow?" She says

this quickly, as if I'll change my mind. "I mean, it doesn't have to be anywhere fancy or anything. I could cook you dinner, I make a mean spaghetti Bolognese, but my parents are…well, I mean I live with them so that might be kind of awkward."

"I would love to meet your parents," I tell her.

Her chin jerks inward. "Really?"

"Absolutely. Love to meet these interesting artists who raised such a talented daughter. But how about we save that for later this week? Tomorrow, I'll take you out. Top of the Mark if you wish, or any place you choose."

"No, that's fine," she says. "It would be fun to go somewhere nice. I'd love it."

"All right. The least I can do is drive you home, then."

Through all my research I've been unable to get the McQueen's address, but I'm not surprised to find they live just a couple of blocks over from Sins & Needles in a narrow three-story row house that must cost well over a million dollars.

I glance at Violet as we pull up to the curb. *How do you think your parents can afford this place? Through tattoos and fancy photographs?*

She looks at the house anxiously as she opens the door. "Thanks for everything."

I should follow her to the door, tell her I'm just looking out for her. I should insist on meeting her parents. I should drop the charade.

But I don't drop anything. I'm becoming the charade.

I tell her I'll see her tomorrow.

Then I drive off.

Javier

Sinaloa

J AVIER BERNAL STANDS AT THE EDGE OF HIS PROPERTY, where the lush lawn starts to peter out into the thick jungle that continues all the way down to the ocean's edge. He narrows his eyes at the lumps of rocks that scatter along the grass and feels his heart rate go up a notch.

This was where he was going to put in his beloved koi pond, one of the first things he vowed to do when they took over this land a few years ago. But time, as usual, got away from him. Now there is just a pile of rocks that represent the best of intentions.

He's surprised at the bitterness welling in his throat. It

seems the older he gets, the more his intentions lose their hold. It's been a nonstop climb back to the top and he's getting tired. He needs someone with new life to run the show.

Someone like Vicente.

But Vicente hasn't yet been broken. Javier knows you have to break the boy to create the man. And there's no one to break him but Javier. Sometimes you have to hurt the ones you love to make them stronger, and while Javier would fight to the death to protect his son, he also knows he's the only one who can make Vicente the man he needs to be, even if it destroys both of them in the process.

It breaks Javier's heart.

Having to do this to him.

"Javier?" Luisa calls out softly from behind him. He doesn't turn around but he relaxes slightly when he feels her thin, soft arms wrap around him from the back. "What are you doing?"

"Dreaming," he answers. The more in the dark his wife is, the better. She wouldn't quite agree. Then again, she babies Vicente too much. "Do you remember when we were first together, that old compound? I would find you down by the pond, staring at the fish."

"I was planning my escape," she says mildly.

He nods. "Do you think you would have been better off, in the end?"

"Are you serious?" She lets go and comes around in front of him. The dire puzzlement on her face is a tonic to him.

He gives a half-hearted shrug. "If you had escaped, you would never have had to live the life of a wife of a drug lord."

Her puzzlement turns to annoyance, which makes him chuckle inside. There's no one more beautiful to Javier than his wife, yet when she gets feisty and riled up, her beauty is increased tenfold. He's nearly in awe of it, even still.

"Need I remind you that for the last twenty years or so, I've been an equal partner in these operations, not just your damn wife," she says viciously, poking a long-fingered nail into his chest. "I'm not like the rest of those fucking women, sitting around with the other wives and talking gossip and discussing your mistresses. Without me, you never would have risen up."

Javier raises his brows, wondering briefly if that's innuendo or not. She does tend to get turned on when she's on fire. "You're very right, dear Luisa." He grabs her finger and raises it to his lips, gently sucking on it.

She tries to glare at him but her eyes soften into liquid pools, dark as teakwood, and he can see her pulse moving delicately along her throat. He's been worried about her lately so to see this zest return is nothing less than comforting.

"And need I remind you," she says, hesitantly taking her finger away, "that I chose not to escape. I chose to stay with you. I chose you and all of this, all the ups and all the downs. If I had left, we wouldn't have Vicente or Marisol. I would have never known this peace."

"Are you at peace?" he asks curiously. He's not sure if he's felt peace for more than a minute of his life. Maybe while he's coming inside Luisa and the seconds afterward, or the moment he pulls a trigger, ending someone's life. That peace is fleeting though.

But Luisa doesn't seem so certain either. She looks

away, toward the rocks where the pond should be. "I have moments of it. That's enough."

"Javier," Oscar Barrera's voice comes from behind them.

What fucking now? Javier thinks. *Can't I stand here and admire my nonexistent pond in peace?*

But when he turns around with a heavy sigh to face Barrera, he sees he has news.

"Vicente's card has been used at the Intercontinental," Barrera says. He's Javier's right-hand man now that Vicente is gone, and has been monitoring his whereabouts when he can. Not that there have been any whereabouts to go by.

Javier wasn't that surprised to lose contact with Tio and Nacho though he admits it happened rather quickly. It only made him admire his son more.

"Oh, thank god," Luisa says, hand to her chest. "Can you be sure it's Vicente using the card and no one else?"

Ever since they lost Tio and Nacho, she's been worried, *too worried*, Javier thinks, that something happened to Vicente as well. She doesn't seem to understand exactly what Vicente is capable of, and it's quite clear by now that their son has no problems disposing of the people who were meant to protect him.

Then again, Javier knows they were never meant to protect him at all, merely watch and report. Vicente doesn't need protection over there, not yet.

"We can't be sure," Barrera says patiently, "and Vicente is most likely booked in the hotel under another name. The hotel was booked through a website. Two thousand dollars a night."

"Jesus," Javier swears, exchanging a look with Luisa. "The girl better be worth it. All right, well. This is good news. It tells us he's still in San Francisco. Let's send Parada out on the first flight tomorrow morning."

"Why tomorrow when he can go now?" Luisa says.

"Patience," Javier says, giving her a slow smile. "These things take time. You know this by now."

She lets out a ragged sigh and heads back toward the house with Barrera. Javier turns back to face the rocks and starts mentally landscaping the place all over again.

Dear son, he thinks, *let's see how alike we really are.*

Violet

MUST BE GETTING PLAYED.

There's no other explanation.

I mean, seriously.

Vicente is handsome as hell, loaded, beyond charming, and exceptionally smooth. Half the stuff that was coming out of his mouth yesterday would have made any girl groan at the inherent over-the-topness.

But I didn't groan. Because I know they aren't just lines. He means them.

Doesn't he?

I'm staring at myself in the bathroom mirror this morning, trying to figure out what he could possibly see in me. Don't get me wrong—I might be a snowflake but

I'm no Mary Sue. I know I'm attractive in my own way, it's just that way doesn't always attract the right men, at least not the men I want. I'm not tall, skinny, blonde and tanned with big lips, flat abs, and perky boobs. Okay, maybe my boobs are on the perky side, and so is my ass, but that's from all my kickboxing and training. It's big, all muscle, as are my thighs, and I do have strong arms and a strong stomach (covered underneath a layer of pinch-worthy flab, of course).

Body aside, I do have a good face. But it's not sunny, sexy, and open. It's the face that either makes men shrivel away from me or prompts them to say, "Smile, it's not all bad." I wish I had a clever comeback for every time I've heard that.

I honestly have never had a man so into me and so bold about it, and who also makes my heart do somersaults.

I know I shouldn't question it. I should just accept it.

Easier said than done.

"Violet!" my mom yells from downstairs. "I'm going!"

I glance at my phone. My mother is driving me to school today on the way to the studio. My makeup is only half done, so I shove the rest into my makeup bag and pull my hair back into a low ponytail. I don't know exactly what I'm expecting tonight other than dinner, but I did shave my legs and bikini line, so there is that. Just before I'm out the door, I grab a couple condoms from my drawer and put them in my purse.

Just in case.

I totally just jinxed myself, I know.

My mom is waiting impatiently by the door with her arms crossed. She looks more stressed than usual, her mouth set in a firm line. When she sees me, her expression softens.

"You look nice," she says, eyeing me up and down.

"Thanks," I tell her as casually as possible as I walk out the door and down the steps to the street. I'm wearing pointy studded black boots with kitten heels, probably the nicest boots I own, having haggled on eBay for them, black leggings, and a maroon long-sleeve dress with a low and lacy neckline. I left my beloved leather jacket behind since it's probably too faded and banged up for a fancy restaurant, and I have a black satin bomber jacket on instead (a cheap find but it doesn't look it).

"Going somewhere after class?" she asks, suspicious, wheels turning.

I shrug as I stop by the passenger side of our grey Jeep, waiting for the doors to unlock before getting inside. Dad has an old muscle car similar to Vicente's, a black '73 Challenger, but it's in our tiny garage and he never takes it out.

"Why so secretive?" she asks as she starts the engine, not letting it go.

I give her a look that says, *Are you kidding me? You should talk.*

"What?" She wiggles her fingers around me. "You've got this mysterious aura about you. I'm just curious. It's a good thing."

"That you're curious?"

"That you've got something going on."

"I never said I have anything going on."

I'm not even sure why I'm keeping Vicente from her. I mean, he did say he wanted to meet my parents, which is both crazy and promising all at once. I guess I'm afraid that since I just met him and we haven't really been on a date, I don't want to jinx anything. I feel like I'm already doing that with my shaved legs and matching bra and panty set.

My mom doesn't say anything else. She looks a little crestfallen as she drives down the hill, enough that it makes me feel bad. It makes me shove my animosity over my grandfather aside for now and try and reach out.

"I met a guy," I tell her, resisting the temptation to pick at the edges of my nail polish.

"Oh?" She sounds surprised. I can't blame her. I think at one point she assumed Ginny and I were dating, and it probably made her happy.

"Yeah. As in literally just met him. So don't worry, I haven't been keeping you in the dark."

"That explains why you're looking hot," she says, glancing at me with a small smile.

"Mom."

"So when did you meet him? What does he do?"

"I met him on Monday. He's an aspiring photographer and he was trying to get Anderson to accept him into the school."

"Oh, really?" Now she sounds impressed. I usually dated musicians. This would be the first time for a photographer.

And you're not dating, I remind myself.

"And did he get into the school?" she asks.

"I don't think so. He was willing to pay his way in, but Anderson wasn't having it. But I said I would teach him what I know."

Now my mom is grinning at me. I wish she would do it more often since it makes her look a decade younger.

"That's my daughter. Hey, maybe you'll find that teaching is your calling."

"Maybe."

"So what's his name? How old is he?"

"His name is Vicente. I'm not sure how old he is, maybe mid-twenties?"

"Vicente," she muses, then shrugs a shoulder. "Nice name. Very poetic."

"He's Mexican. Born in the U.S., so I guess he's a dual citizen, but he spent most of his life in Mexico."

Her posture stiffens at that. Her jawline twitches. "Do you know where in Mexico he was raised?"

"No idea. I know his dad is like a farmer. Or something to do with selling avocados."

She nods at that, seeming to relax. I guess she's back to acting odd again. "And he's here for the school or…?"

"I don't know. He said he came here to discover his roots, where he was born, and that it's the perfect city for photography."

"That's very true. Well, I'm glad you've met a nice guy." She gives me a sideways glance. "He is a nice guy, right?"

"Yes," I say, exasperated. "Very nice. Very…smooth. Says all the right things."

She cocks a brow. "Oh yeah? You better watch out for guys like that."

"Are you speaking from experience?" I look at her. "Is that how Dad won you over? Smooth lines?"

She laughs, loud. "Oh Jesus. Violet. You've met your father, haven't you?"

I can't help but laugh too. "I guess since you met him in high school, he probably wasn't the coolest." I'd seen photos of my parents back then. Dad looked like a Marilyn Manson wannabe with nerd glasses to boot.

"Hey, your father would surprise you in more ways than one," she says.

The image of the newspaper clipping pops into my head. "I have no doubt about that," I tell her.

"Anyway, I just want you to be careful with this guy. That's all."

"Why? You're always badgering me to go meet someone."

"First of all, I don't badger you. Second of all…I know you can take care of yourself. That's why we rarely worry about you in these kind of situations. It's just…trust me, sometimes the guys who have all the right things to say have the right things to say for a reason."

"I'm pretty intuitive. I'll back out if things get weird."

She nods a few times, chewing on her lip. "I know you are. And I'm glad. But…trust me. All the intuition and intentions in the world can go out the window when you sleep with someone. Especially if you're stupid enough to fall in love."

"Mom…"

"Just try and keep your mind intact, that's all. Don't let a few orgasms shield you from the truth about someone."

I scrunch up my nose. "Who said I was going to sleep with him?"

"Violet, you have a whole bunch of condoms in your bag and you already have that glow going on."

I glance down at the purse at my feet, the condoms visible. Damn, she's observant.

"And, sweetie, it's fine. I just know how easy it is to be

charmed by someone."

I stare at her oddly. "Other than Dad, you mean? Because you were high school sweethearts…"

She swallows. "Yes. But don't think other people haven't come and gone in my life. Everyone meets a silver-tongued serpent at some point."

Silver-tongued serpent. I know the phrase is supposed to make me feel wary about Vicente but instead it only turns me on. I envision him licking the glass the other day and wonder what it would feel like to have him lick up the sides of my legs, those intense eyes staring right into mine.

I'm not even sure I can handle that. That's where my mom has pegged me wrong. She thinks that I'll lose all control over my emotions and judgment the moment I sleep with Vicente. The fact is, I almost wish for that happen. With all the guys I've slept with—and there's only been three—I've never been able to disconnect from my brain and logic, which unfortunately means I've never experienced sex the way it should be.

Unless things change with Vicente, I think. But as smooth and sensual as he may be, I think he's going to have an uphill battle.

Once at school, I have a hard time focusing on the tasks at hand. Usually I'm such a perfectionist in my work, but my thoughts keep drifting to Vicente, and the more I think about him, the more nervous I get. He said he was going to come get me when class is over at four, which barely gives me any time to prepare.

Even Ginny, who is normally oblivious, picks up on it. "What's going on with you?" she whispers to me, leaning across the aisle. "You're jumpier than normal. And that's saying a lot."

"It's nothing," I tell her, trying not to fidget and to concentrate on whatever the hell Anderson is talking about.

"Nothing, my ass," she says. I feel her eyes on me, staring. "What's with all the cleavage?"

"Why, am I turning you on?" I say dryly.

"Phhfft, you wish."

At least that gets her off my back.

But when class is finished, I'm drowning in my nerves again. If he doesn't take me for a drink before dinner, I'm going to insist.

Ginny still knows something is up because she's hanging around me as I grab my books, eyeing me like a detective on a case. I can only hope that Vicente is across the road.

Nope.

The moment we get out the door and onto the street, Vicente is right there, breaking into a gorgeous grin when he sees me. I swear I can feel it all the way to my toes.

"Hey," he says, coming over to me. To my complete surprise, he leans over and kisses me on the cheek. I can feel that deep inside too.

I nervously look over at Ginny who's staring at us in both shock and annoyance.

"Hi, I'm Ginny," she says, roughly sticking her hand out between us for Vicente to shake.

"Ginny," Vicente says, taking it in stride. "I'm Vicente. Violet's friend."

Friend? Well, at least he's not assuming anything.

"I'm also Violet's friend." She shoots me a glance through narrowed eyes. "Though apparently not a very good one since this is the first I'm hearing of you. *Vicente.*"

"Perhaps she didn't want to make you jealous," he says lightly.

She snorts. "Right. You're obviously new in town, aren't you?"

"Yes. Violet has been kind enough to show me around. Tonight I'm taking her out for dinner to return the favor."

"Top of the Mark," I tell her gleefully.

"Nice," she says flatly. "Anyway, I suppose I should let you both go on your way." She pokes me in the arm. "If you don't text me tonight, I'm showing up at your door. Got it?"

I wait until she has walked away and is out of sight before I turn to Vicente. "Sorry about that. She can be a bit abrasive."

"I like her," he says. He nods to the hill. "Shall we?"

I look behind me at the bar, wondering if it makes me sound silly to suggest getting a drink. I don't want him to think he makes me nervous.

"I have champagne chilling in the room," he says.

My brows shoot up. *What?*

It's like he already knows me on another level.

He watches me, an amused smirk coming across his lips. "Don't worry. We can go to the bar if you want. I just figured you might want to be somewhere a little more comfortable to have a drink before dinner. Somewhere where we can control the lights, the music, the scene. Somewhere you can feel in control."

He knows the right things to say, that's for sure, because the longer I'm around him, the more I feel control slipping out of my fingers.

We head up the hill, my cheek still tingling from where

he kissed me while we talk about the weather (it's supposed to get hot and sunny tomorrow, which often happens in the fall) and the Hardly Strictly Bluegrass festival in Golden Gate Park over the weekend.

"I'm not a fan of country music," he says as we approach the hotel, "but I would love to take you."

"My brother Ben is coming up with some of his friends," I tell him. "We could all go. And they don't just play country or bluegrass, there's a range of different music. A billionaire puts it on every year and it's free for everyone and anyone."

"You want me to meet your brother? Sure."

I realize that Vicente must think I'm using Ben as a buffer, but I'm not. There's no need for that, especially as I'm going up to his hotel room right now.

Once I'm in the hotel and we're going up the gilded elevator, I'm nervous again. I got a glimpse of myself in the mirror as we stepped inside and it's burned into my brain. My face staring back at me, white and clear. Not quite fearful, just…alive.

"Here we are," Vicente says as we stop outside his room. He swipes the keycard and holds the door open for me.

It's like stepping into someone's apartment. I've been in houses smaller than this suite.

There's a huge marble kitchen with stainless steel appliances, a dining room, living area, two bathrooms, and two bedrooms. While I wander about taking it all in (how the hell does he afford this?), Vicente pops open the champagne. He wasn't kidding about that either.

The most stunning thing about the whole suite is the floor-to-ceiling windows with the city and bay laid out at their feet. The fog is lighter today, and we're mostly below it, giving us a full view.

I could study it for hours. In fact, I barely notice that I've perched on the edge of a plush armchair, one hand against the glass, both afraid to get closer and wanting to feel more.

Vicente stands beside me. "Quite the view," he says.

But when I manage to tear my eyes away, he's staring at me, holding out a glass of champagne.

"Thank you," I tell him, taking a small sip. It's hard not to chug the whole thing, but as much as I want to relax I also feel like I should stay on my toes.

"Do you mind if I ask you a favor?" he says as he walks back to the kitchen to grab the champagne bottle.

"No," I tell him, my heart thudding loudly in my ears.

He brings the champagne over to me and sets it at my feet. "Do you mind if I take your picture?"

I frown. "Like, now?"

"Yes. Now. Just…like this." He waves his hand in the air, gesturing to me, to the city. "But without the jacket. I want to see your tattoos."

My throat feels thick. I try to swallow another sip of champagne. "Why?" I manage to say.

"Because you inspire me," he says before turning around and going through his camera bag on the coffee table. I watch as he pulls out a brand-new Nikon, the kind of camera I've been saving up for.

He notices my envious gaze because he raises it up. "Tell you what. You let me take your pictures, you keep the pictures and the camera."

"What?" Now I'm doubly confused.

"It's only fair," he says, flicking it on and going through the settings.

I chew on my lip for a moment before guzzling back half the glass of champagne. "But why do you want to take my picture if you're going to give the pictures to me anyway?"

"Because I want to show you what I see. You said that's why you love photography, because you can expose the light in all the darkness. I want to do that with you. I want you to see the beauty that you can't. See what you look like through my eyes."

Damn Vicente. Just, damn.

I don't even know what to say. This man is getting under my skin like no one has before. So I grab the champagne and pour another glass because I think I'm going to need it.

"I don't need the camera," I say softly, the bubbles from the glass tickling my nose.

"It's yours, whether you take it or not," he says, walking over to the light dimmer switch so the room is filled with a soft rose glow that seems to stretch out into the endless grey of the city.

"What do you want me to do?"

"Just take off your jacket," he says, coming closer. "Or I can take it off for you…"

"I can manage." I put down the glass of champagne and slip my jacket off, tossing it onto the chair cushion behind me.

He makes a sound of disappointment as his eyes rake over me.

"What?" I ask.

He's shaking his head slightly. "You had to wear a dress that covers everything."

"We're going to a fancy restaurant," I explain. "I didn't want my tattoos to be on display. Not that I have many on my arms."

He's watching me carefully, his eyes gleaming dark in the low light. He lifts the camera up to his face, and suddenly I feel his gaze magnified through the lens.

But he doesn't take a picture. There's no click. He's just observing, bringing the focus in and out, the lens in and out.

Oh god. I've never felt so on display before and I'm fully-clothed. I feel like he's reading me, sorting through the layers, trying to reach the bottom. He doesn't realize he won't like what he finds.

I let out a shaky breath and bring my attention back to the cityscape outside the large windows, trying to relax. "Is this all you want me to do? Just sit here?"

He doesn't answer me at first, just keeps watching. Like he's waiting for something and I don't know what it is.

"How do you feel?" he asks. "Right now."

"Right now?" I repeat. My veins feel hot, warming my body from the inside. My cheeks have to be flushed red. "I feel...stupid."

"And?"

"And? Well, I don't know. I want to finish the champagne."

"Then finish it." He comes closer, the lens still at the forefront. I've never felt such scrutiny before, never been the subject like this.

I pick up the glass and drink the rest of it, holding it

between my fingers, feeling the cold fragility of the stem. I try and concentrate on that feeling instead of everything else that's going on.

"How do you feel now?"

"Buzzed," I admit. "Better. But I still don't know why you're not taking any photos."

"Because I don't believe in wasting shots. I'm waiting."

"For what?" I ask thickly. He's shooting on fucking digital.

"To see you."

I rub my lips together nervously, watching as a low cloud skirts the top of the Transamerica Pyramid. "You don't see me?"

Again he doesn't answer. He puts the camera down gently and walks over to me until his thigh is pressed up against my arm.

My breath stills in my throat. I slowly raise my head to look up at him, trying to steady myself so I don't fall backward onto the armchair.

He reaches down and carefully runs his fingers across my collarbone, soft like feathers, until his hand slips behind my neck. He holds it gently, firmly.

I can barely breathe. Not because he's choking me, but because the feel of his palm at my neck is rendering me incapable of anything. Any thought. I'm just here and he's here, and I'm feeling everything sink into my skin.

"There," he murmurs, his voice so rich and low that it coats me from head to toe. "This is you. No thoughts. No inner world. No voices. Just you. Here with me. This is the you I want."

"You want?" The words leave my lips in a whisper.

"*Si*," he says. His hand goes up to the base of my ponytail and the other holds the back of my head still as he slips the elastic band off until my hair is cascading loose around my shoulders.

I have to admit, I feel better with it down, like it's armor.

He then crouches until he's just below me and reaches for the hem of my dress, slowly raising it above my leggings.

"What are you...?" I start to ask but then realize there's no point.

"I want to see all of you," he says softly, his eyes meeting mine as he brings the hem of the dress to my waist.

I should ask him what time dinner is. I should tell him things are getting out of hand. I should probably stop him.

But I don't want to.

I want things to get out of hand.

I'm scared to death of everything that's happening.

And I've never wanted it more.

His hands slip under the dress, hitting my bare stomach, and I gasp. My skin is sensitive, feeling the warmth of his palm like a searing sun.

He keeps his eyes on me as he moves them up, stopping just short of my breasts.

"Lift up," he whispers, tugging at the dress again.

I take in a deep breath, a long pause, before briefly raising my hips off the arm of the chair as he pulls the dress up. I sit back down then raise my arms straight up.

Vicente stands, lifting the dress up and over my head, over my arms until I'm sitting on the edge of the armchair in just my bra. I automatically lean over, trying to shield my stomach rolls from his eyes, even though my leggings are high-waisted.

"These too," he says, going for my boots now. He crouches down at my feet and unzips them, one by one. He does it all with such patience and ease, like he's enjoying every second. "Don't feel self-conscious in front of me. Let all of that go."

Easy for him to say. It's been forever since I was half-naked with a man.

"Trust me," he whispers, pulling off the boots and setting them to the side. Large hands run up my calves, my thighs, until they settle around the waistband of my leggings. His fingers curl around it as he slowly pulls them down.

I'm breathless as I watch him teasingly expose me to the room, to the city, to him. My skin erupts in goosebumps from head to toe, a contrast against my bra and underwear, gold silk trimmed in black lace.

What am I doing?

"Just like this," he says, his voice still low and settling over me like velvet. He picks up his camera and peers through it.

Finally, a *click*.

I don't even know what face I was making.

"Just relax," he says again. "Tell me about your tattoos."

Tattoos? I can barely remember them. I have to look down at my body to see them.

"Uh, I just got this dinosaur. Thought he was pretty cute."

"Dinosaurs," he muses gently.

"I was pretty obsessed with them growing up."

"Mmmm. Tell me about the snowflakes," he says. "On your shoulder. Do you think you're an ice queen?"

I give him a shaking smile, looking over my shoulder at the small ones that ink down my back.

Click, click, click.

I try my hardest to bury the self-doubt and I take a deep breath. "I was tired of being called a special snowflake for most of my life."

He lets out a small laugh but keeps shooting.

"You don't seem so cold to me, Violet."

"It's not because I'm cold," I tell him, staring off into the distance, hoping he's getting my profile and not a double chin. "In America, we call someone a snowflake if they're especially sensitive. Because snowflakes are seen as fragile and weak. And I'm, well, you know…"

"Snow is rare in Mexico. I've only seen it in other countries." This makes me wonder how many countries he's been to. "To me, a snowflake is precious and beautiful. Not fragile, not weak. You have enough of them, you create an avalanche." He pauses. "And besides, even if they're delicate, even if you're delicate, how is that an insult at all?"

I give a half-hearted shrug. "I don't know. But that's why I wanted the tattoo. To show them, the world, that I own the title. They can't insult me if I don't take it as an insult. I wanted to take the power back."

He comes closer to me and I inhale sharply as his fingers brush the hair off my back and trace over the snowflakes with the gentlest touch. I can't help but close my eyes, giving into it, my neck arching back slightly.

Another *click.*

This time, I don't mind.

"I hope you realize the strength in it. In what you have. In what you are."

I open my eyes and watch as he comes around to the front of me, his back to the windows, the camera aimed at my body.

"I rarely see the strength," I admit, my limbs tensing before the lens. "As I said the other day, it would be nice to turn the world off. To have nothing bother me. To let everything go."

"What do you think I'm trying to get you to do?" He eyes me over the camera and I'm struck by the intimacy of his gaze.

"You think taking my photo in my bra and underwear is a way to make me let go?" I let out a decidedly unsexy snort laugh.

Click, click, click.

Oh for the love of…

Now I'm hoping that I still get to keep the camera because these photos have to be the absolute worst.

"You're halfway there," he says. "I'll bring you the rest of the way."

I can only stare at him. Blink. Blink.

A grave look comes over his face. He gestures to the seat of the chair. "Slide back into it. Ass on the seat, legs over here."

Okay, now he's directing me. I do as he says, sitting in the seat with my legs hooked over one arm and my back against the other. Somehow this makes me more comfortable. Maybe he knows that.

But then he walks off into the bedroom and disappears.

At least it gives me a moment to get my bearings.

Which actually isn't the best because the more I think about what I'm doing—I mean we haven't even kissed yet—the more nuts I feel.

That feeling peaks when Vicente comes back out of the bedroom holding a tie loosely gathered in one hand.

He stops by my head. "Close your eyes."

"Why?" I stare up at him.

"Trust me."

"Why do you have a tie?"

"You'll see. Close your eyes."

But I don't. Not right away. My eyes lock with his as my heart spins faster and faster. His expression says to trust him.

I probably shouldn't.

I close my eyes.

Violet

THE SOFT SATINY FINISH OF THE TIE IS LAID ACROSS MY eyes. I try not to flinch. And fail. My nerves are all over the place.

Vicente just blindfolded me with his tie.

So much for fucking dinner plans.

I swallow anxiously as he knots it around the back of my head.

"Keep it on, try not to move much," he murmurs as he steps away. His voice sounds extra rich in the dark, his light accent making everything inside me dance.

The camera clicks away. I can't tell where the lens is aimed. I can't tell how close the shot is. I don't know what he sees.

"How do you feel?" he asks me.

"Um…weird." My throat feels parched.

"Good weird?"

"I don't know." I try to swallow. "Maybe?"

"What is your mind doing?"

"It's going a mile a minute," I admit.

Are the photos flattering?

Thank god I'm not hunched over anymore.

Where is he looking?

What is he going to do next?

Are we going to make the dinner reservation?

Is this tie his, and if so, does he have a suit? Is that what he's wearing tonight?

Vicente would look amazing in a suit.

Vicente looks amazing in everything.

Vicente is taking pictures of me while I'm half-naked and blindfolded, just laid out on his hotel chair like a piece of art, the city of San Francisco oblivious to all that's going on.

"Can you shut off that world?" he asks gently. I feel him move down toward my waist. "Can you make it go away?"

I shake my head and stop when the tie begins to slide. "No. I can't."

It's why I've always sucked at yoga.

That, and I prefer to punch things instead of stretch.

Click, click, click.

The camera fires, followed by the sound of it being placed on the glass coffee table.

Everything is heightened now. The sound of his breath. The *whoosh* of hot blood in my head. The dull roar of the city traffic below.

111

His fingers brush against my stomach.

My breath hitches.

He doesn't say anything.

He moves his fingers just below the curve of my belly until it runs along the band of my underwear.

Oh my god.

His finger teases along the underside of it. So simple, not even touching anything but a slice of skin, and yet it's terrifyingly intimate.

Everything in me tenses. My teeth grind together. I've never felt so on edge. Never felt so in the moment.

The moment.

It's wrapping around me and holding me in place.

"That's it," he says roughly. "Just be." His voice trails off as his other hand moves to my hips and his fingers curl under the satin edges.

He starts to pull my underwear down. I lift up my hips without him asking.

All at once the moment starts to lose hold of me, the voices come back in my head, the worries, the guilt, the shame.

I hope I didn't fuck up my bikini trim.

I hope he didn't expect me completely hairless.

I hope my thighs look okay.

I hope he likes what he sees.

I hope my…

My thoughts fail me as my underwear hangs from one foot and his hands go between my thighs, parting them.

Oh god.

Oh my god.

His thumbs press into my inner thighs, his fingers on

the outside, a firm hold on both legs. He stands between my parted knees.

Every single part of me is on the razor edge of anticipation, waiting, waiting, waiting for him to do something.

What does he want from me?

He murmurs something in Spanish, something that makes his voice go all throaty, like it's choking with lust.

My heart tries to climb out between my ribs.

The world slows its spin.

It's like all the planets are fixed to this place, a new orbit.

It's pretty obvious what he wants from me.

"So beautiful," he manages to whisper in English. "Violet…if you could see what I see."

I don't want to answer that because I'm pretty sure I know exactly what he's looking at. Every pink bit of me, spread for him and on display.

I have never, *ever* felt so vulnerable and exposed in all my life.

His hands start to move up my thighs, squeezing my skin as he goes.

He lets out a low moan followed by a sharp intake of breath.

I feel his gaze burning over me. I suck on my lower lip, my lungs constricting.

His hands skirt down my thighs now, to my knees.

I feel him going lower, a shuffle as he adjusts himself.

I gasp as his tongue licks at the soft skin of my inner thigh.

It feels like wet silk.

Electric.

His tongue slowly moves up, his hands gripping my

thighs, then my hips, then scooping underneath to grab a firm hold of my ass. The brush of his stubble on my skin feels unreal.

Is this really happening?

But the thought doesn't stay because all I can think about is exactly what's happening.

All I can do is *be.*

He gently kisses the softness between my legs and then I feel his tongue slide, wet and long, among my barest parts.

My body is washed with prickles from top to bottom, a heady mix of hot and cold that makes my eyes roll back into my head, my tongue want to loll out of my mouth.

With his fingers digging into my hips, he moans into me, the vibrations sending me to the moon while he shrugs me forward an inch so his mouth envelopes my clit.

Holy fucking hell.

I groan, my body completely swept away by the feeling as his tongue laps me up in long languid strokes, each one pushing my nerves to the edge. With the blindfold on, everything is heightened, and whatever shock or shame or embarrassment or vanity I had has completely disappeared and is replaced by one thing:

Need.

I want more. Need more.

His tongue is impossibly skilled, working me up and down before swirling in circles around my clit. Every second that passes, I feel my legs opening up more and more for him as I hold on to the chair cushions, as if they'll keep me from flying off this ride.

He wants me to fly off. This was his whole point.

He sure has a way of doing it.

"You taste like heaven," he murmurs, his mouth pulling away briefly while I feel his finger prod my entrance. "Better than heaven." He pushes his finger in slowly and I automatically clench around it, wanting more.

He makes a sound of amusement, like he knows what I want and he's going to take his time giving it to me.

He's a tease.

He's really taking his time.

It's…torturous.

Then, two fingers follow.

Three.

I suck in my breath, stretching around his fingers. My body might want it but it's not used to it.

"Relax," he whispers. He lifts my leg to get around to the side of the chair, his one hand still inside me, his fingers moving in and out in an aching rhythm. He grabs my bra and pulls the cup down so my breast is exposed. My nipple hardens in the air before his lips close over it.

He sucks it in, my nerves shooting in firestorms all the way to my toes.

"Oh god," I cry out as he takes my nipple between his teeth and pinches it. Bursts of hot pain radiate outward, fizzling into a heady bliss.

He soothes the pain by licking it tenderly, too tenderly. I'm practically squirming beneath him, his fingers still thrusting inside as his thumb presses over my clit.

Everything is building up, up, up.

Vicente stars licking a hot path away from my breast, up to my collarbone, which he grazes gently with his teeth.

Then nips my shoulder.

My neck.

Small bites before he starts sucking right below my ear.

I'm the lit wire at the end of dynamite, fizzing and sparking and...

"Kiss me," I manage to say as he devours my neck. "Please."

He grunts, breathless, and pulls away. I can see the shadow of him come over me, feel his hot breath on my cheek.

Nothing happens. Even his fingers have stilled inside me.

He removes them and now I am empty, aching for him. I've never felt so ravenous, so hungry, so starved. I had no idea how deprived I was for this.

But Vicente seemed to know. Says all the right things, knows all the right things.

Does all the right things.

He runs his finger over my mouth and I can taste myself on it, salty, musky, sweet. Then he reaches up and slides the tie off my eyes.

I blink up at his face, trying to focus, squinting at the light.

My world went from darkness to golden brown eyes. His gaze is so direct, so abrupt, so penetrating.

It's a vibrating line between the two of us.

Connecting, tightening.

Waiting.

Then the look in his eyes smolders, drunk with desire, and he grabs my face with one hand, the other hand going behind my neck, and he's kissing me.

Hungrily.

I can barely react. I'm overwhelmed by his mouth, by

the feeling of *him*, his warmth, his need.

If I was already standing it would be knocking me off my feet. His tongue is insatiable, explicit as it thrusts into my mouth ravenously, his lips crazed and needy. It's wet and violent and makes me throb, hot and desperate. His hand at my head is gripping my hair as if he's holding on for dear life, and each tug shoots fire through my nerves. Every part of my being feels alive, soaking it all in, desperate for more of his touch, more of him, more of everything.

I'm so fucking starved for him.

For this.

All of this.

He pulls back half an inch, just for a second, just enough time to let out a moan while his other hand holds my face in place, captive. His heavy-lidded gaze fixates on my eyes, then my lips, as if I'm some sort of apparition.

I grab his collar and yank his lips back to mine. The need in me builds and builds. I'm dying to wrap my legs around him, to feel every inch, to feel his want for me. I think I whimper. I gasp. I kiss him with the same kind of abandon as he's kissing me, his mouth all-encompassing as if wanting to swallow me whole.

I need him inside me. I'm aching, dying for it.

He knows this. He rips his shirt off over his head, tossing it to the ground then starting to undo his jeans, pulling a condom out of his pocket.

I try not to stare but I'm staring, watching with wide eyes and shaky breaths as his jeans fall to his ankles and he's wearing just his boxer briefs.

Jesus.

His body is un-fucking-real.

His skin glows, tanned from top to bottom, like he's dipped in gold, his every muscle from his thick and toned thighs, to his rippling six-pack abs and the sharp cut of his hip muscles, stands out. He looks carved by a famous artist, every single inch of his body molded to perfection.

And while my eyes roam over his wide, smooth chest, the rounded strength of his shoulders and the bulk of his biceps, they can't help but focus on his package. I couldn't tear them away even if I tried.

His boxer briefs are small, on the tight side, and red. The thin cotton material shows every single vein and the hard line of his cock as it bulges out of them, ready to burst the flimsy seams.

If I thought his fingers were too much, I'm going to have to re-evaluate things because Vicente looks like he's smuggled a python into his underwear for safekeeping.

"I guess it's only fair," he says, his voice rough and low. I manage to look up at him, at the smug expression on his face. "I got to memorize your body with my eyes. You should be able to do the same."

He slowly shifts his briefs down over his hips until his cock springs loose, dark and formidable in his palm. He strokes it from length to tip, staring at me with such heat that I feel I might burst into flames on the spot. The condom is rolled on expertly, shiny and stretched.

Then he's at me again, like a viper. He bites at my neck until I'm moaning his name and then he's picking me up off the chair, as if my legs aren't heavy with muscle, as if I weigh nothing at all.

I'm spun around, picked up, and my back is now against the glass window.

I gasp in fright, the cold pane of glass pressing into my back, while my legs wrap around his waist and my nails dig into his shoulders, holding on for dear life.

"I've got you," he murmurs into my neck.

But I can't breathe. The fear is unreal. I might go through the window at any moment. My lungs are tensing, waiting.

"Breathe," he tells me, pulling back to kiss me softly, tugging at my lower lip with his teeth. "I said I've got you. The glass will hold."

And if it doesn't? We're twenty floors up, more so because of the angle of the hill we're on. I'm starting to shake. I can just imagine the fall.

Down.

Down.

Down.

I gasp, trying to get air.

"Violet," he says softly but sternly as he reaches down, priming his cock against me. "Keep your eyes on me. Watch me. Just me."

And yet that's somehow more terrifying.

The moment he pushes into me though, it doesn't matter.

I cry out sharply, my eyes pinching shut as he enters. Everything inside me tightens, a closing fist. I'm pressed so hard against the glass, I'm afraid it will shatter, that I'll shatter.

Vicente groans, the sound making me even more wet than I already am, his lips brushing against mine. "That's it, so perfect, so sweet. Just breathe."

I try. I gulp for air and dig my heels into him, holding

on tight as he slowly pushes deeper and deeper inside. My hands grab the back of his neck, feeling the strength in his straining muscles. He kisses the length of my throat and moans into me as his hands pull my breasts out of my bra cups and his cock thrusts in.

"You're so sweet," he whispers hoarsely. "So good. So fucking good." He pulls out slightly and drives back inside, pushing me harder against the glass until I start to melt. My dancing heart leaves the fear behind. The pleasure starts to take over, a wash of warmth all over my body, making my skin feel tight and hot.

"You know how you feel to me?" he whispers.

I shake my head.

He grabs my chin with his fingers, holding my face in place. "Look at me," he commands.

I open my eyes to see his tiger eyes boring into mine. I feel like prey. I feel like a tiger myself. I feel everything as he comes at me again, arching his hips up, his cock so thick and rigid, filling me to the brim. I can feel his ass flex against my legs as he pounds deeper and deeper with intense, animalistic thrusts.

"You're everything I've ever needed," he says through a lustful groan. He bites his lip, the corded muscles of his neck straining. "I was famished, starved for you. For this."

Good god, this is too much. Being fucked against a window by this man, this man who seems so in control and yet absolutely undone by me.

"I want you starved for me," he says, voice raspy and broken. His hand slips away from my face, down to my clit, and he presses his thumb there, rubbing with each thrust. "I want you to come for me," he murmurs, kissing me quickly—hot, wet, and sweet, his tongue teasing the seam of my mouth. "I want you to come so hard, you'll swear you're falling. Again and again." He groans, his eyes fluttering closed. "Fuck."

Something changes in his pace, like a switch being flipped. He quickens, his hips like pistons, firing again and again, my whole body slamming against the glass until I'm calling his name without even knowing it.

In this moment, I fear nothing. Not my bare ass pressed against the window, not the glass breaking, not the fall. I don't fear the unknown. I don't fear anything because all I can do is chase my relief, down and down and down the spiral, desperate for it.

He is starved for me. I am starved for him.

And then it hits, generating from my core, spreading outward like a supernova, gaining speed in waves and waves and waves of stardust until it lets go, thundering in aftershocks. I'm babbling, holding him tight and letting go all at once. I stare into his eyes, I look away. I feel everything and feel nothing. I ride it out, muscles jerking, body shuddering in sharp waves.

I'm not sure I exist anywhere.

Then Vicente comes with hoarse grunts, his hips driving into me while every muscle in his body strains. With sated eyes I watch as he arches back, exposing his strong neck, his fingers gripping my hips so hard I think they might mark me forever.

Our chests rise and fall, and the room is filled with the sound of our ragged breathing.

Vicente looks at me. His dark hair clings to his forehead, the glisten of sweat lines his upper lip. His eyes have taken on a quality I haven't seen in him until now.

Vulnerability.

I feel like I'm looking at a Vicente that's rarely revealed.

Like he's sharing the inner reaches of his soul with me and me alone.

His mouth quirks up in a lazy smile.

"My Violet," he says softly, reaching up to brush the damp hair off my face. "That was a lovely appetizer."

"Appetizer?" I can barely get out the words.

He murmurs, "Yes," as he gently kisses me, slowly pulling out. "I'm only getting started."

Grabbing my waist, he steps back from the window and carries me all the way to the bedroom where he throws me down onto the bed. I bounce with a little squeal before rolling over. My heart has barely had time to slow, my head is still swimming against the tide, unable to pull itself out of the post-orgasmic bliss.

I manage to take off my bra that's somehow still on and prop myself up on my elbow, watching as he leaves the bedroom. His ass is firm, ripe like a fucking bronzed peach, and I can see why he was able to fuck me like a madman.

When he comes back, cock still long and swinging as he walks, I'm reduced to warm clay again.

He's got the tie in his hands.

He stops at the foot of the bed and stares down at me.

"Raise your hands up, above your head," he says with a quick nod.

I lie back, arms over my head, trying not to smile.

He comes over and I watch his face as he gently ties my hands together at the wrists. There's a determined slant to his brow, the way they arch and come together, but at the same time there's something so achingly gentle about it all, tying me up like he's trying to soothe me.

This man is nothing short of a mystery to me. There are so many facets, so many sides, and I never know which one I'm going to get. The man in the other room just fucked me mercilessly against the glass for the whole city to see. The man in here has nothing but quiet movements, tying me up like he's doing me a favor.

Maybe he is.

Honestly, I've only had vanilla sex before. I haven't had anything except blow jobs, missionary. Occasionally a boy-friend went down on me, sometimes we did it doggy-style. That was it. We never played with sex toys or sex games. I don't even have a vibrator (which Ginny makes fun of me relentlessly for since it's like mandatory for every female in the city).

"Are you going to be good?" he whispers to me when he's done, staring down at me, searching my face earnestly.

"What would be considered bad?"

He smirks at me. "You're already questioning things. That's off to a bad start. Perhaps I should restrain the rest of you."

I raise my brows and glance at the corners of the four-poster bed. I have to wonder if it was by accident that he got a room with a bed like this.

My heart has started racing again. I'm getting wet at the thought of what lies ahead. Maybe I'm kinkier than I thought.

"Yeah," he says, looking me over. "I think I might. You can't be trusted."

I let out a laugh, both nervous and girlish. "I think you

might have our roles confused."

"Oh, you can trust me," he says, heading over to the wardrobe. He opens it and rifles through it. I'm still staring at his gorgeously naked body.

He brings out two long loops of nylon rope.

What the…?

"Why do you have rope with you?"

He grins at me, standing at one corner of the bed. "It's for tying up hostages, of course. No Mexican travels without it."

Thankfully I know he's joking. "Where's the duct tape?"

"In my toiletry bag," he says without missing a beat, wrapping the rope around my left ankle and securing it to the bedpost. Like he did with the tie, his movements are slow and self-assured which calms me.

Kind of.

Because, oh my god.

He's fucking tying me to the bed!

"Relax," he whispers to me. "Give up control. You'll learn to love it."

While I don't think Vicente uses the rope to tie up hostage victims, I'm starting to think that with his confident ease, he has the rope with him for exactly this.

I try not to think about it, about the other women he might have been with.

He walks to the other post, tugging on my leg slightly so I'm more spread eagle on the bed, and starts tying up that ankle as well.

Any thoughts about other women are totally obliterated because now all I can think about is how fucking crazy this is.

Don't think, I remind myself. *Just be.*

I take in a deep breath and watch as Vicente slides his hand up the length of my leg and then crawls onto the bed between my thighs.

The most devious expression lies on his lips, like he's not sure what to do first.

"I thought it would be rude if I didn't finish what I started," he says, bracing his elbows on either side of my shoulders. He smiles down at me, and once again I'm unnerved at how gentle it is. It softens every rugged thing about him, making him look, just for this moment, like he might not be any older than I am.

He runs his fingers over my nose, down the hills of my lips, looking at me like he's *seeing* me, just as he did earlier, only there's no camera lens to capture it. It's his eyes that take the photos, and he's taking in evidence.

"I want to suck on every inch of your body," he murmurs. "Is that all right?" He licks along the rim of my ear, the sensation causing my skin to tingle.

I make a sound that's half yes, half begging.

He continues to move his lips and tongue down the length of my body, caressing my collarbone, my breasts, sucking hard at my nipples until I'm dizzy and nearly mad with sensation. The fact that my legs are tied and spread, my hands above my head, just adds to it, like pouring gasoline on a fire.

And I have no choice but to succumb to the flames.

My stomach shivers under his tongue, and my hips jerk under the tickle of his stubble, the sweep of his soft lips.

Finally his head settles between my legs, already parted wide for him, thirsty with anticipation. Naturally, he takes his time. He parts me open, slowly letting the rough pad of his fingertip brush over my sensitive flesh.

I'm already gasping, unable to keep quiet, to contain myself.

Then his tongue snakes out, sliding along my clit and setting off more fireworks that flame the fire inside me. My breath shakes, unstable, my fingers clawing at each other, trying to grasp the sheets. My hips lift up, wanting more of him.

He obliges, putting his mouth and lips into it. He's watching me. Those tiger eyes are watching my every movement as he gives me more and more pleasure, his teeth grazing over my clit, his tongue plunging deep inside. His head between my legs is the world's most beautiful sight, and I know I'm looking dumbfounded and crazed as I stare back at him.

The air between us crackles, lightning in a summer storm.

This is dangerous.

The thought sweeps through my head before I can hang on to it.

Maybe I need dangerous.

I can't hold his gaze any longer. I throw my head back and the world becomes hotter, tighter, as if my universe were built of a million burning stars. It grows and grows and grows, this impossible force inside me that gathers every single nerve and piece of my body until it's wound over and over again.

The slide of his tongue pulls the trigger.

"Fuck," I cry out, and he murmurs into me, his groans vibrating deep inside and kicking me over the edge. I'm going over, falling from the bridge, whistling through the wind, and my body quakes endlessly, until I'm quivering, boneless, and lost to him.

I can barely catch my breath, my chest heaving and covered in sweat. He gets off the bed, grabbing a condom from the drawer beside us.

Then he's back on the bed and he's grabbing my thighs, positioning himself. He pushes inside, still hard through all of that. I'm so wet and spent that he slides in easily, though still as huge and thick as he was earlier.

He shoves himself into me with pressing urgency that borders on profane.

I'm one hundred percent in his hands. I have no control. I'm at his mercy.

Vicente grinds into me, his hips circling as he pistons himself in and out. He is merciless, grunting hard with each thrust, this rough, animalistic noise that gets louder and louder the closer he gets to coming. It's such a gorgeous, raw noise that causes the heat to build in my core, coaxing the last bit of flames I have left.

Faster, harder, deeper. His pace is relentless. It slams me hard into the bed, the rope around my ankles digging sharply into my skin with each thrust.

Pain never felt so good.

So, so good.

And obviously good for him too. I can see him starting to lose control, dipping over the edge. His eyes burn into mine, and then he's in deep, so deep that he's shaking and muttering my name in low, guttural tones.

Before he totally loses it, he sticks his fingers in his mouth and then places them at my clit, rubbing, swirling, faster, faster.

It sets me off in a hot second, and once again I'm floating, flying, but this time I'm with him, and we're riding it together, our bodies joined inside and out. For this moment, we are one, falling together.

Vicente collapses against me, his hard body sweaty and sliding against mine. His breath is rough and steady in my ear, and his lips brush my neck briefly. I want to hold on to him, to feel his skin as it calms, but I can't move. I think my arms are asleep.

Once he catches his breath, he places a soft kiss on my forehead, then pulls out. He takes the condom off, disposing of it in the trash before he comes back and starts to undo the tie around my wrists.

He moves to my ankles, slowly unwrapping them.

He makes a *tsk* sound and I look up, shaking out my arms and trying to get the feeling back into them.

He gently runs his fingers over the welts the ropes made on my ankles, then kisses the red marks. It only stings a bit.

"Sorry," he says softly, placing my feet back down.

"Worth it," I tell him. And I mean it.

He smiles at me and holds out his hands to pull me up.

"Now, how about we get some fucking food?"

I laugh, letting him pull me to my feet. Holy shit. My entire body feels brand new.

"I have to admit, I'm not sure I feel like going to a restaurant after all this," I tell him.

"Room service?"

"Yes, please."

"Only if we can eat naked though. And maybe if I can eat dessert right off of you."

My god. This man doesn't stop.

I don't think I'd want it any other way.

I watch as Vicente drives off, the lights of the Mustang disappearing into the fog. The chilled air rushes against me as it passes, but my shivers aren't from the cold. They're from the impossibility of everything that just happened.

I look up at the house and see the light on in the living room but no shadows, no movement. I immediately start walking down the street, smiling into the night. I need time to process everything that happened. I can't be alone in my room, trying to contain myself. I can't talk to Mom and Dad. I just need to be free.

I head down to Haight, the only place that feels remotely safe at eleven at night. A lot of the bars are still open and tourists still walk the streets. I move anonymously among them with no direction in mind.

My body is humming with electricity. I feel his lips between my thighs, his teeth at my nipples, his hard length inside me. I can see his eyes, relive what it was like to lose all sense of self. It was like the opposite of time travel. No past, no future—there was nothing in those moments with him except for what was happening, sweaty second by sweaty second.

God. We were fucking animals.

I'm still in shock. There's only the new camera at my side and the sweet stiffness between my legs to tell me that what happened was real.

I was thoroughly fucked by Vicente.

Over and over and over again.

In a way I never imagined.

He made me step away from myself. He pulled me out of that prison. He opened my eyes to a reality I didn't think I could be a part of.

He made my weaknesses my strengths.

He made them raw and beautiful.

I don't see how my life can possibly go back to normal after this.

I must have walked up and down the main five blocks of this street a few times before my phone buzzes.

In a stupor I pull it out, half-expecting it to be Ginny following up on her earlier threat (my god was that only today?) but instead it's Ben. Not exactly who I want to talk to when I'm still recovering from post-coital bliss, but he rarely calls.

I pick it up. "Hey."

Even though I sound pretty fucking cheerful, he answers with a stiff, "Hey."

I decide to cross the street at Masonic and head back up the hill. "What's wrong? Are you okay?"

"Yeah. Yeah, I'm okay. I…um," he clears his throat, "was doing some research on Dad."

I can feel my orgasmic glow drain out of me and I suddenly stop in my tracks. A man in a dark blue coat who must have been walking closely behind me, bumps into my shoulder, spinning me around.

I grumble at the man who turns to the right and keeps walking down the hill. "Sorry," I say to Ben. "What did you find?"

Silence fills the line but then I hear him breathing. "Ben?" I prompt. I stand at the corner, wondering if I should head down the street or up. It's then that I notice the man that bumped into me. He's stopped, waiting a few stores down, collar up and hat down, partially obscuring a very pale face.

The hairs at the back of my neck rise.

Something's not right.

"Yeah," he says. "Sorry. It's…I found another clip online. Just something short. From 2014. It wasn't about Dad so much as about something else. He was mentioned at the end as being falsely blamed for the kidnapping of a…of a woman and her three-year-old son. But it wasn't him, it was these two brothers with ties to the mafia."

"Mafia?" First Mexican gangs, now Italian ones.

I'm aware that people are starting to crowd around me waiting for the lights, so I decide to cross with them and back across the street again, remembering to lower my voice.

"Yeah. The woman he kidnapped, I mean, who he was blamed for kidnapping. Her name was Sophia."

"Sophia?" I repeat, walking back up Haight.

I make the mistake of looking over my shoulder and see the pale man in the blue coat running across the street as the traffic starts up, a cab honking for him to get out of the way.

"Does it ring a bell?" Ben asks, but I barely hear him.

The man starts walking a few yards behind me.

My mouth goes dry.

Am I being followed?

"Are you there, Vi?" Ben asks.

131

"Yeah," I whisper into the phone, turning back around and quickening my pace. "I think someone might be after me."

"After you?"

"Following me."

"Where are you?"

"On Haight. Just about to cross to Club Deluxe."

"Who's following you?"

"I don't know. I don't recognize him."

"Cross the street again. Just make sure before you get all paranoid."

I grumble under my breath and quickly dart across while there's a gap in the traffic, ignoring the lights. Cars are honking at me now but I don't care. "Okay."

"Is he following you still?" he asks.

I look across the street and our eyes meet. His are dark, shadowed, hidden beneath a fedora. It makes his bone-white face look like a skeleton from the Day of the Dead.

I watch as he walks up to the lights at Clayton and waits, wanting to come over to my side. His dark gaze never drops from mine.

The walk signal lights up. He begins to cross.

"Shit," I swear. "He's coming across."

"Go inside somewhere busy," Ben says.

I start jogging up the street, but it's late and so many shops are closed. I glance back to see him right behind me, coming up fast.

I could run across the road. I could make a run for it all the way home. But the streets around my house are dark. I'd be safer in public. The man can do nothing to me here, right?

Or can he?

"Vi?" Ben sounds panicked.

"Yeah, going into the Rock Shop," I tell him, ducking into the massive tourist shop that sells anything to do with San Francisco, drugs, and psychedelic rock. The lights inside are bright fluorescent, the kind that normally hurt my eyes and make me feel sick, but now I welcome them.

It's not empty either, which is a relief. People are scattered among the racks of t-shirts and posters and glass cases full of patches and bongs.

"What are you doing?" Ben asks.

"Hiding. To see if he's coming in here," I whisper.

I head toward the back of the store where the rows of posters are and hide behind them, watching the front door through the cracks.

It opens.

The man in the dark blue wool coat walks in.

I suck in my breath.

In the garish lights I can see him more clearly. The brim of the fedora still casts long shadows over his face, but it's a face I can't forget. Pale, like milk, with no eyebrows. He must be albino or wearing white stage makeup. Large swaths of raised scar tissue cover his cheeks and lips.

Even the clerk behind the counter notices him, and that clerk is always stoned out of his mind. His glazed eyes follow the white man as he slowly walks inside, scanning the store.

Looking for me.

"Ben," I say in a hush. "He's in here. He's looking for me."

"Can he see you?"

"No. I'm behind the posters. I can see him through a crack."

And the minute I say that, he moves out of my sight.

Fuck.

Part of me realizes how ridiculous this is. There are at least five other people in the store, people who would help me if I needed it.

But would they?

Too many times I've heard stories of people being attacked in front of others, people who yell for help, and no one comes to their aid. People these days are too afraid to stick their neck out and help each other. There are too many guns, too many crazies, too many criminals. Even in the most liberal city in America, I wonder how many San Franciscans would take the chance.

But I can't think like that. I have to believe in the good in people, even as the world spins to an even worse future.

Run for the door, I tell myself. *The people in here will protect you. The scrawny clerk probably has a gun beneath the counter.*

Do it.

"I can't see him anymore," I tell Ben. "I'm going to run."

"Violet," Ben warns.

"Hold on." I move the phone away from my ear, clutching it in my hand like a weapon. I can hear his muffled voice telling me not to do it.

I don't care.

I need to know.

And I need to go home.

I take in a deep breath and jump out from behind the posters.

The man is ten feet away, his back to me.

He'll see me run out, but I don't care.

I start running down the aisle, bumping into t-shirts that swing on their hangers, until I'm almost out the door. I give the clerk a look, one that I hope says "stop that man if he comes after me" and not "I just stole a bunch of your merchandise."

Then I'm outside on the street and running across traffic again, almost getting nailed by an SUV, before I round the corner about to head home.

But I have to know. I pause, turn back, and go to the corner of the building, half-hidden, watching the door to the shop, watching for the man to come after me.

I raise the phone to my ear. "Ben," I tell him. "I made it outside. He hasn't followed me yet."

"Fucking just go home now. Or I'll call Dad to make you."

"I'm going, I'm going, I just have to see."

And I stand there and watch for at least another minute as my heart rate returns to normal.

Finally the door opens and the man steps out.

"There he is." I shrink back against the wall and peer out.

The man looks up and down the street then slowly starts walking up Haight toward the park.

"What's he doing?" Ben asks.

"He's walking up to Golden Gate Park. It took him forever to leave the store. He doesn't seem to be looking for me anymore."

"So maybe the whole fucking thing was in your head again?"

"Maybe," I admit.

But thinking that doesn't make me feel any better.

"I'm going home now."

"Good," he says. "I'll see you this weekend. And I need to talk to you some more…in person."

"Okay," I tell him. "See you Friday."

I hang up and take in one long inhale as the fog starts up again, sliding past me down the street like a ghost.

I'm in no mood for this film noir atmosphere.

I go straight home and try to push the last fifteen minutes out of my head.

I think of Vicente instead.

And smile.

Vicente

'M DREAMING.

I can't remember the last time I dreamed.

It feels so long ago.

Maybe I was a child.

Twelve years old, tossing in my bed, welcoming dreams to take me away from the days where I yearned to hold on to my childhood while learning how to shoot a gun.

But like in those dreams, I'm fully aware. Not in control, just an observer who quietly watches the world crash and burn.

In this dream I am in a safe house, one of the many I was shuttled into growing up. For a while there, things got pretty bad. My father didn't know who he could trust around his family.

So Marisol, my mother, and I were under watch of a family friend, Diego. Diego was the closest thing I ever had to a father. He was always old, always had a swoop of thick grey hair and a mustache I used to liken to a caterpillar. He's dead now, passed away from cancer, which in a way seems like a rarity when so many die at the hands of another. Sometimes I wonder if it was better to go like Diego did, old and in pain, having lived a long life, or to die younger with a bullet to the head.

My father was visibly upset after Diego died—he was one of his most trusted friends and certainly the one who stuck around to the bitter end. But even then, I remember my father put his hand on my shoulder and told me it was better to live like a king and die young than to die at an old age without having lived.

I always thought that was an odd thing to say, especially as my father also taught me how important family was, and how without it, a man truly had nothing.

Just another thing I'll never understand about him. Family, blood, was everything, and yet he sometimes acted like it would only get you killed in the end.

In my dream, a bare lightbulb hangs in a dark room, swinging, casting harsh light on our faces. We all sit with our backs against the wall, hands tied. Normally the safe houses are nice places, but this one has no furniture, no windows. It barely seems to be a room—it stretches into black infinity.

We are waiting for something horrible. We are no longer hiding. We are no longer protected.

Diego starts murmuring a prayer to Santa Muerte, the

Saint of Death. When I look over at him he starts crying blood, shaking his head so it flies everywhere. It lands on my cheek with a hiss.

Then the shape of a door slowly appears, a glowing white outline, like someone shining a spotlight from the other side.

The light turns red.

Violet.

The brightest purple.

The door opens and I have to shield my eyes.

A figure walks in, taking careful steps. The light blinds everything except the silhouette. Tall, in a long robe that drags as the figure walks.

It stops right in front of us. Diego's prayer fades into nothing.

This is Santa Muerte.

I stare at her feet in black combat boots before I slowly gaze upward to where bone-white skeleton legs disappear under a purple gown.

I blink into the light until I see Santa Muerte's face.

I wish I hadn't.

Though her face is just a skull, blackened with ash, with long thick black braids that hang down on both sides, her eyes glow within their dark pits.

I can feel them on me, burning through.

These are Violet's eyes.

She has become the Saint of Death.

Tonight, she has come for my family.

With revenge from her family.

"You caused this, Vicente," my mother hisses to me, and when I look at her, she's nothing but skeleton too. "You caused this."

"You caused this," says the skull of Marisol.

"You," says Diego. "For what purpose?"

"For love," I say, looking back at Death. "I did this for love."

Santa Muerte leans over, her heavy braids swinging forward until her ghoulish face is right in front of me. My eyes are locked on to her sockets, where I know Violet is, where I can feel her radiating outward like damaging rays.

Ultraviolet.

"Didn't your father ever teach you," Violet's voice, rough and demonized enters my brain, taking over my head, "that love is what gets you killed?"

Then she kisses me with cold bones.

And I am swept away into the black.

The sound of flapping wings takes over.

Then fades.

When I wake up, I'm shaking and covered in cold sweat. I can't remember the last time I had a fright like that and it takes me a moment to figure out how to breathe.

I'm in bed, in my hotel room. It smells like sex from earlier and I breathe it in deep.

Violet, Violet, Violet.

My hands can still feel her skin yielding to me, the breathless gasps from her mouth. The way she writhed underneath my tongue, her eternal sweetness filling my mouth.

The tight, wet slide as I pushed myself into her. Over and over again.

I move my hands over my cock, hard and thick already, slowly stroking up and down.

What are you doing? a voice whispers in my head. It's loud, commanding, swirling up from the deep.

I ignore it. I keep stroking myself, desperate for thoughts of her.

It persists.

Why are you even here?

What good will this do when your fun is over?

What do you really want?

Her. I want her. For now, I just want her.

I tell myself I'll figure the rest out later.

Even though I know there is no later.

Not for us.

Not ever.

Violet is the means to an end. She's a pawn in a game I'm not sure how to win.

Why are you here?

To win the respect of my father.

Why are you here?

To understand my father.

Why are you here?

To distance myself from my father.

Why are you here?

To find out how to beat my father.

And then what?

To take over the cartel. With no interference.

To become king.

To rule my way.

Then you know what you must do.
You must plan.
You must execute the plan.
Use Violet to get to her mother.
Befriend the McQueens.
Learn from them.
Then kill them all, except for her.
The reason you thought you came here.
Then take her to your father.
She's collateral.
She's a bargaining chip.
She's an offering.
And if it all falls through?
Then you're no better than he is.

I wake up again. A dream within a dream. Motherfucking inception.

I blink at the grey dawn slowly coming into focus through the open curtains and dig my nails into my arm until they bleed.

It hurts. It's enough to tell me I'm awake this time.

The voice still resonates in my head.

Reminding me of why I came here to begin with.

It was never about Violet.

And yet here I am.

I slowly get out of bed and head into the kitchen to put on a pot of coffee. While it percolates, I flip through the room service menu for breakfast options. The dishes from last night are laid out on the coffee table, and the memory of us eating it, naked, stirs something inside me that I don't wish to wake up.

We made rough plans last night to meet today after her class. Part of me wants to cancel and take the time to get my head on straight, to think about the plan and what to do next.

But the other part of me realizes that this is what I have to do next. Get to know Violet better. Earn her trust. Fuck her pretty little brains out.

It's not my fault that I want this, that I enjoy this.

I wonder if this is how my father felt?

Or was it Ellie that played him?

I'll find out soon enough.

Violet is lost in her own world.

I should just let her be.

Respect her space.

Don't get involved.

Not now. Not ever.

I have a feeling that whatever she's stewing over and the way it's translating into her stabbing her maraschino cherry with her straw repeatedly as the two of us sit side by side at an outdoor patio, along a high-top table overlooking the bay, has got nothing to do with me.

But the more information about her life she gives me, the more I can use it.

"What's on your mind?" I ask her.

It takes her a few moments to look up. "Huh?"

"You're stabbing that cherry like it's wronged you. Has someone wronged you, *mirlo*?"

"*Mirlo*?" she repeats. It sounds so cute coming from her mouth.

I run my hand over her dark hair that's shining in the sun. "You have blackbird hair. *Mirlo*, in Spanish."

"Oh." She attempts a smile but fails. Her lower lip pouts slightly and I take the opportunity to kiss it, licking the cherry juice from the inside rim.

Her eyes are closed when I pull back and she slowly flutters them open. Every time she looks at me like that, right after I fuck her, right after I kiss her, it undoes something inside me. Something that should never be unraveled and yet I'm helping her pull the strings.

"As I was asking," I remind her, running my thumb over that sweet lip.

She squints at me and then pulls her sunglasses over her eyes, a barricade. It could also be that this is the first truly sunny day since I've been here, so the sun is extra impactful, and everyone around us is dressed in summer gear. I guess that's the thing about San Francisco, all their seasons are ass-backwards.

"Wronged is a strong word," she says slowly, her attention back to the ferries darting across the bay. She's back to stabbing the cherry again. "Or maybe it's the right word, I don't know." She sighs. "Can I ask you a question?"

"Anything," I tell her, displaying my palms.

"Do you have a good relationship with your parents?"

I nearly laugh. "Do I?"

"Yeah." She's totally serious.

"Well," I begin, not sure how much to share. Then I decide, fuck it, I'm all in if she gives me her truth. "Not really. No."

"Why not?"

I open my mouth then close it, thinking, *because they aren't good people*. "It's just always been that way," I finally say. "My childhood was very…unusual. Because of my father's business."

"Selling avocados?"

I give her a half-smile. "*Si.* The avocados. My father was very busy and the job is very stressful, so I rarely saw him."

"He was away on business a lot?"

"Hmmm. Not that often. The business came to him. We lived in a big property. He was always in his office or one of the secondary houses. My sister and I were always elsewhere. We were kept very separate from what he did."

"You have a sister? How old?"

"Three years younger than me."

"And how old are you anyway?"

"Young enough to get away with everything and old enough to know better."

She frowns but I continue. "Anyway, my sister, Marisol, she was babied a lot by my mother but I wasn't so much. She got most of the love, I got the tough version of it. I guess because I was the boy. Was your brother treated differently?"

"Not really, no."

"It doesn't matter. It is what it is. My father is a man who…well, honestly, at times seems incapable of love. Which is an odd thing to say because I know he loves my mother and he loves his children. I just think it's different for him."

Just as it's different for me.

"And your mother?"

"My mother did her best with me, but as I got older I could see...things were changing. She became more distant, like she wasn't sure how to be a mother to me." I pause. "She began to fear me."

Violet stops stabbing and gives me one hell of a look. "Why would your mother fear you?"

"Because she thought I would grow up to be like my father."

"And did you?"

"I don't know yet. Time will tell, I guess."

"And...that's a bad thing?"

I shrug with one shoulder, palming my beer. "It depends who you talk to. My father is one of the most respected men in the whole country. He is also the most feared. Some might call him good because he has done a lot of good for the communities. *Avocados* are a popular business, and that business keeps a lot of people employed, and a lot of excess money goes toward funding villages and towns. Those people see him as a savior. Without him, many would suffer. Ironically, with him, many suffer as well."

"And the other people?"

"The other people want him dead."

She blinks at me. Whispers, "Dead?"

"If he's dead, they can take over the business and get all the power. Right now he doesn't have all the power. At one time, he used to. But since then he's lost a lot of it. It's been fractioned and we need to figure out a way to unite the, uh, businesses. But many still consider him *el jeffe* of *el jeffe*. He certainly does."

"Your father isn't a farmer. Is he?"

I look her dead in the eyes. "Is your mother really a photographer? Is your father really a tattoo artist?"

She swallows hard, her gaze caught in mine, eyes flecked with fear, but manages to nod. "Yes. They are."

I believe her. She knows nothing at all.

"At least…that's what they do now," she says slowly, cautiously, like she's uncertain that once the words leave her mouth, they become truth. "Sometimes I wonder… who they used to be."

"What do you mean?"

"I can't really explain it."

"Try."

Her brows knit together. "I don't know…"

"You can trust me," I tell her. "You know this."

Trust me.

She nods. "Okay. I trust you."

I supress a victorious smile.

She takes a deep breath. "This will all sound weird."

"It can't possibly after what I just told you."

"I don't know about that. My brother and I were always told that my grandfather, my dad's father, died a long time ago. He never talked much about him but we knew that much. My grandmother, of course, apparently died long ago too."

"Apparently…"

"Yeah. Well, now I don't know. Because a few weeks ago I found a letter addressed to my father. There was no return address, but it was stamped in California. Mailed locally. Inside was a newspaper clipping." She takes her phone out of her jacket pocket and quickly scrolls through it before placing it next to my drink.

I pick it up, shielding the glare from the sun, and eye the photo on the screen.

A picture of a newspaper article.

I quickly read it.

I'm surprised.

I glance at her. "Do you know what Mexican drug cartel it was?"

"No," she says softly. "I don't know any of this. Why? Do you think…do you think you could help find out? Because my brother Ben has been looking into it and…"

"What did he find?" I ask a little too sharply.

She doesn't seem to notice. "He wouldn't tell me everything. Says he needs to talk to me this weekend. But he said that he doesn't think it was a Mexican cartel. He thinks it was the mafia."

This is new. "The Italian mafia?"

"I guess. He said he found a news report from 2014 that mentioned our father in conjunction with a kidnapping attempt."

"Kidnapping?" Jesus. That wasn't in the files I found. Then again, most of the information my father had was about Ellie, not Camden.

"But my brother said it was cleared, like a mistake or something, and it was actually two brothers who had ties to the mafia that kidnapped a woman and her son."

"Violet." I put my hand on her thigh, squeezing it lightly. "When did you find all this out?"

"Like I said, I had the article for a while but Ben called me last night to tell me the rest."

"So you have to confront your parents…"

She shakes her head. "No, I need to know more. Ben can find it out. You can find it out."

"Why me?"

"Because you're Mexican."

I let out a sharp laugh. "Just because I'm Mexican doesn't mean I know anything about drug cartels."

Wry disbelief is etched on her face. "Oh, please. You can't tell me all about your father and his so-called business and not have me thinking a few things."

"But the article your brother found—"

"I know. But the article I read, the one here," she picks up her phone, "mentioned a Mexican cartel. I just want to know something, anything."

"And then what happens? What if you find out it's the Sinaloa cartel? Or the Zetas? Or who knows what fucking cartels existed way back when. Then what? You going to stroll down to Mexico and go knocking on their doors?"

And then, as I'm saying those words, it dawns on me.

Shit. Has Violet been playing *me*? Has she let all of this, all of us, happen, because she thinks *I* might lead her to the truth?

If only she knew how close she was.

I can never let her know.

She sighs, shaking her head, eyes getting watery.

Fuck.

I rub my hand up and down her thigh. "Hey. Look. I'll…ask my father. How about that?"

Oh, if only you fucking knew.

"No, no," she says. "You just said you don't get along. I'll just…it doesn't matter. I'm just scared."

"It's natural to be scared when you're presented with a

lie. Especially when it turns your world upside down."

She sucks in her lower lip, staring across the bay. "Someone was following me last night."

"What?" I jerk to attention, my fingers digging into her leg. "When?"

She frowns at the pressure and I ease off. My heart is starting to pound.

Following her? Could it be one of my father's men already?

"Last night," she says. "When I was on the phone with Ben."

"I dropped you off at home," I tell her roughly, angry she didn't go straight in.

"I know, but I was too…excited. To sleep. So I walked up and down Haight to burn off the energy."

"You should *never* walk there alone."

Her withering stare cuts into me. "Oh, come on. Sorry, Vicente, but I've been taking care of myself just fine before you came along. You don't even know the city. I do. It's my home."

"Two bodies were found shot in the head in the park close to your house," I tell her. "The person who killed them is still out there. You just said you were scared."

She rolls her eyes. "People always die in that park. Drug overdoses or drug deals gone wrong, there's no difference. And those people, they were just passing through…" She trails off. "They were Mexican, weren't they?"

"I don't know, the news never identified them."

"It doesn't matter. And the guy who was following me wasn't Hispanic at all. He was white. Very white. Like, albino white. Not that it matters, I guess."

Albino? If anyone should be here and on my case, it's Parada or maybe Barrera. Definitely not an albino.

This isn't good.

If she's honestly being followed, it makes my job that much harder.

"How do you know you were followed?"

"Because where I went, he went. Up the street, down the street, across the street, back and forth. I ducked into a store and hid, and he came inside too. I had to wait for the right moment and then I ran out. He stopped following me at that point but he was definitely following me up until then."

This guy isn't from any cartel, not my father's anyway. He sounds too sloppy. And I haven't been followed at all. I would know. It's what I've been trained for.

So why would someone follow *her*?

This is getting messy. I need to simplify things.

"I wouldn't worry too much about it," I tell her. "I'll worry for the both of us."

"Yeah, right. Okay. Sure."

"You told me yourself that you're sensitive and overly observant, and I know those things are true. I'm not saying that this didn't happen to you, but for now, you have to keep in mind that it could be a by-product of your imagination. That this man wasn't following you. That it was a coincidence."

"That's one hell of a coincidence."

"I've seen bigger coincidences, and in the end that's all they are." I put my hand back on her thigh and move it inward. She stiffens. "You're safe with me. You understand that, right? Whether someone is following you or isn't, I've got you." I slide my hand up between her legs, under her skirt. "I've got you."

She looks around tensely. Not because she thinks she's being followed, but because my fingers are further up, teasing the edge of her underwear.

"I don't think you should wear underwear anymore," I tell her, leaning in so my mouth is at her ear.

"What are you doing?"

"You know what I'm doing."

"We're in public."

"If someone is following you, let's give them a show."

The truth is, there's a potted palm tree right behind us, partially obscuring us from the other tables at our backs, we're seated at the edge of the deck right above the water, and the next couple seated down the long bar from us are too busy staring at the bay views to pay attention to what I'm doing. There isn't much of a show, unless you look for it.

I wouldn't mind either way if people watched.

I'm just watching her.

I slide my finger under the edge of her panties and find her hot, wet cunt. Her legs automatically part slightly, her lips doing the same.

Fuck. This is everything.

I love how trusting she is with me. I know that I push her boundaries. I know she hasn't had this kind of experience with men. I know she overthinks and her heart is wildly soft.

But she's willing. She's learning what she wants.

And what she wants is me.

My finger slides up over the swell of her clit, gently

rubbing in circles.

I watch her closely as my finger goes around and around. Her pulse ticks along in her throat—her heart must be racing. Underneath her sunglasses, I bet her eyes are closed, rolling back in her head.

"You like this?" I whisper, leaning over. I lick the edge of her ear before taking her lobe between my teeth and tugging.

She gasps, breathless. She can't answer. But yes, she likes it.

I lean in closer, moving my fingers down slowly, teasing her inch by inch, until I tease her cunt. "You've soaked through your underwear," I murmur. "I told you you shouldn't wear them anymore."

"Vicente," she says. My name has never sounded better. She offers it to me like a prayer.

I thrust my fingers inside, feeling her clench around me. Her whole body tightens. God, she feels so fucking snug. It's unbelievable. I'm harder than rebar, my dick straining against the fly of my jeans.

Now would be a terrible time for the waitress to stop by.

But she doesn't. It's just me and Violet and the gulls that wheel above the bay, their cries for food masking her breathless little ones as I slyly pump my fingers in and out of her, building in a quiet rhythm.

When I know I've worked her up to a certain point, I take my fingers out and drag her wetness back to her clit, sliding it over, slick and fast.

"Oh god," she says, nearly choking on her words.

She comes in my hand, pulsing, her fingers grasping

onto the table, trying to keep her body from rocking out of control.

We're in public, after all.

When she finally calms down, I take my hand away and make a point to lick each finger in front of her. She has no idea how good she tastes to me. Better than dessert.

"I can't believe you just did that," she whispers to me, clearing her throat a few times.

"Lick my fingers or make you come on my hand, surrounded by people?"

She gives me a wry, sated smile. "Both."

"Well, you should start believing it," I tell her. "Or I'll have to prove to you over and over again just how wild and crazy you make me."

"That doesn't sound like such a bad deal."

"Oh, it's not."

I pick up my drink and raise it to hers. "Now hurry up and finish your drink so I can fuck your brains out properly."

The couple down the table both look over at us in shock when I say that.

Guess it was a little bit loud.

I just give them a wink.

Fucking prudes.

Violet

"**P**UT YOUR ASS IN THE AIR."

Vicente's words slide over me like silk and I don't even have to tell my body how to act, it's already acting.

I arrange myself so my ass is raised, my head down, cheek pressed against the cool sheets.

I know I probably should have gone home after we had our date at the bar. I mean, he got me off in public. Not just in public, in broad daylight. Surrounded by people! If that's not a sign that I should probably go home before things get crazier, I don't know what is.

Plus, I have homework I need to do and it feels like I haven't seen my parents for days. But the truth is, I'm nervous about seeing them. I'm nervous that I'm possibly being fol-lowed—I don't care what Vicente says, I know what I saw and my intuition is always right.

I'm afraid for a million reasons.

And I know that he's the man who will take my fear away.

By replacing it with another fear.

A good fear.

Anticipation.

Because when the man you're sleeping with and totally infatuated with tells you he wants to fuck your brains out, it's nearly impossible to say no to that. We couldn't get back here fast enough and I was barely in the door before he was stripping me naked.

"You must learn to shut it all off, Violet," Vicente says, taking me out of my thoughts and back to the fact that I'm on his bed with my ass in the air.

God, his voice does something to me, like taking a bath in milk and honey.

"Let it all go. All of it. Every single thought and worry that's going through your head right now. You need to be in the moment, with me. The world won't disappear the mo-ment you stop holding on to it."

How is it that he can read me so well?

I hear him walk closer to the foot of the bed, feel the warmth of his proximity, the intensity of his eyes. I know they're raking up and down my body, and my skin prickles from the sensation.

"I want you to close your eyes."

My eyes are already closed.

"I want you to listen to the room."

I try and listen. I hear the fridge from the kitchen humming and a door shutting somewhere down the hall of the hotel. I hear my heart-pounding loudly in my chest, a drumbeat without end. I hear his breath getting heavier, raspier.

I hear the sound of his shirt coming off then landing on the floor.

I hear the slide of a belt being pulled out of the loops.

Then the creak of leather.

Something touches my ass and I jump, startled, my heart flying all over the place.

"Easy, *tranquilo*," he murmurs. "The belt is your friend. It will keep you here and now. If I see your brain and thoughts being sucked somewhere else, somewhere other than me, I will whip you."

Oh my god.

I pop one eye open, the other pressed into the bed.

Are you kidding me?

He's going to whip me? First the ropes, and now this?

"I will go gentle on you," he assures me, and the belt moves slowly over one cheek, dipping into the crack, then up and out. "The only pain you'll feel is the pain you want. The pain that will bring you back into the here and now." He pauses. "*Lo entiendes*?"

Fuck, I love it when he speaks Spanish.

"*Si*," I tell him. "Speak to me in your language."

I can hear him smiling. "You won't understand what I'm saying."

"It doesn't matter. I can feel it."

He leans over me, casting a shadow, and the belt trails up my spine and back. Shiver after shiver rocks through me.

"*El amore es invisible y entra y sale por donde quiere,*" he whispers, "*sin que nadie le pida cuenta de sus hechos.*"

It turns out I don't know what it means. Sounds romantic though.

Snap.

The belt cracks against my thigh.

Fuck! I snap to attention. Was I already drifting off?

"Come back to me," he says. "Clear your head."

The funny thing is, that didn't even hurt. It was just the tip of the belt. It was a shock.

"I was trying to figure out what you said."

He says something else in Spanish, then says, "There's no need to figure it out. You said you can feel it. So feel it. Close your eyes."

I take a deep breath and close my eyes again.

He slides a finger between my legs, up to my ass and down again, dipping inside me where I'm still wet from earlier. I squirm, wanting more, wanting less.

I still can't believe this is happening, how I can go from the Violet I was a few days ago to this one, the one who lets this man do anything he likes and—

Crack.

The belt gets my shoulder. Harder this time but the pain is sweet.

"Sorry," I mumble.

"Bring your mind back around. Forget the voices. Forget that inner world. Just live in this one with me."

He makes it sound so easy.

Snap.

A whip to the other shoulder.

My thoughts go dark.

I submit to him.

"That's it," he says, reaching underneath me to my breasts, cupping them with wet and greedy fingers. He gently tugs at my nipples. It's just the slightest bit painful, but more than that, it causes a shower of electricity to hum out from my limbs.

"Fuck," I say breathlessly into the mattress.

He moves away at that, getting off the bed. I hear the crinkle of a condom foil and the slide of it as he slips it on. My ass can't help but wiggle in anticipation.

"Get up on all fours," he commands, voice throaty with lust.

I push myself up.

He grabs my waist and yanks me back toward the edge of the bed.

Teeth sink into my ass.

"Ow," I cry out, laughing at the same time.

"I had to," he says. "Your ass begs for it."

Crack.

The belt comes down on one cheek, making me jump from the sting.

"Sorry, that was all me," he says. "It was begging for that, too."

"Tell me what else my ass wants," I joke.

I can feel the smile on his lips and I look over my shoulder at him with a warning glance.

Sure enough, he's grinning. "I think you know. But we'll save that for later," he adds. "Some things are worth working up to."

"Need I remind you that the second time we slept together, you tied me to the bed?"

"Yes. And that was the second time, not the first. Now look forward," he orders.

I do what he says, just as he moves over me.

The belt slips around my neck in a loop, like a damn collar.

"Vicente," I say quietly.

"Don't worry," he whispers, moving the hair off my back and kissing down my spine. "Trust me."

I'm putting an awful lot of trust in you these days, I want to say, but I don't want to talk with the belt pressed against my windpipe.

I have to admit, it's scary. I know lots of people like being choked during sex but since I never had that done before, I'm not sure.

"Easy now," he says, holding the end of the belt loosely. "If you're uncomfortable, I'll stop. If you don't want to do this, I'll stop. Just say the word. If you want to continue and stop later, we can do that to. The last thing I want to do is hurt you. I just want to bring you to another place."

Another lesson in letting go, courtesy of Vicente Cortez.

I nod. I'll go with it. For now. He hasn't let me down yet.

With one hand holding the end of the belt, causing my neck to arch back, he grips my hip with the other and slowly eases his cock inside me.

Fuck. This feeling is everything and unlike anything. The way I spread around him, how tantalizingly slow he inches inside, drives me wild.

He's opening me to a whole new world.

In other words, he's fucking Aladdin and I'm on one

hell of a magic carpet ride.

"Easy," he whispers through ragged breaths, continuing the torturous push.

But I don't want easy now, not even with the belt around my neck. The slow pace only riles me up. I want him deep, deep inside until I can't see straight.

I tell him so and it brings out a thick grunt from his throat as he grips my waist with his hand, yanking back on the belt.

My breath catches in my throat, choked out of my lungs, as he slams into me all the way. I'm so tight and he's so big and I'm so wet that he slides in like silk.

It feels.

Too.

Fucking.

Good.

The angle is everything, the way he's standing off the bed. He pushes himself in to the hilt and I feel myself expand around his thickness, his cock dragging over every wild nerve inside me.

A long, aching groan pours out of my mouth. I grip the sheets, bunching them in my hands, starting to feel dizzy even though I'm still able to breathe.

But my breath is short and rapid, and growing quicker.

He slams into me again, over and over, his hips circling quickly, hitting the right spot every time. The feeling in my core grows and builds and tightens until I feel like I might pass out. Our skin slaps loudly against each other, a frenzied soundtrack to our animalistic fucking. The belt yanks back on my neck like I'm a wild creature he's trying to tame.

With one smooth movement, he pulls my hips up higher, angling himself down in a long, powerful thrust, and he's hitting my G-spot with the perfect hot grind.

All the tension snaps like a wire pulled too taut.

I try to cry out but the noise dies in my throat.

Every feeling, every sensation is heightened tenfold while the world starts to go grey and staticky, like my vision is turning into an old television.

I think I'm passing out.

And I'm definitely coming hard.

Then with a throaty moan he lets go of the belt and it loosens around my neck and I'm gasping for breath as I pulse around him, washed away in the waves of my orgasm where I can't make sense of anything.

His pace quickens, both hands holding on to my waist as he drives himself inside me, so hard and thorough and brutal, as if he's punishing me again and again, like he did with the belt.

He's savage.

A fucking savage.

And I'm still riding my orgasm, still trying to breathe again, each brutal thrust keeping me going on the wave, like I'll keep coming for as long as he's in deep. I'm up so high, high, high and I can't come down even if I tried.

It's pure, primal bliss.

"You're going to be the death of me, Violet McQueen," he growls, so rough and frantic in his rhythm, and then he slows with one, heavy push. His fingers dig into my skin, hard enough to leave bruises, and his loud, wild groan fills the room, twisting with my own.

He stills against me, drops of sweat falling onto my

back, our heavy breathing in unison, and it feels like he has to pry his fingers away from my hips.

Eventually he pulls out.

I collapse straight down onto the bed, my arms shaking. I reach up for my neck to feel for the welt, hoping it won't leave something like the ropes left on my ankles. My parents won't understand this one.

"Let me see. Did I hurt you?" Vicente asks tenderly, moving up beside me on the bed. I roll over to face him and he runs his finger gently over my neck. "There's no mark," he says.

"It doesn't hurt," I tell him.

"And you were okay with it?"

I give a slight nod. "I came pretty fucking hard."

He gives me a soft grin. "You did." He leans over and kisses along my neck, then up to my chin, my nose, my lips. "Do you find you're able to be more in the moment with me?"

I exhale loudly. "Yeah. Everything is just so…it's different now. Everything is different." I feel awed just saying it. He's opened up a whole new world, a whole new side of me that I never knew existed. It's like finding a door to a place that you'd only heard about and never believed was real.

Vicente is my Narnia.

"Good different, I hope?"

I break into a crazy smile. "Of course it's good different. You're blowing my fucking world apart every moment I'm with you. You're like…magic."

"I'm not magic," he says solemnly. "Just my cock is."

I laugh. "Mexican magic cock."

"There are many legends about it, but only you know

the truth."

"Well, let's keep it between you and I then. I don't want to have to fight off any women."

He brushes the hair from my face. "There aren't any other women, you know that. Just you. Only you."

I hate what those words do to me. Fill me with hope. Make my heart swell. We're not even a couple and yet we're acting like it. How scary it would be for all of this to stop, to fall apart. It's so soon and yet I can't bear to lose it.

"What are you thinking?" he asks, tapping his fingers along my temple. "What thoughts could you have now, after all that and my magic cock?"

I can't help but give him a half-smile. "You know me. Hard habit to break. Might need your magic cock in me at all times."

"That can be arranged. You know by now I don't tire easily." He places his hand at my chest, the expression on his face turning grave, like he's grappling with something heavy. "Sometimes I think I can feel your pain. I can see the softness of your heart."

I don't know if it's all the emotions from the sex or with my family or what's going on, but just those words, just the feeling of his warm palm against my chest, so tender, and I feel tears burning at my eyes and nose.

I take a deep breath.

Shit, Violet, don't lose it now after all that.

"You know," Vicente says quietly. "Just because I want you to escape from yourself during sex and connect with me doesn't mean I don't want to hear about what bothers you. What lurks inside your head. Tell me about your darkest places, Violet. Don't hold them inside."

I close my eyes, the tears falling. Shit. I am so fucking weak.

But he doesn't ask me why I'm crying. Which is good, because if he's going to be around me for a while he's going to find out pretty soon that I cry over a lot of things. Sad commercials, music, cute animals, movies, books, happy or sad. Even an epic sunset can reduce me to tears sometimes.

He rubs his thumbs underneath my eyes, wiping away the tears. "You just need a little tenderness, Violet. I think that's all you need."

I swallow hard, nodding. Because he gets it. He fucking gets it.

"You know what," I whisper to him, biting on my lip for a long moment while I find the courage to go on. "It took me a long time to see this but…back in high school, if my boyfriend broke up with me or we had a fight or if I failed a test or something bad happened at home or friends were mean, whatever it was, I would often drag it out for as long as I could. It was like I wanted to wallow in it, become a martyr or something. I couldn't figure it out, what was wrong with me. I thought that maybe I just liked punishment or I wanted people to feel sorry for me. Like I wanted their pity."

I take in a deep, steadying breath and meet his eyes. He's watching me so carefully, absorbing my words as they fall from my shaking lips. I continue. "But later, I realized that wasn't the case at all. I didn't want people feeling bad for me. I didn't want to forever be a victim. All I really wanted was for what they gave me when I was one. When I was hurting, people were a little bit nicer to me. They were more gentle. Tender. Soft. It's all I wanted. Most people don't realize it when they're being crass and abrasive, because the world teaches you that no one deserves extra kindness or extra *anything*, that there is strength in being hard and tough and strong. It's buck up, pull up your big girl panties, stop feeling sorry for yourself and get over it. Don't be so *sensitive*." Even saying the words choke me up. "And all I wanted was just a little extra compassion. I just wanted people to be nice to me. Not because I deserved it. But because everyone does. And fuck if it's hard to find in this world. Empathy is rarer than diamonds."

There. I've just poured my heart out to him in a way I haven't done with anyone. I've never said those words outside my own head before. I've kept them locked away because there's a world out there that just doesn't understand, and worse than that, will turn on you for it.

And Vicente, of all people, seems to have been born from a tough stock. He's all tobacco and leather and prickly cactus. He's steel and fire and the harsh sun of the desert. He's belts and ropes and ties. He's everything I'm not.

Yet as he's watching me, thinking, as we both lie here on the bed naked, I see that deep inside he knows exactly what I'm talking about.

"You know," he says carefully, "in other cultures, being kind isn't a flaw. And being emotional and open isn't either. Violet…your heart is safe with me. You know this now. Your heart is safe, as is your mind and your soul and your body. I won't hurt you. I won't let anyone else either."

I could cry all over again.

Only this time I don't.

All the softness is turning to heat.

I smile.

Grab the back of his head, my hands sinking into his soft hair, and pull him to me, ready to go again.

I want to stay at Vicente's all night, but again, I know I should go home.

But when his Mustang pulls onto Waller Street, I'm hit with a different impulse.

"Do you want to come inside?" I ask him. I don't know why the question makes me feel like I'm in high school.

He grins, a flash of white teeth in the dark. "Are you sure?"

I nod. "Yeah, if you can find a parking spot."

Luckily we manage to find one less than a block away. As we walk to the door, my heart bubbles up. His arm goes around my waist, holding me tight while he has a few casual puffs of a cigarette. I briefly lean my head against his shoulder as the feelings run away with me, caught up in the scent of sweet tobacco.

This shouldn't feel so good, so fast.

It's *so* fast.

You're just introducing him to your parents, I remind myself. *This stuff happens.*

But that's not what's fast. It's not what's going on, on the outside. It's what's happening on the inside.

Feelings. Motherfucking feelings.

Ridiculous, ludicrous, grandiose feelings.

A whole tree of them, growing at a rapid rate, a canopy above my head.

I can only hope they don't all rain down on me at once. I can only handle one at a time: desire. Lust. Sexual obsession.

And then what happens next?

We pause in front of my house. The light in the living room is on and I can see flashes from the TV on the walls. It's only nine o'clock. They're probably both up and watching television.

Fuck. What am I thinking?

"You think they won't approve?" he asks me, an edge to his voice.

I squeeze his hand and give him my most reassuring smile.

"Why wouldn't they?"

They have no reason not to.

Just because my mother warned me about men who know all the right things to say.

She'll meet Vicente and forget all about that.

He'll win her over like he won me over.

"Just don't…mention what we talked about earlier," I tell him.

"Are you kidding me? I told you that you can trust me." He pauses, peering at me. "And I'm not going to let what you told me cloud my judgment of them. They're your parents and I'm sure they're very lovely people."

Damn. He really can read my mind.

With that in mind, we go up the steps and I stick my key in the lock, opening the door.

It's warm inside. The hallway is dark, with only a faint light coming out of the kitchen. The low murmur of the television sounds from around the corner.

"Violet?" I hear my mom say from the living room.

"Yeah, it's me," I tell her, hanging up my jacket on the coat hook and gesturing Vicente to do the same with his. "Dad with you?"

"He's out with Paul," she says. His friend he often plays music with. It's probably easier that he's not here.

I look at Vicente. I can barely see his face in the dark. I grab his hand and then bring him around the corner to the room.

My mom is sitting down on the couch, her hand in a bowl of popcorn. I'm vainly glad she's not dressed like a dork, not that she normally does but since she wasn't expecting anyone she could have been in a green face mask and mom jeans.

Instead, she's in heather grey cotton shorts, her legs curled under her, showcasing the gorgeous cherry blossom tattoo she has snaking up her leg. She's wearing a thin black t-shirt and probably no bra but she doesn't really need it. Her hair is down over her shoulders, so dark it disappears into her shirt.

It's funny how looking at your parents through another person's eyes makes you realize who they really are. My mom's a fucking MILF, and at this moment, with her dark eyes focused on the TV, she looks like the spitting image of me, albeit a skinnier, older model.

"Hey," I say to her, Vicente standing beside me.

She turns to look at us and to her credit she only flinches slightly when she realizes I'm not alone.

"I'm sorry," she says, slowly placing the bowl of popcorn next to her. "I didn't realize you had someone with you." She's squinting at us—with the glare of the TV and us in the shadows, she probably can't see that well.

I take a step toward her. "Vicente was dropping me off so I thought I'd bring him in to meet you."

So you can stop being so goddamn paranoid.

My mother slowly gets to her feet, rubbing her palms on her thighs before offering her hand.

"Nice to meet you, Vicente," she says.

Vicente steps out of the shadows and grasps her hand in his. "I've heard a lot about you, Mrs. McQueen."

A faint gasp comes out of my mother's mouth as she stares at Vicente in absolute horror.

"Something wrong?" Vicente asks lightly.

"Mom," I chide her. "You're being rude."

What the hell is wrong with her?

She just blinks, managing to clamp her mouth shut while her eyes stay wide open. Vicente shakes her hand and shoots me a sly smile. "She must be shocked by my handsome good looks." He turns back to her and raises her hand to his mouth, not dropping eye contact as he kisses it. "I've been told I have that effect."

I have to admit, it's a really weird moment. I wasn't expecting for Vicente to be so intense with her, and I wasn't expecting her to have a fucking aneurysm.

He drops her hand and looks around the room. "A really nice place you have here."

"Thanks…" she says, swallowing hard. She glances at me and I can still see traces of fear in her eyes. I don't know what her deal is.

"Mom, you look like you've seen a ghost," I tell her. "Chill out. He's not staying. I just thought he'd come in and say hi and you wouldn't act like an absolute loon."

"I get that a lot," Vicente says, coming back to me and taking my hand, squeezing it. I squeeze it back, grateful for his support. "I must have one of those faces."

"You certainly do," my mother says carefully. "What did you say your name was again?"

"Vicente."

"Vicente what?"

"Mom…"

He gives her a charming smile. "Vicente Cortez. Do you want to see my driver's license?"

"ID doesn't mean anything," she mutters under her breath. Then she perks up. "I'm going to go get us some wine for the occasion." She looks at Vicente. "Do you like wine, Vicente Cortez?"

"I prefer tequila, if you have it. Patrón."

"I don't. Wine it is." She walks over to me and grabs my arm. "Violet, I need your help with the glasses."

And then she hauls me out of the living room. I look back at Vicente, trying to shrug, but he just raises his palm and nods, somehow understanding all of this.

"Mom," I hiss at her when we get to the kitchen and I wrestle out of her grasp. "What's your fucking problem?"

"Don't you fucking swear at me," she says, hugging her arms close to her chest.

"What? Since when?"

"Since you bring some fucking strange Mexican into the house."

Whoa. "Mexican? Mom, please don't tell me you're drinking the racist Kool-Aid now."

My mom is the most liberal person I know.

"You don't know him, Violet," she says, pacing between

me and the fridge, her fists opening and closing. "The other day, two men, Hispanics, not from around here, were shot dead in the park."

"That happens all the time," I tell her.

"No. Not like this. It was a clean killing. Nothing sloppy or rushed about it. Not the kind of killing you would do over a drug deal. It was murder and it was planned."

My mind is totally boggled. What the hell is she talking about? "Murder? What? Mom…I think you've been watching too many crime shows…" I trail off, my mind going where I don't want it to.

To the newspaper clipping.

"Why does it matter if he's from Mexico?" I ask carefully. "Do you have bad blood with them? Did something happen once?"

She stops pacing. Looks at me with a pale face. She blinks, trying to take in my words. Finally she says, "No. No." She presses the heel of her palm to her forehead and takes a deep breath. "Sorry, baby. My medication is messing with me these days. I think I need to switch. I just…you're right. I've been watching too many shows."

I exhale loudly, feeling bad. I don't know why, but that's par for the course.

"Let me get the white," I tell her, opening the fridge and taking out an almost full bottle of chardonnay.

"I'll get the glasses," she says absently, grabbing three of them from the cupboard. When she puts them on the counter and I begin to fill them up, I can feel her watching me very carefully.

"What?" I whisper tensely.

"I just want you to be careful," she says in a low voice.

"That's all. You said this was the guy who always has the right thing to say. And I can see that. I don't trust him."

I give her a sharp look. "I don't care if you don't trust him. I do."

She shakes her head slightly but doesn't say anything.

"You going to behave?" I ask her. "Be a normal mom?"

She flinches at that, almost spilling the glasses. "I am a normal mom."

I let out a dry laugh and walk back to the living room. Fucking hell she's normal.

Back in the living room, Vicente is hunched over, hands clasped behind his back, staring at the family photos on the mantelpiece. I have to admit that with his dark grey jeans and black long-sleeve shirt, he does look a little like the bad boy every mother has to warn her daughter about.

"Here you go," I say to Vicente, holding out the glass. "Sorry about my mom. She needs new meds."

"Violet," she admonishes, and I can tell from the tone that I've actually zinged her with that one. But she needs to understand that the honesty is important to Vicente.

Vicente takes the glass from me and raises it at my mother. "Regardless, thank you so much for letting me into your home, Mrs. McQueen. No, that sounds too formal now that we are all friends. What else can I call you?"

"Mrs. McQueen is just fine," she says sternly.

"All right. Here's to you, Mrs. McQueen."

We all raise our glasses in unison, though my mom looks like hers is made of lead.

After Vicente takes a sip and makes a small noise of approval, he gestures to the photos on the mantel. "Lovely family you have here. How long have you lived in San

Francisco? Some of the pictures look further up the coast."

She arches a dark brow at him. "We used to live in Gualala. Up Highway One."

He nods. "Would love to head up there one day. Maybe Violet and I can go, take some photos."

"We could visit Grandpa Gus and Mimi," I say excitedly.

My mother doesn't say anything but she doesn't look happy. "Since we're asking questions," she says. "How long are you in San Francisco for? Violet didn't seem to know."

"I'm here for as long as I want. I'm dedicated to photography now and I think the city is a special place to stay."

"You're not heading back to Mexico anytime soon?"

He takes her question in stride. "I have no reason to go back."

"Things tough down there?" She almost sounds like she's mocking him.

He shrugs and takes another sip of wine. "Not particularly."

"Violet says you come from a family of farmers."

"We export avocados," he says. "But we don't farm them."

"Can't be much money in that," she muses, her eyes narrowing slightly.

"Mom, have you ever bought an avocado? They're like ten bucks a pop," I remind her. "Avocado toast is like currency in this city."

She ignores me. "So, if you don't mind my asking, Vicente, what is it that you do? Since you're not a student at the school and you're taking lessons from my daughter."

Jesus. She's really grilling him. Now I wish Dad was home. Surely he'd go easier on him.

Maybe.

"If you're wondering how it is that I can afford to live in San Francisco, I'll just say I have a lot of investments that are slowly paying off. And no, you can't have the name of my financial advisor. He lives in Mexico City."

"And where did you live in Mexico?"

"Oh, around. Places you've never heard of."

"Try me."

"Have you been to Mexico, Mrs. McQueen?" he asks, slowly walking over to her.

I'm about to answer for her and tell him no, but she says, "I have."

I balk. This is news to me.

He stops a few feet away, wine glass at his lips. "Where did you go?"

She doesn't take her eyes off of him. I feel like they're in some sort of sparring war. The overprotective mother and the boyfriend who won't be intimidated.

Boyfriend.

I have to remind myself that we're not official yet.

Even though he's acting one hundred percent like he has a lot of stake in this.

As is my mom.

"The east coast," she says. "Spent a lot of time in Veracruz."

"Oh really? Dangerous town nowadays."

"It was back then, too." She briefly notices me staring. "Dad was also in Mexico."

Interesting.

"And what did you do in Mexico?" Vicente asks, his voice lower, eyes searching hers. I have a feeling that he might be trying to get to the bottom of that article. "What took you there?"

"An old friend," she says.

"Who?" I ask.

"No one you know." She doesn't look at me when she says it. "It was a very long time ago. Before you were born."

"How old was Ben?"

"Three."

"Did he go with you?"

She doesn't answer. Instead, she takes a gulp of wine and breaks the staring contest with Vicente, going over to sit on the couch, her eyes on the TV. Like we were never here at all.

Well, this is awkward.

Vicente looks over at me and gives me a look to say that he tried. And did he ever. Then he looks back at my mom. "I should be off. Thank you so much for the wine." He finishes the rest of the glass. "Next time I'll have to ask you all about your tattoos. Especially the one on your leg. The cherry blossom and that moon. Very unique. And the one on your arm. The music notes."

She glances down at her bicep, the bottom of the music notes just poking out from under her sleeve.

"It almost looks like an old song my father used to sing," he says softly, as if reliving a memory.

My mother looks at him sharply. That fear again. She really does need new anxiety medication because this is getting a bit ridiculous.

"Goodbye, Mrs. McQueen," he says, heading out of the living room and back into the hall. I quickly put my glass down on the mantel, shooting my mother the dirtiest of looks, and run after him.

He's shrugging on his jacket and we don't speak until we're both out the door and on the steps.

"I am so sorry," I cry out, hanging on to his arm. "I don't know what's wrong with her. Usually she's *nice*."

"I'm sure she is," he says. "Some people just have off days and a lot of people don't like it when others drop by unannounced. I'm pretty sure you don't. That's part and parcel of your hyper-sensitivity. Leads to you being overwhelmed."

"Phhfft. My mom isn't hyper-sensitive. She's tough as nails."

He shakes his head. "No, my *mirlo*, she isn't. Just because someone looks and acts tough doesn't mean they aren't a mess on the inside."

The name he gave me, *mirlo*—blackbird—dances in my heart. I try not to trip up over it but I can't help grinning. "Okay, well, you're tough. I doubt you're a mess inside."

"You're right," he says with a cheeky smile. "I'm not a mess. But I can recognize the softness in others. Cut open a weathered leather chair and you've got feathers inside." He looks down the street toward his car. "I should go. I'd still love to have dinner with your family, but I have a feeling that won't be happening anytime soon."

"What? No, seriously. My mom is having an off day. Come over tomorrow. I have to head back here to do some work, but if you drop by at like six pm, that's enough time to have a drink beforehand. You can meet Ben too. Ben's great."

"And your father? Is he anything like your mother?"

"Not at all," I say emphatically, though the article quickly crosses my mind.

"All right. Well," he says, hands cupping my face as he kisses me softly on the mouth. My eyes flutter closed and I sink into the kiss, the feel of his tongue brushing against mine, sending champagne bubbles down my spine. God, I want to go back to his hotel with him and make everything go away. No more thoughts, no more worries.

Just his body and mine.

"See you tomorrow, *mirlo*," he whispers as he pulls away. He gives my hand a squeeze and then he's walking down the street. I stand on the bottom step and wait until his tall figure disappears.

Then I slowly trudge up the stairs and back into the house.

Ellie

A MOTHER'S WORST NIGHTMARE.

No, Ellie thinks, slamming back the glass of wine. *My* worst nightmare.

She doesn't know what to think, how to act. She knows she might be going crazy.

Like, fucking crazy.

In a way that her anti-anxiety medication can't handle.

Because there is no way in hell that that's Javier's son.

It can't be. There's no reason for that to be him.

She doesn't even know if Javier has a goddamn son.

And yet, she looked into those eyes and that's all she saw.

A ghost from her past in another form. A specter with

179

a glowing amber gaze.

The front door slams, making Ellie jump. Violet has come back inside.

She knows that she was a total bitch to him and that Violet is angry. She has every right to be.

I'm a fucking terrible mother, she thinks. *The first time in forever she brings a guy home, a guy she's happy about, and this is how I act?*

Why does it have to be someone that reminds me of Javier?

She has to push past this.

"Vi," she says to her, patting the space beside her. "Come here."

Her daughter glares at her in that way she does so well. She knows she's hurting inside at the way she acted. Violet gets bruised *so* easily.

Yet another reason why she has to be careful.

Ellie needs to talk to Camden before she loses her mind.

"Mom," Violet says, crossing her arms and leaning against the wall. "I can't believe you."

If only you could see what I see.

"I'm sorry," Ellie says, because it's what she has to say. Everything she says next is what she needs to say in order to make everything okay again. "I'm…"

"Yeah, you said you needed new meds. But what am I supposed to tell him?"

"Other than the fact you just told him I needed new meds?" she says snidely, because yeah, she's pissed off about that too. This isn't a family where everyone throws each other under the bus.

"Look, you were being a bitch."

"Violet," she says, but she's too tired to yell. And fuck, she *was* being a bitch. She has to own that.

She takes in a deep breath, feeling all too fragile. "I'm sorry. This caught me off guard. I wasn't feeling well and you came home with this guy, and I guess he just reminded me of someone."

"Mr. Smooth Moves."

Smooth Moves? She almost laughs. Smooth never quite explained it. But he had moves all right.

That thought makes her feel like dirt on the inside.

"Mom?"

Her daughter is eyeing her in a strange way. Concerned. Ellie doesn't know what's showing on her face. She straightens up and shoves a handful of popcorn into her mouth, chewing while she gathers her thoughts.

"So why were you and Dad in Mexico?" Violet asks over her shoulder as she heads to the kitchen. Ellie can hear her rifling through the fridge, and when she comes back, she has another bottle of wine.

It's an expensive one but she's not complaining. She needs this and she's sure Violet does too. She watches her daughter as she unscrews the cap and fills both their glasses before settling down in the armchair. She's watching her with such wariness that Ellie feels like a caged animal.

"Well? Why? I never heard you mention it before?" Violet is as stubborn as her mom. Ellie would normally feel a twinge of pride, but right now it's hindering to be put on the spot like this.

You used to be so good at lying.

"As I said, it was a long time ago."

181

"Like, how long? 2013"

That gets Ellie's attention. How did she guess the year so exactly?

She watches Violet.

Violet watches back.

Goddamn it, she's becoming wary of her own daughter now.

She's ashamed at that. Her daughter is everything to her, has been everything. Violet doesn't deserve this.

Ever since she found that letter telling Camden that his father had died, she's been on a razor-thin edge. She still doesn't know who sent the damn thing or what it means.

Camden doesn't know either.

He wants to believe that it's someone he knew, maybe an old client, someone still in the community of Palm Valley that somehow found out where they lived and wanted to let them know what happened.

Anonymously.

Of course, Ellie isn't too sure.

"Around then. That's a good guess," she says carefully.

Violet shrugs. "Well, you said Ben was three…"

Ellie relaxes a little. Violet's mode of deduction is fast. She's always been quick.

God, she's proud of her daughter.

"Me and your father went to Veracruz to see an old friend of ours. Ben stayed with your Grandpa Gus in Gualala."

She hates having to lie like this, but it's better than the truth.

The truth that Ellie and Camden have spent their children's lives trying to protect them from.

The fact that they aren't who their children think they are.

They're bad people.

Criminals.

Especially Ellie. Camden only did what he had to do in the past to protect Ben, then later to protect her. Camden has always been the good one.

Ellie has always been the bad one.

A wounded animal that can't stop biting back.

But that's not who you are anymore, she reminds herself as she sips the wine, ever so grateful for the numbing affect. *The person you were is long gone.*

She has to remind herself of that.

Often.

And when the memories become too much, when the past creeps into her veins and blackens her heart, that's when the medication kicks in.

It keeps the past at bay.

She hasn't conned anyone in twenty years.

Hasn't killed anyone in twenty years.

Life has been a set of three parallel paths.

She's managed to stick to the middle one.

Knee-deep in the grey.

Violet doesn't stick around for much more conversation and soon gets up to leave. Ellie feels bad. She knows her daughter wants to talk about Vicente. She knows she's absolutely smitten (she can almost feel it—god, it brings her back), and that she should be happy that her daughter is glowing for once.

She has to make the effort to move past this.

Vicente is not Javier's son.

He's far too tall and rugged looking. Javier was on the shorter side and as slick and elegant as a snake. While Vicente's mannerisms are similar, there's an impulsiveness to him, a roughness that would probably worry any other mother.

So when Violet pauses before heading up the stairs and asks, "Is it okay if Vicente comes over for dinner tomorrow?" Ellie knows she has to say yes.

She just has to.

Luckily Camden will be there. Camden will see. When he gets home tonight, she'll explain to him about Vicente and what she thinks, and he'll dismiss it all with a kiss as he usually does. She can say the craziest things but her husband will always keep her grounded.

But tomorrow he'll meet Vicente and then he'll probably agree with her.

That he looks like he could be Javier's son.

"Of course," Ellie says to Violet through a forced smile.

And if he tries anything, I'll kill him.

It stings to know she's not even joking.

Vicente

I SHOULDN'T TAKE A GUN TO THE McQUEEN'S HOUSE. Though my father would be proud, my mother would chide me for being a terrible dinner guest. Expensive alcohol, yes. A gun, no.

But I have a feeling that in that elegant old Victorian, a multitude of guns lie hidden along with a multitude of sins.

Ellie—Mrs. McQueen—knows who I am.

At least, she thinks she does.

And I made no effort to dissuade her.

I want her to think it.

I want her to slip up.

I want her to know I have the upper hand.

And unlike my father, I always will.

The meeting went exactly as I hoped it would. She was on edge, afraid of me, afraid that her daughter might go down the same path that she did.

And what path was that? The path where she chose her husband over my father?

I'm not upset about it. If Ellie hadn't married Camden, my father would have never married my mother and I wouldn't be here. My father, in the end, made the right choice just as Ellie did.

The choice that brought Violet into the world.

To be fair, when I try and imagine Ellie with my father, I just see two writhing snakes trying to bite each other, reminding me of the symbol caduceus. The pairing seems like it would have been a mistake from the start.

But for whatever she's worth, she got under his skin. She knows things about him that I don't.

Things I want to know.

She beat my father at his own game.

And won.

I wash my face in the bathroom sink and glance up at myself in the mirror. I do have my father's eyes and his brow, but everything else is all me. I run my hands through my hair, pushing it up and off my face, and quickly trim down my beard, attempting to look more respectable.

I can hear my father's voice in my head, telling me to be more clean-shaven, to dress better.

Fuck it. For once in my life I'm actually going to follow his advice.

I shave my beard off until my face is smooth, slick my hair back, and then grab a black linen suit jacket and white dress shirt from the closet, pairing it with a pair of dark blue jeans.

Now I can almost see him staring back at me.

I grin at my reflection.

Time to go have some fun.

I grab my .45 and shove it in my ankle holster, grab a bottle of booze, and then I'm out the door.

It's foggy again, making for a wonderfully dramatic drive up the hills and into the clouds. This city just screams noir from every shadowy crevice. Part of me wonders if I could actually settle down here. I for damn sure wouldn't be a photographer, but if you know the right people and make the right deals, you could rule this place with ease. It's too liberal. Its citizens are used to progress and safety. I could burn the city to the ground and no one would see it coming.

I find parking off of Haight and walk the block over until I'm standing in front of their house.

Violet, my blackbird, my *mirlo*, she has no idea at all.

Kept in the dark all these years.

Locked in her head.

Made to think that her intuition has been lying to her when it hasn't at all.

One day she will find out the truth.

It might be tonight.

It might be next year.

But when she finds out who her parents really are, that's the day she'll find out who I really am and what I'm doing here.

What I'm doing with her.

I hate to say it, but in some ways I hope that day never comes.

And if it does come, I hope to god she won't hate me.

Not hate you? I counter. *She'll want you dead.*

Santa Muerte.

I take a deep breath and head up the stairs.

I don't even have to knock at the door before it's flung open.

Violet grins at me, white teeth against bright red lipstick, and then her face falters for a second.

"Your manly stubble is all gone," she remarks, marveling at me.

I rub my jaw. "Believe me, you'll thank me later when you don't have rug burn between your thighs."

She giggles at that, shutting the door partially so she's out here with me. "Shhh," she says, leaning in for a kiss. "Remember, this is meet the parents part two."

"Horrible movie."

She giggles again, and now I realize she's a bit tipsy. I try and look over her shoulder and into the house. "Is everyone here? Your brother? Your father? Are they armed?"

She laughs, smacking my shoulder. "Stop it. But yes. They're here."

"I'll be on my best behavior."

"You know it's not you I'm worried about."

And yet she should be.

She straightens her shoulders and opens the door wider, then we both step inside.

It smells like cooking. Pasta sauce and garlic. A deep male voice is laughing.

We go down the hall and step into the open kitchen that overlooks the dining table, the settings already in place.

Her father and Ben stand side by side by the counter, a box of spaghetti beside them. Her father has a beer in his hand and is showing something to Ben on his phone, probably something on YouTube. It sounds an awful lot like goats screaming. Whatever it is has them both laughing, although Ben's laugh seems stiff and forced and purely for show.

They both look up when we approach them. In my hands I have a bottle of the most expensive sipping tequila I could find. It's nothing like the stuff at home, but I figure it will help win favors and fuck things up a bit.

Speaking of fucking things up, the look on Camden's face is priceless. The same slightly gaping mouth and wide eyes that his wife had when she saw me. Only he recovers quickly. So quick that Violet doesn't seem to notice.

But I did. I give him a half-smirk while she makes the introductions to them both.

Camden McQueen is taller than I thought he would be and in great shape, judging by his shoulders and arms. Every visible inch of him is covered in tattoos, which is no surprise. Based on the old photo I saw, I expected him to be wearing glasses, but he's not, and grey and silver threads through his dark hair. He's lucky, like my own father, that hair loss doesn't seem to be an issue.

Ben is a miniature version, and by miniature, I mean he's maybe two inches shorter. That's about it. Otherwise, they look extremely similar, down to the build and the tattoos. Violet had mentioned he's an MMA fighter so that explains the thick neck.

Honestly, they both look like wannabe tough guys. For all their muscle, they wouldn't last a second against me. Meatheads pound aimlessly. I've always got a strategy.

Just like tonight.

Poke, poke, poke the beast.

Ben is the first to offer his hand and a genuine smile. "Hey, man," he says. "Nice to meet you."

"I've heard many things about you," I tell him. "All good."

Ben gives Violet a quick smile, even though there's still something strained about his actions. Something is on his mind.

But it's none of my business.

Camden, however...

I stick out my hand toward him and am so fucking tempted to give him a little wink, but I manage to control myself.

"Hi," he says in a deep voice, his eyes narrowing slightly as he shakes my hand. At least he gives a good shake. Holding a tattoo gun must be good for something. "You must be the guy who came into the store asking about getting a tattoo."

"What?" Violet asks.

He's a suspicious one, isn't he? I give her a smile and shrug, covering up fast. "After I found out what your father did, I had to go check it out for myself." Thankfully her father doesn't realize I came in there before I even met Violet. "Your father wasn't there, of course."

"It was Lloyd," he says to Violet before looking back at me. "What were you thinking of getting?"

"I'm not sure," I say. "I thought a *mirlo*. A blackbird." Violet starts to grin. "Mixed with Santa Muerte, the Saint of Death." Her grin falters.

"Charming," Camden muses.

"Sounds fucking rad," Ben says. "Dad, you would do a hella good version of that. You should do it for free."

Camden gives him a dirty look.

I try to look appeasing. "I'm still thinking about it, don't worry. Perhaps we'll talk more after dinner."

"Camden." Ellie's hushed yet urgent voice comes from the living room. "Can I talk to you for a minute?"

Camden nods at us and then tells Ben to get me a drink before walking down the hall, disappearing into the living room to be with his wife.

I can't hear anything beyond their hushed murmurs, but I know exactly what she's saying to him.

Doesn't he look just like Javier?

I smirk to myself.

"Do you want a beer or should we perhaps crack open that bottle of tequila?"

My attention goes back to Ben who is nodding at my hands, eyes looking brighter than they have so far.

I give him the bottle. "Here. It's for you. Go nuts and I'll have a glass too."

Ben happily takes it and sets about getting glasses. "How about you, Vi?"

"Sure," she says, letting out a light sigh. "Getting drunk should help this awkward bullshit."

Ben laughs, setting the glasses out. "Oh, come on." He nods at me. "Vicente seems to be handling it fine. Sorry, man. We should probably have warned you ahead of time that our parents can be fucking weird."

"Weird is good," I tell him, noting that his hands shake slightly as he pours the drinks.

"He's already met Mom," Violet says. "And that didn't go well."

"Fuck," says Ben, handing us our drinks. "Well, bottoms up, then. The only way out of this night is through."

I gulp the tequila down. It burns beautifully. It reminds me of drinking with my father in his office, the only times he's ever shown me his humanity.

I push those memories away into the dark.

"I should probably tell you now," I say, wiping my mouth and holding out my glass for more. "That it's supposed to be sipping tequila. It's no Jose Cuervo. Add a bit of ice and go slow."

"Whoops," Ben says, opening the freezer. "Sorry, man."

"Not a problem. I think we all needed that."

"Fucking right," Ben mutters to himself, placing a few cubes in the glasses.

The three of us end up drinking and talking in the kitchen for a good thirty minutes or so, Ben taking care of the cooking, before Camden comes back to the room, this time with Ellie beside him.

I shoot them a quick glance over my shoulder. They've both got determined looks on their faces, as if they had a long chat and decided to be grown-ups about the whole thing.

Ellie, he only looks like him. And not even that much. He's not Javier's son. He's long gone out of our lives.

I can just imagine the conversation.

Let's go in there and have a nice dinner. Violet deserves to be happy.

I give her hand a squeeze.

She does deserve that. And so much more.

With the dinner ready, thanks to Ben, we all sit at the table. Violet and I are beside each other across from her parents with Ben at the end. The tequila is put aside for later, and a few bottles of red are laid out along with the food.

Ellie looks very beautiful tonight, just like her daughter, but I enjoy it so much more when I'm watching her squirm. Her thin brows come together, her jaw locking every time she glances across the table at me.

I pretend not to notice for the most part, but every now and then our eyes meet and I give her a look that makes her nostrils flare.

What do you think you know? I ask her silently. *Am I the big bad wolf at your door?*

Camden seems to have eased off a bit, which I suppose is good. While I don't think too much of the man, he's not really my concern anyway. Though it has to piss off my father that he's the one who won in the end.

Then again, my father was the one who won the country. Too bad in our line of work it never matters how well you did in the past or how respected you were. All that matters is what happens with the here and now. The past is just ground beneath your feet, there to hold you up or be left behind.

"Vicente," Ben says, bringing me out of my head. "Where in Mexico are you from?"

I clear my throat with a sip of wine "Outside a small town, just north of Mazatlán."

"Is that the good part of Mexico or the bad part?"

"Oh, they're all good parts." I smile at him.

Ellie seems to grumble at that and I'm pretty sure Camden just kicked her under the table.

193

"Did you know Mom and Dad went there when you were three?" Violet says to him.

Ben stares at his parents. "I didn't know that. Does that mean I've been there?"

"No. You stayed with your grandfather," Ellie says quickly before busying herself with her wine.

"Where did you go? Near where he's from?"

Ellie gives me a poignant look. "No, I think we got stuck with the bad side."

"But there are bad sides to every country, Mrs. McQueen," I remind her. "Even in your fair city of San Francisco, I bet behind every smiling, rainbow-painted face, there's something dark and dangerous." I gesture to the house. "I bet inside these walls there are untold horrors. I bet beside your bed you keep a gun."

"Yeah right," Ben says with a snort. "You must mean my bed. I'm the one with the gun. My parents are very much against owning one."

I eye them. "Is that so?"

Camden clears his throat. "It doesn't mean I haven't handled one back in the day. I just don't believe in them now."

"Back in the day?" Violet asks. "Seems like there's a lot you guys did back in the day. Secret trips to Mexico. Guns…" She pauses and I know she's trying hard not to mention the article. "Silver-tongued serpents…"

That's a new one. I raise a brow, wanting to know more. "Silver what?"

Ellie abruptly gets up, her chair noisily sliding back on the floor. "I think it's time for dessert," she says, avoiding everyone's eyes as she grabs her plate, hastily tucking her hair behind her ear.

"Can the dessert be the rest of the tequila?" Camden asks before he gets up and starts to clear the table.

"Yes, please," Ben says.

I know I should play the part of the dutiful boyfriend (fuck, does that word sound foreign) and help clear the table, but when Violet volunteers, her mother insists that we all go relax elsewhere.

There's nothing like a cigarette after a big meal, so I excuse myself and sneak outside alone, sitting down on the bottom step and taking in the damp air and nicotine. Though the traffic of Haight hums nearby, here it's quiet. You can almost pretend you're not in a city at all. It's the suburbs on crack.

Such a nice little life.

A nice little lie.

I don't know why it is that I'm so determined to shake this family up. Aside from the obvious, for what I came here for.

But now that I'm here, I want to expose them for what they are. I want to show Violet that her instincts have always been correct. At least I was raised in a house where everything was laid out on the table, for better or worse. I watched my father torture and kill a man when I was eleven years old. I learned how to shoot an AK at fourteen. I've been with him when he's put bullets in people's heads. I've watched him make deals that I knew were based on lies.

And I turned out just fine.

Violet, on the other hand, has been raised to believe that something is off about her life. She's been sheltered from who her parents truly are. And because of that, she doesn't know what she truly is.

The Bernals aren't good people.

The McQueens aren't either.

The sooner Violet knows this, realizes it, the better off she'll be. That sensitivity she has will be her strongest asset once she learns to let go of who she thinks she is.

She could be whatever she's been afraid to be.

Blackbird singing in the dead of night.

Take these sunken eyes and learn to see.

The only problem, of course, and it's a big problem, is that when she does see, and she will, she'll see me for every lie that I am.

The door opens behind me and I look up over my shoulder.

It's Camden. He closes the door behind him and stands there, the lights from the house causing shadows to fall over him.

I ease to my feet and stare up at him, taking a long, lazy drag of my cigarette.

He watches me as I exhale, not saying a word as the smoke billows around me.

I hold out the cigarette. "Do you smoke?"

He seems to weigh that question. He walks down the steps until he's right beside me and takes it from my fingers. "Sometimes," he says, inhaling deep. Too deep. He coughs and hands it back to me. "I remember now why I don't."

I watch him carefully as I take another drag. Though there's something very genial about him, when you look past the build and the tattoos, I think it would be wrong of me to underestimate him. There's a flash of something in his eyes, a way that he moves that makes me think he's a man with a lot of demons, and those kind of men are nothing if not unpredictable.

"You play any music, Vicente?" he asks me, eyes searching the street as if there's something out there other than fog and darkness.

"No," I tell him.

"Don't have a musical family?"

"Not even the slightest. You?"

He nods and then grimaces. "Yes. No. I did. Used to have a band. But who didn't? Growing up in California, especially in the Coachella Valley, it was practically a rite of passage."

"That must have been a long time ago."

His gaze focuses on me sharply. "It was," he says, then relaxes. "Anyway, I jam now with some buddies that live in Twin Peaks. You know the area?"

"Just the TV show." I notice him staring at the cigarette and hand it back to him, wondering where he's going with all this. He doesn't strike me as an idle chit-chat kind of man. "I'm still getting my bearings in this city."

"And how long do you plan on staying here?" He takes another drag, the look in his eyes hardening.

Now I see.

"I don't know," I admit.

"Vicente, may I ask you a question?" He exhales slowly while waiting for my answer, the smoke blowing in my face. It's hard to read if it's intentional or not. From the way my hackles are rising, I'm going to assume it was.

"Sure."

"What are your intentions with my daughter?"

I crack a smile. "Intentions? What is this, the 1950s?"

"Just answer the question."

His voice isn't so jovial anymore. I want to remind him that Violet isn't a teenager and can make her own decisions, and their input into our relationship is nonexistent. But those demons of his are winking at me, daring me to slip up.

And he's holding on to my cigarette like a hostage.

"My intentions for Violet are pretty much what you would expect. I like her a great deal and wish to keep seeing her."

"And then what? Why are you here?"

"Why am I here?"

"I've seen your type before, you know."

I squint at him, my voice growing rough. "My type? Do you mean Mexican?"

He wants to say yes, because of my father. I want him to, just so I can call him racist.

"I mean the type who use sweet, trusting girls like Violet."

"No offense, Mr. McQueen, but it's up to your sweet, trusting daughter to make those choices for herself. Also, if I were you, I'd get to know her a little better. She might be sweet but she's no broken bird. Her wings are mending and soon she'll fly the fuck away from here."

He flinches slightly. I've got him where it hurts. He knows this, deep down, that she's lost and looking for any excuse to leave and spread her wings. He knows she'll leave one day and never look back.

And I'll be the one to give her the push.

"What are you guys doing?" We both look up to see Violet poking her head out the door. "The tequila is getting cold," she jokes uneasily.

Camden looks at me and pastes a fake smile on his broad face. "We'll have to discuss that tattoo later." Then he flicks the half-smoked cigarette onto the middle of the street and turns and jogs up the stairs and into the house, squeezing Violet's shoulder as he goes in.

Violet watches him and then comes down the stairs to stand beside me. "I need to ask you a favor," she says, looking up at me with a pleading look in her eyes.

"What?" I ask, grabbing her hand and kissing the back of it. "Anything for you."

"Can I take a rain check on tonight?" she asks. "I'm just going to stay here."

She was supposed to come back to the hotel with me after dinner for a night of long-overdue fucking.

I immediately feel a punch to my gut, a sour arrow digging deep. "Why?" I ask slowly, unable to keep the edge out of my voice. Have her parents turned her against me already?

"Ben just told me something. I need time to process it."

"What did he tell you?"

"I can't say…well, I don't want to. It's complicated and I need to talk to him more. He's pretty upset."

"I can see that."

"Me too. I just didn't expect…anyway, I won't keep you in the dark. I just want to make sure we know what we're dealing with first before I tell you."

I have to admit, this stings. More than I thought it would.

Perhaps she doesn't trust me after all.

Perhaps she sees through everything.

Maybe she knows.

I stare at her for a few fervent seconds before I cup her small, beautiful face in my hands and search her dark eyes for something, anything, still left for me.

"I'm not leaving you that easily," I tell her, my voice growing hoarse.

"Vicente," she says softly, "I'm not leaving you either. It's just for tonight. Family stuff. Please don't take it personally. I have to respect Ben. He told me not to tell you anything."

That eases my heart a bit.

But just a bit.

I kiss her hard, taking her breath away, sliding my tongue over hers and hoping to leave a mark in the deepest parts of her. My need for her seems to grow by the second.

"You're mine, Violet," I murmur roughly against her mouth, my fingers pressing into her cheekbones. "I don't care how that sounds, but it's the truth. You belong to me."

Her fingers wrap around my shirt, holding on tight. I can feel her heart beating against mine and I'm struck by how strong it sounds and how fragile it is.

It frightens me.

The danger she could be in just by being with me.

The danger of loss.

I take in a deep breath and step back. I need to find my footing in all of this.

"Okay," I whisper to her. "I'll go."

Her eyes widen. "You don't have to go now!"

I nod. "I should. Go, be with your brother tonight. I'll

see you tomorrow."

Then I turn and head down the street, collecting my pride.

She calls after me but I just wave my hand and keep going.

If I turned around, I'd see her swallowed by the mist.

Violet

STAND ON THE STREET WATCHING VICENTE DISAPPEAR. When he rounds the corner, the fog drifts in, like it was waiting to roll down the street and greet me. Like it felt safer with him gone. Like he burned too hot for it.

Vicente could light water on fire.

With this thought, I breathe in deep and head back inside the house. As much as I worry about him, that I hurt him somehow (which I didn't think was possible seeing how in control and self-assured he's been), there's something else on my mind.

Not on my mind. Wrong use of words. It's more like it's infiltrating my brain, making sure my thoughts turn to this one horrible thing.

Ben isn't my full brother.

I just can't believe it.

I can't.

I hurry back inside to find him.

While Vicente had gone outside to smoke and Mom was busy with the dishes, Ben pulled me aside and down the hall near the back door that leads to our tiny brick courtyard.

In a broken whisper he told me that the article he found, the one that Dad was cleared for, mentioned the woman's name, Sophia Madano, and her son Ben.

They were once the McQueens.

So he did some searching.

Found out Dad was married before.

Then fucking Mom called Ben into the kitchen to help her with something and now I'm left with information I don't know how to process.

I knew I couldn't go back to the hotel with Vicente, even though he's been so good dealing with my crazy (lying, fucking lying!) parents. I wouldn't be able to leave Ben, I wouldn't be able to leave without knowing more, I wouldn't be able to concentrate on Vicente.

I had to stay and he had to go.

I might have hurt his ego to push him out of here, but right now it can't matter. Tomorrow it will. But tonight, I have to be here for my brother. I have to know the truth.

I look in the kitchen, but I don't see him. I pop my head into the living room to where my parents are just settling down on the couch with the wine.

"Where's Ben?" I ask.

"I don't know," Mom says, looking above her at the

ceiling. "In his room, maybe?"

Oh god, I can barely look at them. How much does she know?

"Where's Vicente?" Dad asks.

I can't look at him at all.

"He left," I say through grinding teeth.

I don't have to stick around to see the look of relief on their faces.

I head down the hall and up the stairs.

My bedside light is on in my room. Ben is sitting on my bed drinking the tequila straight out of the bottle. For a moment, in this strange prism of time, I can see it. See him for who he's always been. His skin has always been darker than anyone's in the family. His nose is Roman and out of place. Even his eyes have a different angle to them.

I close the door behind me and he looks at me through drunken eyes.

"Sophia Madano is my mother. I'm fucking Italian."

I can only shake my head, hugging my arms to chest like the room has grown cold. "Tell me again. Everything. I don't understand…"

"And you think I fucking do?" He waves the bottle around and then laughs sourly. "Look, Vi. I'll tell you what I know. Dad was apparently framed to look like he kidnapped his ex-wife and child. He never did it, which I guess is the good part. It was actually Sophia's brothers, the very infamous, very horrible, Madano brothers. It doesn't matter how much looking I do, I'm searching every fucking thing that was ever put on the web, but all I know is that there was once a Sophia and Camden McQueen and they lived a very happy life until they got divorced. Dad then went to live in Palm Valley and opened a fucking tattoo shop. Three fucking guesses what the name was. I lived with my mom in LA and took the name Madano. Then something happened. Sophia, my fucking real mom, disappeared, but I didn't, and then suddenly I guess Dad moves on, marries Mom, and you were born and one big happy perfect family. Right? Right!?"

He's near tears. My brother isn't emotional in the slightest, not on the surface anyway, so it breaks me in pieces to see him like this. I can deal with my feelings about it later—after all, this doesn't affect who he is to me—but I don't know what to say. I wouldn't know how to feel if I were him.

"Ben," I say softly, sitting on the bed next to him. I put my hand on his back. "I'm sorry. I don't want to make excuses for them…"

"And you never have," he says bitterly. "You know that, Vi. You never have. You always said there was something off, something wrong. You knew. I was the fool. After this, I'm starting to think they might not be our parents at all."

I give him a look. It's very clear that there's a lot of my mother in me and a lot of my father in him. "They're our parents, Ben."

"They're both yours," he says. Then he takes another gulp from the bottle. I'm tempted to take it away from him. "They're not both mine."

Ugh. My heart sinks. "Ben," I say to him softly. "Let's go down and talk to them. Tell them everything. Get it all out in the open and deal with it together."

He shakes his head, staring at nothing. "No. No, I don't want to do that."

"But you have to."

"Why?"

"Because neither you or me can live with this burden of keeping it to ourselves. And we're both probably making it out to be worse than it is. We need the truth."

He hangs his head, making him look like a little boy. "They'll lie again."

"No they won't. They can't. And you know they want what's best for us. I'm sure whatever the explanation is, it's something worthwhile. You were so young."

"I was three. I wondered why I have no memories younger than five. Something so traumatic must have happened to me that I blocked it out."

Well, kidnapping would do that.

I get up. "Come on. Let's go downstairs."

"Violet," he says in a voice I don't even recognize. "Let me deal with this my own fucking way."

Then he gets up, nearly knocking me over, and storms out of the room to his old one across the hall, slamming the door. The tequila went with him.

I exhale loudly and sit down on the bed.

Nothing makes sense anymore.

Nothing except one man.

I know I shouldn't bug Ben anymore, so I go about getting ready for bed. After I've brushed my teeth and washed my face, slathering on moisturizer, I pick up my phone to text Vicente.

With one hand on the phone, about to type, I reach up with my other to lower the blinds.

I gasp.

Outside the window, down below in the courtyard, is the tall figure of a man standing beside my mother's lemon tree. He blends in so well that it's hard to know what I'm looking at, especially as the mist curls around him and scatters the faint light from the back door.

But there's a glowing amber in the darkness. A lit cigarette that moves from being held at the side and then up to the mouth where it burns bright like a star.

It's not just the hairs on the back of my neck that are standing up. It's every single pore of my body, raised, electric.

I keep my eyes on the figure while texting Vicente at the same time.

Where r u?

I press send and wait.

I watch.

The figure seems to be the same height as him with the same wide shoulders, but I can't make out any details or features. For a moment I think my eyes are playing tricks on me, but when I keep watching, the figure moves slightly as if off-balance, the cigarette still glowing.

Who are you? I think. *Are you my Vicente? Are you ghosts from my parents' past? Are you the white man who follows me?*

But the figure gives no answer and I don't dare look away. The longer I stare at him, the more he seems to morph into nothing at all.

And then I realize that visibility is down to a few feet. Fog obscures everything. I quickly glance down at the phone and see the text from Vicente.

Just got to the hotel. Talk to you tomorrow, mirlo.

I look back to the window.

The fog has quickly blown past.

The tree is there.

The man is gone.

I shake my head, trying to blink him back into existence. It must be the wine, it must be the tequila, it must be the stress of dealing with Ben.

He was probably never there.

I shut off the light and get into bed.

I close my eyes.

I know there was someone there.

Ellie

LLIE SITS UP IN BED, IN THE DARK. SHE CAN FEEL THE gun burn beside her in the bedside table drawer. Vicente was right about that, the little fuck, but he doesn't know that there's a gun in the other bedside table as well.

You can never be too careful.

Ellie knows this well.

She waits until Camden comes through the door and shuts it behind him, his tall silhouette approaching the bed.

"They're asleep," he says with a heavy sigh. "I think Ben's passed out."

Ellie nods, holding the blanket up to her chest, her fingers curled over the hem like she's a child all over again, holding on to that one stuffed rabbit she had, the only thing she really remembers from her childhood that signified she ever was a child.

Everything beyond that rabbit—grey matted fur with the stuffing coming out, the one shiny eye and crooked yarn smile, the cliché of every marred childhood—was a blur of lies and pain. She never had a childhood, she just had games she had to play, games that ended with acid being poured on her leg by a madman.

She was so young when she was scarred for life. Scars that traumatized her throughout the years, that reminded her each and every day that she had no one to love her, that she was just a pawn and would always be a pawn.

Her husband's cherry blossom tattoo masks the deformities, but even beautiful art can't hide an ugly canvas. It will always be there, underneath.

"Are you okay?" Camden asks, getting into bed beside her.

"Yeah," she says quietly and hates how weak her voice sounds.

Camden puts his arm around her and pulls her to his chest until her head sinks in there, fitting just right. She can hear his heartbeat—it's her metronome. It's the pulse that her life moves to. Without him, she has nothing.

And without her children, she has nothing too.

This is what scares her. That they're all on the verge of the abyss, and one wrong move will send everyone over. She doesn't know what she'd do if anything were to happen to Violet or Ben. It doesn't matter that Ben isn't hers biologically—she's raised him since he was three years old to be hers, and so he is.

Time seems to slow in their bedroom. The house creaks

on with the night. Finally she says, "I'm scared." Her voice seems to echo in the room, like the room is scared too.

"Don't be," Camden says. "Violet can take care of herself."

"You really don't think it's him?"

"Javier's son?" he asks. "No. You're right about the eyes, but everything else…I don't know. I think you're seeing what you want to see."

She stiffens. "Why the fuck would I want to see that?"

"Because it's your past. Because the past has recently caught up to us, and now we're seeing it everywhere. It's just bad timing, Ellie. That's all. Vicente just happens to look the same as Javier and you're taking that and running with it, assuming he's been sent here for her."

"What if you're wrong?"

Camden swallows noisily. "If I'm wrong, we'll know. And we'll deal with it then."

"That's a big risk."

"I trust our daughter. That's all there is to it."

"But she doesn't know what that man is capable of."

"That's true. But Vicente isn't that man. Even if he does end up being his son, and that's a long shot, he still isn't *that* man. It's been too long. Too fucking long." He sighs. "This is just life. We knew this wouldn't be easy, to keep everything the way it is."

"Keep up the lies, you mean?"

"It's for the greater good," he says. "The only time lies are worth telling." He holds her close to him, kisses her forehead. "It's going to be okay. It will be."

He needs it to be okay. They both do.

Her eyes are wide open, staring into the shadows of the

room while she listens to Camden's breath grow deeper and deeper as he falls into sleep.

Ben was acting weird tonight, she thinks. But she can't bear to bring it up. He'd chalk it up to her paranoia again, her guilt over Sophia, that she's not Ben's real mother.

So many lies, one on top of the other.

A pile of matchsticks about to go up in flames.

Vicente

THE DREAM COMES BACK AGAIN.

Santa Muerte.

But this time she has blackbirds instead of hair, swirling around her in a gathering storm.

I'm alone in the desert, wide open and stretching as far as the eye can see.

There is no life here.

Only death.

This is the home of Santa Muerte.

The Saint of Death with Violet's eyes.

I want to ask her what she wants from me, but I cannot speak.

She's not alone.

She has a man with her.

Or the remains of one.

She drags him behind her on a leash made of frayed rope.

But though the man is nearly skeletal, his suit hanging off him in dirty, wet tatters, he's not dead. He's still alive.

She moves, throwing her arm out, birds flying forth from underneath the endless void of her cloak, and she whips the man around until he's lying at my feet.

For one horrible moment, as the dust rises and falls, I think I'm staring down at my father.

It *is* my father.

Younger. Ten, twenty years younger. But still him.

Then it quickly fades and morphs, as faces do in dreams, and becomes the face of Juan Alvarez.

The first man I ever killed.

I had known him for years. He was the man who drove me to school in the mornings. He was the driver for our family, in charge of making sure Marisol and I got to where we needed to go. He watched over us, protected us.

Then one day my father found out that a *federale* had bribed Juan for information.

Juan would never give us up. I believed that even as a child.

But what he told the *federale* led to a bust on one of our shipments.

My father doesn't take betrayal lightly.

And because Juan had been in charge of driving me to school for years, I was to be the one to end Juan's life.

I still don't like to think about what happened that day. My father had Juan down on his knees, naked, hands bound in front of him, in front of the wall that wrapped around the courtyard where my mother liked to have her coffee in the mornings.

In Juan's mouth was an apple, shoved so far back against his molars that he couldn't spit it out.

My father, dressed in a white linen suit, handed me his gun and told me to shoot the apple out of Juan's mouth as "punishment."

I was fourteen at the time. I knew how to handle all weapons. I wasn't a bad shot. I knew that if I aimed for the apple, I would shoot the apple. I would shoot him clear through his head.

That was the moment in my life when everything changed. When I took the step from child to adult. When I realized that tears couldn't save me. A good heart couldn't save me. That I could never go back to the way things were, that I would call for my innocence but it would never return.

Despite being a good shot and handling all guns, this gun in particular felt heaviest to me. A brick of lead. I almost dropped it. Who knows what would have happened if I had. It would have probably gone off and killed my father.

Sometimes I wonder if that's what should have happened instead.

But it didn't.

I took the gun and raised it with shaking hands, squinting at Juan over the barrel, the Juan who would drive me through the heavily guarded roads on the way to school and give me sips of his coffee from the thermos. The Juan who would offer me a smile before he offered anyone else one. The Juan who sometimes acted like he cared about me more than my own parents did.

I shot that Juan right in the head.

A part of me died that day with him. Maybe all of me did.

I try not to think about it.

Until it's looking right back at me, a figure from the grave, a reminder of how far off the path I've strayed.

Even though it's a dream, a song lyric floats into my head.

The righteous part is straight as an arrow
Take a walk and you'll find it too narrow.

And it was too narrow. Too narrow for the likes of me.

In the dream, Juan looks up at me from the desert floor. A rotten apple rolls out of his skeleton mouth.

Santa Muerte laughs as more blackbirds fly from her eyes, her hair, her lips.

"Good job," my father's words ring across the desert. "You've done me proud."

And I think that's all I've ever wanted.

Until now.

I'm tired the next day. The dream did a number on me. After I woke up, I tossed and turned for hours, wishing Violet was with me to keep the nightmares at bay, both the living ones and the ones in my dreams.

She wants to see me at her house today. We're going to this damn music festival, which is the last thing I want to do.

What I really want is her here in this room. On her knees. On her back. That gorgeous face staring up at me, promising all the good in the world, even if it's locked inside her.

And yet for all her softness and kindness and bleeding heart, I want to make her stronger, better. Something more like me.

God forbid.

But that won't happen today, so I make do with what will. I'll see her and that's the most important thing right now.

Plus, I'm hoping she'll confide in me what happened with Ben. When I got back to the hotel last night, I thought I would dig around a bit online and see what I could find about Ben McQueen, but there was nothing. Ben's obviously got some mad hacking skills to pull up the stuff he did.

Since the festival posters promised lots of alcohol along with the free music, I have one of the hotel's private cars take me to Violet's door.

She and her brother are already waiting on the steps, sitting on the stoop like the poster for an old sitcom I used to watch on *Telemundo*. Except instead of cheesy grins, they look like they're going off to war.

"Hey," I say to them, shoving my hands in the pockets of my jacket. "Ben, you look like shit."

He does. Too much tequila and something else.

Whatever it is I'm supposed to find out.

He just dismisses me with a pained wave, getting up off the step with a pathetic whimper before staggering down the street.

I turn to Violet and hold out my hand, helping her to her feet.

"How are you, *mirlo*?" I ask her, running my hand over her silky head.

"I've been better," she says, standing on her tiptoes for a kiss.

I want to ask. But I keep it to myself. She'll tell me in time.

With my arm around her waist we head off down the street until we catch up with Ben who seems to be in his own tortured world.

Violet controls the conversation, putting on a brave face and leading us through the bands who are playing, the ones who are worth checking out, the history of the festival, and the philanthropist who started it. Her voice is high, speaking fast. She's nervous and even gives me the occasional pained look that tells me she notices it, too.

Things change as we enter the festival grounds, however. Tens of thousands of people, all drunk, stoned, or something else, are joining the pilgrimage with us into the tall, fog-shrouded trees of the park. Somehow, two of Ben's friends appear from the crowd and manage to find us.

I don't pay them much attention and don't even recall their names. They look like college boys, young and naively self-assured. They think the world is their oyster, but they'll find out pretty quickly just where they stand.

The guys want to check out this classic folk band that used to be the pioneers of indie rock, but Violet's stomach is growling and I've seen her get hangry before. We tell them we'll catch up and head to the nearest food trucks instead.

I have to admit, it takes me a moment to let everything

sink in. In fact, it's all catching me off guard. The festival, all these people here, young and old, all races, all religions, filling up the space, here to listen to music and live and be.

I've never been to anything like this before. My childhood was strangely sheltered, in the sense that I was never allowed to have a normal one. Though I went to school, it was a security risk to have me hang out there and make friends, so Juan would shuttle me there and back, and that was the extent of my social life.

I used to have friends when I was younger, but I was about ten when that stopped. Gone were the sleepovers or the camps or the parties. I understand now that there was only an illusion of freedom, that wherever I went there were guards, that I was only allowed to be friends with the boys and girls of the people who worked for my father (which, at one point, seemed to be everyone).

As I got older, my friends were taught to respect me, maybe fear me. They realized I was different from them, that I stood above them and apart.

Vicente was the son of *el jefe*. You couldn't be friends with him. You could only keep your distance and watch your mouth. I learned how to use their fear to my advantage, even if it made me feel hollow inside.

High school followed a similar pattern until I was fifteen.

I got in a fight with a former friend, the son of one of my father's henchmen (for lack of a better word).

I'd slept with his girlfriend.

I was completely in the wrong and I knew it.

Didn't care.

I was young, ready to fuck anything that walked.

219

She was there.

She wanted me.

The power.

It was the first time I really understood the cards I'd been dealt. I had a royal flush. Everyone else had nothing. I knew then that for the rest of my life, I could have everything I wanted.

Almost, anyway.

So the next day at school, the boy punched me.

Nearly broke my nose.

The funny thing is, it didn't piss me off. Everyone was sure he would be dead, that I would kill him right there with my bare hands and no one could or would do a single thing about it. The Bernals owned everyone.

But I let it go.

Maybe because I knew I deserved that punch.

The next day, his father was found in a ditch with a bullet in his head.

A henchman no more.

And my parents kept me away from school. I was to be homeschooled from now on by a matronly teacher— Marta—who would teach Marisol as well.

It was safer that way.

But it meant that both my sister and I were cut off from the rest of society. We only knew the world within the compound. Isolation was control. But Marisol was the luckier one. She often went to be with our aunt Alana in the Caribbean, or with Marguerite in Manhattan. She was able to escape. My mother made sure of that.

I, on the other hand, was stuck. When I left, it was always on business, always for the business. The more control you have, the more you are controlled, and I was a wheel that had to keep spinning for the sake of the cartel.

I had always thought that having power meant having freedom, but I'm not sure if that's true.

No, I don't think it's fucking true at all.

"Are *you* okay?" Violet asks.

I blink, steadying my gaze at her. I think I've been staring at the chalkboard menu for this chicken and waffle food truck for a good five minutes.

"Would you believe it if I told you I'm a bit overwhelmed?"

Her forehead crinkles in surprise. "You?"

"I guess it happens to the best of us." I pretend to study the board.

I feel her lingering attention on the side of my face, wanting me to elaborate.

Sighing, I say, "I've never been to a music festival before. Or even a concert."

"What?" she cries out. "How is that possible? You like music, don't you?"

"*Si,*" I tell her. "But…it just never worked out that way." I look around, at the mix of people eating, laughing, drinking, the thump of faraway acoustics. There's an awful lot of happiness here, and it's nearly disorienting.

No one here thinks there's a price on their head.

No one here is worried that their life is in someone else's hands.

No one here thinks they might be kidnapped and dragged to Mexico as a peace offering, a way to earn favor and respect.

Not the person who should probably think that, anyway.

221

Fuck.

Violet places her hand on my shoulder, making me flinch.

"Vicente," she says softly, her voice filled with concern. "Do you want to leave?"

I shake my head. No. No, please keep me distracted from the things I need to do.

I don't even know if I want to do them anymore.

I just want her.

I'm a motherfucking fool.

And I'm in way over my head.

I fix my eyes on her, determined to put things back on track. "Tell me about your brother. What happened last night?"

She nearly shrinks at that, rubbing her pink lips together. I wish she didn't turn me on like a light switch at the most inappropriate times and for no real reason other than being her sweet little self. "Can I eat first?"

I wait while she gets a paper plate of sliced fried chicken covered in maple syrup with a giant waffle bun. I don't know much about American cooking, especially from the South, but it's pretty fucking good.

We eat and walk down the gravel road, away from the food trucks and stages. I smoke half a cigarette before she starts talking.

"Ben isn't my full-brother," she says abruptly.

Hell. This is news to me.

"Our dad was married before he met Mom. Ben is from that marriage."

Camden, you snake, I can't help but think. "How did you find out?"

"Well, that article that Ben found. That was the big thing he needed to tell me in person. The child in the article was him, the mother was his mother, Sophia Madano."

"And for your whole lives this Sophia was never mentioned?"

She stops in her tracks, holding out her hand and counting off on her fingers.

"Look, this is what Ben and I have known all our lives. Our mom and dad were high school sweethearts that grew up in Palm Valley in the desert. They moved to Gualala before I was born. We moved to San Francisco later. My grandfather on my mother's side is Grandpa Gus, who lives in Gualala with his wife Mimi. She's not my biological grandmother—I mean who knows if anyone is fucking biological anymore—and I don't know much about my supposed real one, other than she's dead. The same goes for my dad's side. Both of his parents were supposed to be dead. For a long time."

"And now you know that's not true. I'm assuming you've seen Ben's birth certificate and it doesn't mention Sophia."

"I know he has seen it. And I've seen his passport."

"All those things can easily be faked."

She opens her mouth to say something, then shuts it, frowning.

"What?"

"I was going to say I can't believe my parents would fake his birth certificate but then…"

"But then you remembered your instincts and that you can somehow believe all of this. Because your parents aren't who you think they are."

Her eyes are sharp as she glances at me. "What do you know?"

I raise my palms. "I know nothing. The same as you. I'm just going on what you told me. Hey, I'm sorry about Ben. I really am. That's got to be rough on him." I pause. "You know you have to tell them now."

"I know I do," she grumbles, folding her arms across her chest. "Believe me, I really want to. But I'm waiting on Ben. He's the one who has a mother he knows nothing about."

"And you're the one living in a house of lies."

She glances at me, thinking that over. The wheels in her head seem to turn for a long time. "What are you doing with me?" she finally says.

I balk, caught off guard. "What?"

She sighs, running her hands over her face, turning away with a low moan. "I mean it, Vicente. What are you doing with me? What do you want with me?"

I don't like these questions. I don't like the heaviness they're adding to my heart. It makes breathing just a bit harder.

"I don't understand…"

"I'm a fucking mess!" she yells, eyes blazing as her hands drop away from her face. "Look at me! You just met me and I'm sure you wanted a quick fuck and now you're roped up with all this…this…ridiculous fucking drama! From my family! I mean, how perfect is this timing? You show up, finally a guy who gets me, who really fucking gets me, and then my family just explodes into shit!"

I watch her, completely enthralled at the anger pouring out of her. I want to see more of it. I want her to own it.

"Everyone has problems with their family," I tell her. "Even me."

"Not like this! You know who your parents are, don't you?"

I swallow, nodding.

Unfortunately, yes.

"Now you're going to leave me and I'll be stuck with them, stuck here in this life I don't fucking want anymore."

I ignore the stabbing sensation in my chest. "I'm not leaving, Violet," I say as patiently as I can. "I told you that last night."

"Yeah fucking right. You're saying that because you're too nice."

I burst out laughing. "Nice? You just called me *nice*?" That's a new one. Vicente, the *nice* guy.

She recoils at my laugh. "Well, you are. You've been more understanding of all this shit than anyone else should be. Right now, it should just be about you and me. Us. That's it. My family should have nothing to do with this."

Oh, my blackbird. That will never, ever be the case.

Our families would die before they ever let us be together.

"What if I were to tell you that I'm not as nice as you think," I say to her, grabbing her hand and pulling her to me. I run my fingers over her cheeks before placing my palm against her throat, my fingers gripping around her neck. "Would a nice boy tie you up and choke you? Would a nice boy encourage you to leave all of this and your family behind?"

She stares up at me warily. Her throat is warm and presses against my hand as she tries to swallow. "What do you mean?" she whispers.

"You want it to be about just you and just me?" I lean in, kissing the side of her mouth. "Then you come away with me. You leave their bullshit and their lies behind and you become the Violet McQueen you were always meant to be. You become free."

Images of blackbirds fill my mind, flying away, singing into the dead of night.

Her eyes shimmer as they gaze up at me. I find it impossible to look away, impossible to let her go. "Come with me," I whisper.

It will be so much easier this way.

Her mouth drops open for a moment, sucking in air. "Where?" she finally asks, shaking slightly. This scares her. It thrills her. Even the fucking thought of it all. I can practically smell her getting wet over it.

Escaping.

With me.

To a place far, far worse than here.

"Anywhere you want to go," I tell her and I'm not lying. Not right now. I do want to take her where her heart desires. "We can leave tonight. Drive to Seattle. Drive to LA. Go to Vegas. Go to New York. Just you and me and the car and, *mirlo*, I promise you you'll see things you've never seen before. I'll open your eyes to the world."

"Vicente…" she trails off, breaking her gaze. I tighten the grip on her neck until she looks back at me.

"I'm serious. You say the word and we'll go."

There's a flash of pink tongue as she licks her lips nervously.

That does me in every time.

My cock hardens. I push it against her thigh.

"I don't…I don't know." She closes her eyes. "I…I have school. I have no money, you know, and I don't want to depend on you."

"Just think about it," I murmur in her ear, releasing her neck and sliding my hand down over her breasts, pressing my cock harder against her.

"I'll think about it."

"Promise?"

She nods. "Yes…if you promise me something."

From the glint in her eye I know it's going to be something I'll like.

"What?"

"Fuck me."

I blink at her, unable to hide the grin. "Right here?"

She doesn't say anything but I can see the determination on her brow. She's in need of a distraction from all of this, wants to get out of her head.

She turns and starts to walk for the trees, a faint path winding away from the festival.

I follow, grabbing her hand, letting her know I'm there for her. She keeps walking, as if leading me and we wind our way through the forest in silence. The wind is picking up, whipping long sections of clouds through the trees. Giant grey whales of mist that float past and disappear.

She brings me to a grove of eucalyptus trees, the smooth bark peeling off in greens and greys and rust, and we go behind them, leaving the crowd in the distance. The music is now reduced to a dull thump, like it's happening in a dream.

Her hands go to my face, fingers so soft and cold, and

she stares at me, her eyes searching mine through a million different feelings and I'm torn in a million different ways, ways I shouldn't be.

One minute I think I know what I need to do.

The next I'm not sure I can do it.

"Everything is going to be okay," I tell her. A lie. And I can tell from the fire in her eyes that she doesn't want to hear it.

"It doesn't matter," she says. She pulls my face down to hers and kisses me, hard, deep, as if she's suddenly afraid that she won't survive without my lips on hers, my tongue lost in her warmth. She really believes I'll leave her, that her family drama and her messy life is far too much for me.

It all comes out in desperation as her hands slip down over my dick, pressing hard against my firm length and coaxing a deep moan from me.

She wants to escape.

I will gladly do what I can.

I move away from her hands and undo the button on her jeans before unzipping them. I pull them down to the ground and her lacy underwear along with it.

"What did I tell you about wearing these?" I say, like I'm chastising a child.

I kiss her hard and then drop to my knees, removing her boots and tossing her jeans aside. Without saying a word, I start licking up her cold, bare, naked thighs until she shivers and moans, until goosebumps erupt all over her sensitive flesh. I slide my fingers into her cunt, wet and wanting, just as I thought. She's practically melting into my touch and I melt into her.

"Look how wet you are," I moan, kissing briefly down

her legs. "You're ready to come in my mouth already."

Once she begins breathing hard, swaying her hips for more, I keep her pressed back against the tree and bring up one of her legs, hooking it over my shoulder. She grabs the top of my head for stability, her fingers sinking into my hair as I leave soft, wet kisses from the side of her knee all the way up her inner thigh. My lips and tongue tease her mercilessly, one of my favorite things to do.

Her body tenses and relaxes from my touch, and I grab hold of the sides of her hips, hard, as I bring my face between her legs. My lips meet her swollen ones and I tease her clit with the tip of my finger before sliding my tongue along her cleft and plunging it inside her.

Jesus.

So hot, so tight, so wet.

She's unbelievable.

Her exquisite, heady taste dances on my tongue, reaching deep inside of me and igniting this primal layer, the caveman at my core.

I want to devour her until there's nothing left. I want to make her scream and squirm and moan into oblivion.

I want to be all there is for her.

She cries out, her fist in my hair, yanking hard as she sinks further into me, hips rocking for pressure, for purchase. I give it all, my fingers going in deeper, sliding along the right places, my tongue working her clit overtime, her sweetness running down my chin.

I'm not sure I can ever get enough of her. Of this.

I'm doomed in the most maddening way.

No matter what fucking happens between us, I'm not going to walk out of here a winner.

Neither of us will.

We might not even make it out alive.

She's close to coming now and I swear, somewhere in the distance, I can hear people talking as they make their way through the trees.

It doesn't matter.

She comes hard into my mouth, her clit pulsing beneath my lips, and I drink her all in, keeping her coming until she moans for me to stop.

I pull my head away and look up at her serene, pleasured face, wiping my lips with the back of my hand.

"Not fucking done with you yet," I growl at her.

I grab her by the waist and hoist her up, pressing her back against the tree. She lets out a lazy yelp before hooking her legs around my waist.

I don't have a condom. It doesn't matter.

I quickly unzip my pants, take my throbbing cock out and push into her with one quick, brutal thrust that wrings all the air from my lungs.

She gasps, my mouth biting at her neck, my hand yanking at her shirt, trying to get at her skin. After all I've devoured of her, I still want more.

She has no idea the hold she has on me.

This sweet hell she's dragged me in.

"Fuck," I groan, slamming her back again, my pumps becoming faster and faster, like I'm trying to nail her to the god damn tree. We kiss and it's messy, teeth clacking against each other, lips and tongues trying in wild desperation to win.

Everything inside me is swirling, a black pool of turmoil with no end in sight. I want to ravage her, fuck her, screw her, keep doing this to her until all these feelings go away.

I'm angry. I'm so fucking angry that my heart feels something for her.

That she's getting under my skin.

That she's making me question who I am.

"Vicente," she gasps and I think maybe I'm just fucking her too hard. Her head is starting to slam back against the tree, her nails are digging into my jacket.

But when I look at her, her eyes are focused over my shoulder in surprise.

"People can see us."

God, I almost blow my load right then.

"Oh yeah?" I ask, breathless as I fuck.

"They're watching us," she says, her words twisting into a moan.

I don't bother turning around. If there are people there, I know what they'll see. Me, naked from the waist down, my bare ass squeezing as I relentlessly ram my cock into her, her legs clutching around my waist.

"Let them look," I say, grunting into her neck as my pace picks up, sweat dripping from my brow and onto her chest. The fact that strangers are watching only heightens the sensations, makes me extra aware of her sexy little gasps as I slide my fingers over her clit, aware of the mist as it chills my bare legs. Everything is magnified.

This must be what it's like to be blindfolded.

Only now I can stare into Violet's eyes, searching for her release. Her lids are heavy, her gaze is languid. She trusts me. She trusts me so much.

I can barely handle the thought.

I suck her bottom lip into my mouth, like she's candy.

"I'm coming," she moans, eyes closing, head rolling to the side.

For a moment I think she'll stifle her cries – she knows people are watching and she has a tendency to be loud. But she doesn't. She lets it all go.

"Fuck, fuck, Vicente!" she yells hoarsely, her fingers holding tighter and tighter as she pulses and jerks around me. "Oh, god, oh so fucking good."

"*Si?*" I ask but then my words choke as I'm caught in the riptide. My orgasm sneaks up on me, like being hit from behind.

It's devastating.

It stuns me in a way I never saw coming.

I feel like I'm being fileted and for the first time she might see who I really am.

My eyes pinch closed, shutting her out. I'm loud when I come, my cries rising into the trees. I can't control myself, not right now, not anymore.

Is this what it's like to dance on a tightrope, one end slowly unravelling?

And then, like a switch, the dance is over.

I collapse against her, sweat dripping off my brow and over my nose. I can hardly breathe but I don't care. I'm shuddering on the inside, completely unraveled.

Completely frightened.

And I don't scare easily.

She starts to slip so I gently lower her to the ground and pull out, my cum dripping down her legs.

Got to admit, it's a deliciously sexy sight.

"Sorry," I say, clearing my throat. "Looks like we need

Plan A."

She gives me a small smile, nearly falling over on shaky legs. She leans against the tree and after I do up my pants, I help pull hers back on. "It's called Plan B," she says. She looks in the distance and my eyes follow her.

There's a couple of guys a few yards out, peering between the trees.

Perverts.

I stand back up and wave at them. "Get a good show?"

At that they start running off. Luckily none of them had a camera or phone aimed at me, otherwise I'd have to hunt them down and kill them.

And how would I explain that to Violet?

Then again, I already have a lot of explaining to do.

"Well," she says, blowing a piece of hair out of her eyes. "I didn't see the band Quick Fuck with Vicente on the festival lineup."

"No? They're very underrated." I smile and I grab her hand. "Come on, let's go find your brother."

Violet

"**C**AN I JUST SAY YOU'VE BEEN A REALLY SHITTY
friend?"

Ginny's voice is all business but from the way
she's holding out her bright orange cocktail toward me and
the pleading look in her eyes, I know she doesn't mean it.

Which kind of makes it worse.

I pick up my lychee martini and clink it gently against
hers, looking her dead in the eyes. "I'm sorry. Honestly."

She takes a sip as I take mine. "It's fine. I'm just teasing
you. You're getting the D you've always needed. Hey, I get
it."

I nearly choke on the drink. If only she knew what kind
of dick I was actually getting. Sex with Vicente is about as

wild, adventurous and dirty as it gets.

I give her a look. "No, you definitely don't get it."

"You're right," she says. "I'm pretending. But I can and will tell you that Vicente is a fine looking man. Even *I* turned into a heart-eyed emoji when I saw him."

I roll my eyes. "You were borderline rude, Ginny."

She shrugs. "Whatever. You were keeping me in the dark, after all that talk about getting you laid." She scans the stage. "Where's my girl at?"

We're at a cabaret turned open mic show in the Castro. Normally I find these shows delightfully colorful yet a little too loud for my ears. But Ginny's girlfriend Tamara is the MC and so I'm here for support.

And yeah, I've been a shitty friend. Ever since I met Vicente I've ignored Ginny and everything else around me, including school. I'm way behind in everything and the terrifying thing is…

I don't care.

It's been two weeks since I met Vicente and the hold he has on me is only growing stronger. I can't get enough of him. He occupies my thoughts, my body, my heartbeat.

The sex, that dirty crazy sex, has been amazing.

Incredible.

And constant.

I'm actually a bit afraid.

The edge is in sight, clear as day, and I can see myself going over it.

Maybe just to see what it's like to fly.

But like my fears of walking across the Golden Gate Bridge, the fall scares me. Those moments of life flashing past you, knowing it's all going to end.

Because that's what happens in these kinds of relationships, right?

It has to end.

Only the lucky keep going.

As rock god Josh Homme once said, it's called falling in love because you hit the ground.

"So, are you in love yet?" Ginny asks, hammering the nail on the head, like I'm so easy to read.

Love.

Just the sound of the word is terrifying.

I try and swallow but my throat feels too thick.

I can only shake my head.

No. Not love.

It's too soon. Those are the rules.

But the truth is, as much it scares me, I'm desperate for it.

I want to fall in love. Roll around it. Wrap it up and wear it until it's tattered and torn. I want to be reckless with it and baby it and let it define me.

I'm mad.

This is madness.

Utter chaos of the heart.

A herd of horses in the soul.

Ever since he said I should run away with him, leave my family behind and all the lies and nonsense, I haven't been able to get it out of my head. And the crazy thing is, I think going with him might be the right thing to do.

I mean, it's the wrong thing to do…my parents paid a lot for my school and as much as I'm not concentrating on it right now and as much as I kind of hate them at the moment, I don't want to do that to them. It would be the epitome of being ungrateful and I'm truly not.

But the little voice inside my head, like a chirping bird calling and calling and calling for something, that voice won't go away. I just want to be with Vicente. I just want to shut ourselves away in a place where we're the only thing that exists.

"No, huh? Mmmm, you just wait," Ginny says, her eyes glued to the stage as Tamara, in a sparkling blue jumpsuit that sets off her black skin, introduces the next performer. "You'll be unable to stop thinking the word. Then you'll make excuses for it. Either way, you're doomed. Once love starts, it's impossible to stop. You'll make them your whole world." Her voice drifts off, nearly disappearing in the raucous cries of the crowd. "Your whole fucking world."

I wish I didn't relate. My heart is so much more sensitive than it should be. How can I trust that what I feel is real? How do I know it's not just me pulling a Violet, being hyper-sensitive? For crying out loud, my heart fucking cries and bleeds when I accidently kill a bee.

There are no answers. I have no past to navigate by. The boyfriends I had I thought I loved at the time, but in comparison to Vicente, I realize that they were just comfort and crushes. There was none of that tear your hair out, tear your clothes off, I have to be with you now and all the time and always. That just didn't exist before him.

It was a whole other life before him.

One where I was drowning and didn't even know it.

Vicente's mouth against mine is a lungful of oxygen, his body a life raft. He might be the only thing saving me lately.

Ben still hasn't confronted our parents. To be fair, it's been a week since he found out about Sophia Madano and he's been at school in Santa Cruz. I haven't seen him or talked to him since – my texts have gone unanswered, which isn't unusual when I know he has exams.

I've just been trying to get by, trying to ignore it. Without talking to Ben, there's only so much I can do, so much I can think. I don't want my imagination to run away on me without knowing all the facts, the facts that either he or my parents should provide. Until then though, there's that perturbed feeling of knowing nothing at all.

And then there's Vicente himself.

I want to chalk it up to paranoia, but I swear he's pulling away, just a bit.

It's nothing he's done or said to me. Just what I'm observing when he thinks I'm not looking. The way his eyes drift off into space, the flashes of pain in them, some inner torment that he has to face. How in the middle of the night he'll wake up from nightmares he won't tell me about. Nightmares that have him saying "*Lo siento, lo siento, lo siento*" over and over again.

He's sorry about something. Whatever it is, I want to know about it so I can take it away from him. Set him free.

Maybe it will set us both free.

"Hey," Ginny says, nudging me. "Snap out of it. Join me in the now."

I give her an embarrassed smile. It's one thing to be a crappy friend from afar, it's another thing to be a crappy friend up close and personal.

I do what I can to push Vicente from my brain. The drinks help. And I talk with Ginny and enjoy the rest of the mayhem that is tonight's "entertainment."

I actually have fun, once I learn to let go a bit and start living outside of my head. The best act of the evening was the drag queen with the monkey who would braid her hair. That monkey could have a nice little gig doing hairstyles outside of Powell Street station.

But when the crowd gets too loud and boisterous, I've had enough. I'm drunk and horny and Ginny and Tamara are making out and Vicente isn't anywhere nearby.

I decide to walk home but once I get a few blocks up the hill and away from the hustle and bustle, I chicken out and try and get a Lyft through the app on my phone.

Shit.

Phone's dead.

At least there's no fog for once. Foggiest October on record, I swear.

As I walk down the street, the moon is nowhere to be seen. It's pitch black and the clear air brings a chill as I hug my jacket and scarf close to me, peering in the windows of the Victorians as I pass them by. For some reason the sight of people inside, watching TV or reading by the windows, lights on, brings small moments of comfort. It's like they let you know that the world is chugging along as normal and nothing is as bad as it –

I can't finish the thought.

A hand goes over my mouth. Cold pressure to my temple.

Oh my god!

I'm grabbed from behind and before I can do or say anything I'm twisted off the street and into an area beside a dumpster, shoved into the shadows.

The person holding onto me doesn't say anything,

my mind goes wild trying to figure out who it is. They smell like bad cologne, so strong it makes my eyes water. Their breath is loud and raspy, like they have breathing problems. From the way their belly pokes into my back, I'm guessing they're out of shape.

But they have a gun to my head.

A gun.

And that's when all instinct inside me, the one that tells me to fight back, that knows how to fight back, takes a moment to breathe. To think.

But I can't think.

I can only moan against the person's gloved hand and stare at the street. This street that only a few seconds ago brought me comfort and security.

I'm so fucking *close* to home.

I didn't even pick up on someone following me.

I didn't pick up on anything.

"Violet McQueen," the man says in my ear. A strange voice, hoarse and echoing. No accent, no interesting dialect. A voice I've never heard before.

I can't say yes or no to his question.

I can't do anything at all.

I'm useless.

"I don't want to hurt you but I will," the man says. "I'll need you to come with me. Be a good girl now."

He starts moving, taking me out of the shadows and to the black van parked nearby.

Once I'm in that van, I'm as good as dead.

I know that.

The fear is unreal.

It's a bear inside me, growling with fangs, hovering

above my heart, ready to tear in. Terror is sweating out of my pores, perfuming the air with something metallic.

My tongue tastes like nickels.

I think of Ben. I think of my mom, my dad. I think it's something to do with *them*.

I think of Vicente.

I think it's something to do with *him*.

But I know if I get in that van, I'll never be able to tell them.

I'll never be able to tell anyone anything.

He drags me foot by foot and each inch I move across the rough sidewalk I pray for someone to walk past, maybe with their dog on a nightly stroll, maybe drive by dropping off a friend or returning home from a late shift. I pray for someone, anyone, to tear their eyes away from the TV and look out the window.

I know prayers still need a boost.

He seems to be alone. He has to open the door of the van and he's either going to do it with the hand that's over my mouth or the hand that has the gun. I'm betting it's the latter. It's too much of a risk if I scream, too many houses around, too many eyes.

He reaches out with the hand with the gun.

I don't even have to think.

My body moves on instinct, forged in training, an automatic reaction.

I bite into his hand over my mouth and while his head whips toward me in shock, just a flash of his eyes boring into mine, I raise my elbow and clock him right in the face.

I've never hit hard like that before, with the intent to

maim, not even when I was attacked outside Buena Vista park.

I like it.

I like the sound of his bones crunching from the hit.

I like the feel of my body as it spins, stepping back as my hand jabs up, getting him on the nose and breaking it, blood spilling on the street, moonlight reflected in the splatter.

I like the violence of my results.

I like it to the point it distracts me.

He flies at me, butt of the gun crashing into my cheek bone and temple.

I cry out, shrill. The pain is like stars and gunpowder inside my skull.

But my body moves like the pain is fuel. It silently thanks my father for making me fight all those years.

I try to kick at his face, but I'm too short, the ground too uneven, my legs not as flexible as they used to be.

The tip of my boot catches his chin.

It's enough.

He drops his gun, his body momentarily slumping against the van.

But he's not a weak man and he'll come after me harder than I can come after him.

So I scream.

I open my mouth and I scream my heart out.

Loud.

So fucking loud, like a million banshees are soaring out.

You know when you have those dreams where some-one is after you and you try and scream and run but you can't? Your screams die in your throat and your legs move like molasses?

Well those are just that – dreams.

In real life, you can scream until the whole city hears you.

Until every house turns on their lights, opens their doors.

And you can run.

Oh, yes.

I'm running like the wind.

My legs are pumping up and down as I book it down the street and around the corner. It's almost effortless. I feel like I can run forever, like I'm Tom Cruise out for a jog.

But I know it's adrenaline that's propelling me forward, all the way to Haight.

Past my house.

Because even though I should go there after what happened, I don't.

I'm afraid.

I'm afraid that whoever that was, they have something to do with my parents. Or Sophia. Or whoever sent my father that envelope.

I don't feel safe.

I get in a cab instead, breathless and fidgeting in the backseat. The music the cabbie is playing it too loud and jarring yet I can't find the words to tell him to turn it off. I feel like I'm in a video game, except the pain on my cheek reminds me that it's very real.

I should go to the cops. Should file a report.

Should do this, should do that.

But I can't. Because I feel there's only one person who

can help me, one person who is unbiased and impartial.

The outsider looking in.

Vicente.

Vicente

THINK EVERYONE HAS A LITTLE THING THEY LIKE TO DO when they get nervous.

With Violet, she likes to pick off her nail polish. Or play with her hair. Or scratch her arms until they're red.

With me, I like to clean my guns.

It's as soothing and banal as I'm sure doing the dishes is. If I ever feel the itch of worry, if I'm unable to ignore the anxiety building in my chest, I just take out my guns. Admire them. Then take them apart. It shows that something can become a total mess, rendered powerless, but all you have to do is clean them, make them more efficient, and put them back together again. It's a puzzle with the same results every time.

I have them laid out on the bed, my .45, my 9MM, and .38, when there's a knock at the door. I freeze and stare at the .38 in pieces. I don't have time to put it back together, so I grab the 9MM and keep it at my side as I quickly exit the bedroom, shut the door, and creep down the hall to the main one.

I half expect to see my father on the other side, smiling at me through the keyhole. It would be about time he showed up, actually.

I'm shocked to see Violet. We didn't have plans to see each other tonight – she wanted a break to be with her friend and I needed the time to think.

I quickly shove the gun into my waistband, pulling my shirt out over it, and swing open the door.

"Violet?" I say as she pushes past me into the room, tears streaming down her face.

Her face.

Is she hurt?

Cold swells in my stomach.

I quickly lock the door and follow her into the living room, pulling her to me.

She's in near hysterics, breathing fast and hard, sobs that rip through her body. Her hair hangs in her face so while I grab her arm to steady her, I tip up her chin to look her over.

Terror seizes my throat.

The side of her cheek is red and blue, reaching from the corner of her eye across her cheekbone to her ear and up into the temple.

"What the fuck happened?" I cry out, my fingers reaching for her.

She flinches, turns away. She tries to speak but can't.

I don't know what to do. Part of me is stunned by the horror I feel. Part of me is angry at myself for not being there to prevent this.

Another part, the darkest part, wants to tear the world to pieces and find the person who did this to her. Because someone did.

Someone did.

God help me if it had anything to do with my father.

"Violet." I hold onto her tight. "Please. Tell me what happened."

She can only shake her head.

Fuck.

I leave her and go to the kitchen, wrapping up ice cubes in a dish cloth. I take her over to the couch and sit her down, placing the cloth in her hand. "Here. Hold this to your cheek. Gently." I then grab tequila off of the counter and a glass and pour her some. "Here, straight back."

Her hands shake so much that she has to use both of them to cup the glass and do the shot.

My fucking heart is breaking.

Tiny shattered pieces.

And that's when I realize I am not my father at all.

Not even close.

Because even though I planned to take Violet to Mexico, even though I was fully aware of what would happen to her, seeing her like this, I know I can't do it.

She's been hit in the face and it feels like I'm the one who's bleeding on the inside. What my father would do to her is far, far worse. I've heard what he did to a man called Esteban Mendoza, and I never wanted to hear it again.

I feel vomit rising in my throat and try to keep it together.

She needs me to keep it together.

I sit on the coffee table across from her and grasp her hands in mine, holding them tight, ignoring the jab of the gun into my hip. "When you're ready," I say gently. "Just breathe. In and out. I've got you now. You're going to be okay."

That brings a bitter laugh out of her. "Okay?" she peers at me through sorrowful eyes. "How is this going to be okay? I was fucking attacked walking home and he wasn't your run-of-the-mill random mugger."

"Tell me exactly what happened."

She shakes her head, a whimper escaping her lips. "Okay. Okay I was walking back from the Castro."

"You walked? For fuck's sake, Violet!" I explode, nearly getting up. "You knew there was someone following you a few weeks back and you walked?"

She lifts up her head. Her eyes are blades. "I was an idiot! All right? I walked. And then when I was tired I decided to call a car but my phone died."

I don't care that she's looking at me like she wants to murder me. I can't believe she would put herself at risk like that.

She goes on, looking down at her hands, picking off the olive green nail polish until it rains down on the floor in flakes. "So I was walking and I was just a few blocks from home and suddenly I was grabbed, a gun was held to my head." She pauses, drawing in a deep breath. "I didn't know what to do, I was so shocked. He dragged me over to his van."

"He had a van?"

"Black. No windows. I didn't see the make or the license plate or anything. I barely saw him."

"Was it the same guy as before, the albino one?"

"I don't know. I don't…I wish I could say I saw him but my brain was just figuring out how to live. And I figured he was alone so once he reached for the door to shove me inside I decided to hit him."

Pride knocks into me. "You hit him?"

"I had to. Do or die. We fought. I broke his nose. I was able to get a kick to his face before I ran away."

Good god. I don't think I've ever had a sexier sight in my head, my dear blackbird fighting off an abductor and living to tell the tale. My cock throbs mercilessly and I have to stifle a groan that wants to escape through my lips.

Now is *not* the time.

Still, I can't help myself. "Tell me more about how you fought him off."

She smiles which in turn makes her wince. "Please don't tell me this is turning you on. I know the signs."

I attempt to look innocent. I don't do a very good job.

"While he reached for the door, I bit into his hand and then managed to get my elbow in his face, which obviously caught him off-guard. Then I got him on the nose. Upward strike. Broke it. I felt it break."

I lick my lips. "And how did it feel? To hurt him?"

She takes a moment before she speaks, looking at me, troubled. "Honestly? It felt good. Really good."

A smile slowly slides across my face.

There's a hunger burning in her eyes that wasn't there before.

I would do anything to fan those flames, give her

strength to burn the world to the ground and rise from it.

"Then I kicked him the face. I mean, I almost missed. It's been a long time since I've been in good shape, it's just by luck that I was able to get my leg up that high."

"He must have not been that tall."

"No, he wasn't," she muses, brow furrowed. "Maybe two inches taller."

I think to Parada's height. Like most Mexicans, he's not especially tall. He didn't luck out like I did. But grabbing her on the street and into a black van? Working alone? That doesn't sound like Parada at all. Once again I'm at a loss as to who this person could be.

I do know I'll kill him once I find him.

Drive a gun so far up his ass he'll be spitting bullets.

Then I'll pull the trigger.

"After that, I ran," she goes on, her breathing now returning to normal. "I didn't know where to go. I didn't want to go home, I thought…maybe they were waiting for me there. Maybe it wasn't safe. This has to do with my parents, Vicente, this can't be random."

"It's not random. Nothing that has happened to you is random."

She nods slowly, eyes focused on nothing.

"So these men are after me because of my parents," she says flatly. She brings her gaze up to mine, pain in her eyes. "Or are they after me because of you?"

I stare back at her blankly.

What does she know, what does she know?

Maybe she knows more than she's saying.

Maybe those were my father's men after all.

Changing tactics to throw me off.

"I don't understand," I finally say.

She straightens up, her eyes still searching mine, trying to read me. For once I fear how intuitive she is.

"The moment you showed up in my life, trying to join my class…one minute everything was fine, then you appeared."

I can't let her run away with this.

"Violet, you're scared and looking into things that aren't there. You're overreacting."

"Fuck you!" she suddenly yells, popping up to her feet. "Fuck you, I am not overreacting, I was nearly fucking abducted, this guy hit me with his god damn gun! I'm looking into everything that I can!"

"Calm down."

"I will not fucking calm down!" she throws her arms out and starts storming off.

I jump to my feet and go after her.

By the time I grab both her biceps, twirling her around, I feel the gun dislodge from my waistband. It's too late to stop it.

It clatters to the floor.

Violet looks down.

Recoils.

But my grip on her is too tight.

"Why do you have a gun?" she cries out, trying to get away.

I won't let her. I bring her closer to me.

She struggles.

I'm stronger.

"Violet," I say, my voice soft but firm. "Violet, listen to me."

"Let fucking go of me."

"I will when you calm down."

"Why do you have a gun?" she repeats. Her eyes are awash with fear as she stares at me, like she's never seen me before.

I close my eyes for a second, breathing in sharply through my nose, letting my breath bring me clarity.

"I have a gun for protection. As do most people in this country."

"Protection from what?" She sounds nearly broken from fear. I realize under normal circumstances this might not be a big deal to her. But since she was just held at gunpoint and had that same gun driven into the beautiful bones of her cheek, she's going to overreact.

"Protection from people, people like the ones who did this to you." I loosen my grip on her, put one hand to her face to brush her hair behind her ear, but she turns it sharply away from me.

"Is that your only gun?" she asks.

I hesitate. It tells her enough.

She rips backward out of my grasp and I instinctively reach down to pick up the gun.

"I'll scream," she warns me, backing up into the wall.

I raise the gun in the air, letting it dangle from my finger, a sign of peace. "This gun isn't for you, Violet." But I don't let go of it as I approach her.

She's eyeing it now. She wants to grab it from me. She thinks I'll use it on her.

She's losing her mind.

Our eyes meet.

She opens her mouth to scream.

I quickly place my hand over it, muffling a yelp back into her mouth while I press her into the wall. The gun wants to jab into her side, maybe below her chin. It wants to do its thing. It takes everything in me to fight it and leave it at my side.

"Violet," I whisper to her, my lips at her ear. I can practically hear the blood pounding in her skull. "Don't scream. Don't do anything you'll regret. Just listen to me." I pull back a few inches, staring into her eyes, counting the flecks of gold and grey in the teak. "I have guns for protection, *si*? They aren't to be used against you. They're to protect you."

She doesn't believe me. Her nostrils flare above my hand as she struggles to catch her breath.

"Do you want to see? Do you want to know the truth?"

She nods once, hardly blinking, not daring to take her eyes off mine.

"I'm going to take my hand away. Can you promise not to scream?"

She shakes her head.

For fuck's sake.

I sigh. "Screaming won't help you, I hope you know that. Not because I'll do anything to stop you. I won't. I'll let you leave if you want. But if you scream, people will come for me. And that's very, very bad news indeed. If they come for me, I won't be able to protect you." I lean in closer, my forehead pressing against hers. "Do you understand, *mirlo*?"

She grunts something that sounds like a yes.

I step back and carefully remove my palm from her mouth.

She immediately gulps for air.

"Remember when I said I wasn't a nice guy?" I say. I grab her hand and lead her over to the bedroom, opening the door.

We step inside and she gasps at the sight of the two guns on the bed.

"I have more at home, this is just a little travel kit," I tell her, raising the one in my hand in front of her face, making sure she can see me eject the clip, which rattles across the floor. I toss it on the bed and then raise both my hands. "I'm not going to hurt you and you're not going to hurt me. Deal?"

She walks to the bed, her fingers tracing over the parts I haven't put back together. "Who are you, Vicente?" she whispers, more to the guns than to me.

"You want the truth? Even if the truth will scare you? Even if the truth will make you think differently of me?"

"Yes," she says but she's bracing herself.

"Fine."

I walk over to her and sit on the bed and finish putting my guns back together, as if she hadn't interrupted me at all. "As I am sure you have figured out, my father has nothing to do with avocados. He's the leader of a drug cartel."

I glance up at her. To her credit she doesn't seem all that shocked.

"Oh."

"And I'm the second in command."

She licks her lips. "I see."

"Do you now?"

She shakes her head. "Why didn't you just tell me that?"

I let out a dry laugh. "Are you serious? Tell me you wouldn't have run away or called the police."

She shrugs and sits down next to me, picking up a bullet and examining it. "I don't know what I would have done." I have to admit, it's kind of impressive how she's taking it all in stride. I don't know if it's because of her bloodline, that she's so accepting of my way of life. Or if what's been happening over the last few weeks has been opening her eyes to a new side of things, but whatever it is I'm grateful for it.

"Well I can tell you that it's the kind of thing we keep under wraps. I would be a wanted man if people knew who I was. I hate to sound cocky, but I'm very valuable."

She offers me a faint smile. "You love to sound cocky."

"True. There are a lot of people who want me dead or want me as a bargaining chip."

"People like the ones who have been following me?"

"Honestly, I don't know. But you can see why I need to protect myself."

She glances over her shoulder at the wardrobe. "Those ropes weren't really for sex, were they?"

"Not always, no."

"And let me guess, you really do have duct tape."

"In my toiletry bag."

"And even though you use a tie on me, I assume you have an actual blindfold somewhere."

I shake my head. "No. But back home, we would use a black bag, like a potato sack."

She shakes a bit at that, as if it's all just starting to sink in. "Were you sent here to kidnap me?" the words sound so soft coming out her mouth, I nearly crumble.

"No, Violet. No one sent me here. To do anything. I came here because I wanted to, I needed to…" I'm not even sure if I'm lying anymore. "I wanted to escape, to be a better man. And then I met you…and I realized I could be."

"Am I supposed to believe you?"

"Yes," I say thickly. "You're supposed to believe me."

She exhales and leans back until she's lying on the bed beside the guns. "I don't know what to believe anymore." Her head rolls to the side and she stares at me for a few beats. "I want you to teach me how to shoot a gun. I want you to give me one of them."

My heart swells, fast and warm in my chest. My beautiful blackbird, coming into her own. "That can be arranged."

"I want you to make me stronger."

"I won't have to do much work," I tell her, pushing the guns aside and crawling over to her.

"I want to be able to protect myself," she says.

I climb on top of her, grinning as I run my fingers over her lips. "You'll more than protect yourself. You'll find the guy who did this to you and you'll blow his brains out yourself."

She blinks hard at that, struck by the fear. Maybe the fear of how easily she can imagine it.

I bury my mouth below her ear, licking, sucking, tasting her adrenaline.

"I want us to go far away from here," she murmurs.

"I'll take you wherever you want to go."

"Vegas might be fun."

I laugh as my hands slide up under her shirt, exposing her bra. "Vegas would be fun. I've never been." I pull down the cup and slowly suck her nipple into my mouth in one long draw. She squirms beneath me, her hands running through my hair and tugging.

As I slide her leggings down, she says, "In three weeks.

I want to finish the semester first. I'll feel horrible if I quit right now."

"The last thing I want is you to feel guilty when you shouldn't," I tell her, running my hand between her legs. She's so fucking wet it makes my mouth water. It's going to be hard to take this slow, all the violence and fear and nerves are running wild inside me, dying to come out.

"Is your name really Vicente Cortez?" she asks, her voice breathless, throaty.

I pause, my fingers aching to dip inside her. "No."

"What is it?"

I take my chances. "Vicente Bernal."

She sucks in her breath.

An eternity seems to stretch between us.

Finally she exhales. "Your father. Was he Javier Bernal? That's his name right? I've heard of him."

My fingers slide up and over her clit, then back down again. "Yes."

"H-he…he…" Her breath hitches as I move. "He used to have control over the whole country. He was just as bad as El Chapo, he just never got caught." She writhes back and forth.

"Bad. Or good. Depending who you talk to I say." I hesitate. "Where did you hear that from?"

"The news I guess. I never really paid much attention."

I slowly push my fingers inside her, making her back arch. A gasp escapes her lips.

"Just don't tell your parents," I say, before plunging them into to the hilt. "I don't think they'd understand."

She can't even answer in words, just lets out an achingly beautiful moan.

It undoes me.

I unzip my jeans and bring out my cock, hot and throbbing in my palm, remembering to take an extra second to get the condom out of my pocket and roll it on.

She's below me, waiting patiently, her hair a storm of birds around her, her perky tits with those perfect pink nipples begging to be sucked. My guns lie to the side of her strong, beautiful body; cold, hard steel next to soft white curves.

I don't think I've ever seen a more beautiful sight in my life.

And I don't think I've ever been so turned on.

I will not last long.

The urgency hits me like a hammer and I quickly position my cock before grabbing her wrists and holding them above her head.

I push inside her, a sharp, hard thrust that makes me shudder all over, a hoarse grunt crawling up my throat. She cries out and I bury her mouth with mine as she starts rocking her hips up into me, wanting more.

"Harder, god, fuck me harder," she says in hot little gasps.

I growl and start rutting into her, enough to make the bed shake and the sheets to pop off the mattress. Violet is wet down to her thighs, so wet that I keep slipping out. Every time I push back in, all the way to the thick base, I feel like I'm seeing heaven.

"You're getting my cock so wet," I murmur roughly, dipping my head down to bite at her nipple. "Such a desperate little bird."

Her nails scratch and claw down my back like the

frantic, wild animal she is and I fuck her harder and harder until my arms are shaking, my neck corded and tense as I try to hold everything back.

I don't have to hold on for long.

She comes fast and violent, just like our fucking. Her eyes roll in her head and she shatters beneath me. My own release spirals out of control and I let go, nearly breaking her in half as I pound into her relentlessly, over and over and over until every last ounce of cum has pumped out of me.

Fucking hell.

I collapse onto my elbows, sweat slick between our chests, our hearts clashing against each other like warring drums. I look down at her face, damp and glowing, marred by bruised skin and danger.

She's so beautiful. So precious.

So inherently destructive to everything that I am.

I know my feelings can't be trusted at all. Maybe they never could be.

But I still have that terrifying feeling inside me, like a pill I just can't swallow.

…I think I'm in love with her.

Javier

JAVIER HATES LYING TO HIS WIFE.

He thought after twenty-something years of marriage that he'd be pretty good at it by now. After all, you can't survive more than a day in this business without lying through your teeth about something. You become so skilled at it that you actually believe the lies yourself.

Javier believes nearly every lie he's ever told. He almost believes the one he tells Luisa.

That Vicente will be back soon and all will be well.

It's not that he won't be back…Javier is making sure that he'll be brought back one way or another. And Luisa knows this, that Vicente will kick up a fuss. But she wants him home, safe, and thinks once that happens, everything will go back to normal.

Javier finds this amusing, her need for routine and normalcy. I mean, what the fuck did she expect when she married him? But for all her partnership and influence in the business and his affairs – *their* affairs – Luisa has a soft heart that craves the simple life. A soft heart that he prays his son didn't inherit.

And because of that, Javier has to lie to her.

She doesn't know that it was because of Javier that Vicente set out to California in the first place. She doesn't know she had her own hand in it. She doesn't know it was all part of a plan.

Vicente didn't know either.

Still doesn't.

Oh, to be young and naïve, full of unearned confidence.

Javier feels remorse snake through his body but then it's gone. It never stays for long. It knows it's not welcome.

He's sitting in his office, drinking tequila, and staring into space. He's waiting for news and when he's waiting, he has too much time alone with his thoughts.

Thinking can be dangerous.

He laughs to himself, the sound reaching around the room.

It's true. Too many thoughts mean too much introspection and that's never been Javier's strong suit. If he looks too closely, he doesn't always like what he sees.

Like now.

Sure, he's thinking about his wife and how she thinks Vicente will return when he's good and ready and if he doesn't, her husband will get him back and when he returns he'll be grateful and fresh-faced from new adventures and a sore dick from all the American cunts he's fucking (at least he assumes that's what Vicente is doing since he would do the same).

But as he sits in his office alone and the booze is seeping into his veins like an IV, maybe now he's also eying the cabinet in the room that has a locked box inside.

At least, it was locked, until Vicente broke it off.

Small price to pay. It was proof that it worked.

Javier had told Luisa just before he went out of town that he was looking for old information on the Tijuana cartel. Said there were some people involved and he was curious to remember who they were.

Lies.

He told Luisa that Vicente should look for it. Keep him busy. Keep him involved. He told her it was important he do it.

Truth.

So Luisa told Vicente that morning to go look for the files.

And Vicente, the good son, did as he was told.

He nearly tore apart the office looking for them, determined not to give up.

He found the locked box.

He didn't ask for the key, he just broke the lock off with a hammer because that's what he's been trained to do. Micro-manage. Come up with his own solutions. Get the job done.

In that box, Javier had printed out some information on the Tijuana cartel from back in the day, boring bullshit that no one cares about. There were some files on Evaristo, the *federale* who turned sides, became a priest and went rogue. There were files on old shipments, a few dossiers on a *sicario*.

The rest of the files were devoted to Ellie.

That was the hardest part for Javier. To spend all that time digging around and reliving the past like that. He has to admit, it hurt. He's never taken failure very well, always had trouble with humiliation.

He hates to lose.

And that's exactly what happened with Ellie Watt. It didn't matter that Javier didn't truly love her, not in the way he loves Luisa. It didn't matter that he would be able to get over it with time.

What mattered was that he *lost*.

He lost like he'd never lost before.

That shit has stayed with him.

It's never gone away.

It probably never will.

Unless…

Well, that's for later.

For now, the plan is working. Javier knew that his son was eager for any hint of his father, at who he truly is on the inside. Javier knows this because Javier was once a son himself and the patterns do follow.

History and her bad habit of repeating herself.

He laid his heart out bare in those letters to Ellie. Those real letters that he kept all this time (*but*, he swears to himself, *I never loved her*). He had hoped that those, along with all the information he could currently find on Ellie (now McQueen, fucking *puta*), and the information he hung onto from the past, that it would plant a seed in Vicente's head.

If it didn't? Well, what the fuck ever. He would try something new down the line. No skin off his back if nothing came of this.

But the seed took root. Javier knew it would.

Vicente took the papers and withdrew. Javier knew that he would never approach him and ask about it, ask who she was, why he still had information on her. He would never ask his father about something so glaringly intimate.

Later, when Vicente asked about going to America, Javier could barely hide his smile. He knew the reason why.

Curiosity.

And he knows what curiosity leads to.

It was a gamble, for sure.

It still is.

The loss of Tio and Nacho happened a little quicker than he anticipated, giving Vicente the upper hand for a few days there.

But that's all changed now.

Parada is there in San Francisco watching him, close and from afar.

As in, Vicente's hotel room is bugged.

So is his car.

Parada and Javier know everything he's doing.

Or, more like *who* he's doing.

And doing a lot.

Javier isn't sure how he feels about that one. I mean, in his mind this thing could have gone one of two ways and he would have found out a way to make both work. But from the start, what he really hoped for was another way – the longshot.

One way, and this was probably Vicente's original plan,

was to go and kidnap Ellie and bring her back to Mexico as a trophy of sorts. This plan depended more on Vicente's need to win Javier's respect and approval, to officially be seen as the head of the cartel, to pave the way for his future here.

The other way was that Vicente would become intrigued with Violet and decide to take her instead. Violet would be a lot easier to handle than Ellie and Vicente would probably look for the easiest way out of this mess.

Because it would end up a mess.

Vicente is bold but he's young and overconfident. He'll bite off more than he can chew and mistakes will be made in the process.

Of course, there's the third way and that's the way it seems to be working for now. That Vicente would seduce Violet before bringing her back.

The seduction is important.

Very important.

Because Javier knows firsthand (fuck, he knows that firsthand more than a few times now, huh) that even when you have a horrible task at hand, it's sometimes impossible not to let your guard down. To not become entangled. To not lose a bit of yourself in the person you're supposed to harm.

There will be conflict and turmoil in Vicente's heart when he hands Violet over to his father. And in that conflict and turmoil, Javier will destroy her and destroy him.

He can't pretend it's all for his son's good. Yes, it will make Vicente stronger. It will teach him that you can't be a cartel leader and love like normal people do. It will teach Vicente that if this is the life he wants, people like Violet have no place in it.

Love gets you killed.

But at the same time, it would feel unbelievably good to finally get revenge for what Ellie did. Petty thoughts, horribly petty, but Javier is okay with that. He's more than okay with that.

If revenge is a dish best served cold, then this will be the fucking feast of the century.

No matter what happens at this point, Javier will win.

It will be fucking glorious.

Javier's phone rings and he punches the talk button like a striking snake.

"Parada," Javier says, bringing the phone to his ear.

"I think they're leaving," Parada says from somewhere in San Francisco.

"For here?"

"I don't know. It was brought up like they had discussed it before, elsewhere, so I don't know the details."

Javier sighs, closing his eyes, controlling the rising flames in his chest. "Well tell me what details you do fucking know."

"The girl, Violet, is being followed. She was attacked."

Javier raises his glass to his lips and pauses. "By who?"

"I don't know. Not by one of ours."

"Are you sure?"

"Yes, I'm sure. I've talked to our men. One had been stationed outside her house. He never saw her leave but she must have at some point. The attack happened on her way back from a nightclub."

"Fucking amateurs." Javier's fingers curl around the glass so hard he thinks he could just shatter it. "That's who

I have working for me, nothing but idiots."

"She escaped. Fought him off. She doesn't know who he was either and they brought up that she was followed a few weeks ago by some, I don't know, albino guy? Some white guy. Really white."

"The fuck? How white can these Americans get?"

Parada continues. "She went straight to Vicente after this happened. Didn't go to the police, didn't go home."

Javier manages a cold smile. "So she really does trust him."

He clears his throat. "Yes and no. He told her a bit of the truth."

"And that is?"

"That his father runs a drug cartel."

"Oh fucking hell." He rests his head on the desk.

Vicente, Vicente you stupid, stupid boy.

"Don't worry," Parada says. "It only helped. The honesty. She doesn't care about the cartel, or that he lied, or that he is Vicente Bernal. It means nothing to her. And now they both trust each other. I think they might leave within three weeks."

"Did they say that?"

"She said she wanted to get through a few weeks of school, finish the semester."

"And we don't know where they would be going?"

"I'll find out soon enough. She mentioned Vegas and he laughed. So as it stands, I don't think she knows they're going to Mexico."

Javier rubs at the line between his eyes. It's impossible to smooth out. "And they might not go at all. I obviously can't predict Vicente as well as I thought I could. For once, he's taking his sweet fucking time."

"That's because of all the sweet fucking," Parada jokes.

Javier grows scarily silent for a moment, then says with utmost sincerity, "You know that's my flesh and blood you're referring to."

"*Si, patron.*"

"Right. Well it doesn't matter. Wherever they go, we will follow. If he wants to fall in love while getting his dick sucked, it will only make his own life harder, not mine."

"I'll report back tomorrow," Parada says before hanging up.

Javier sighs and leans back in his chair, downing the remainder of tequila in his glass.

He starts planning what he's going to do with pretty little Violet McQueen.

It won't be easy, especially if Vicente has no plans to bring her to him in the end.

But it will be worth it.

It always is.

Violet

TWO WEEKS.

I just have to make it two more weeks before I can even think about leaving with Vicente.

After the attack, it's all I can think about.

Despite what Vicente told me about him.

His terrible truth.

That he's the son of an infamous drug lord.

He's still the only person I feel safe with.

Maybe because even though I saw his guns and I know his secrets, I know that he has the means to protect me so much more than anyone else has. Not only that, but he has the means to teach me how to protect myself. I got lucky in my fighting. Next time, I want to put a bullet in the man's head.

The only thing that scares me is how good that might feel.

I had to tell my parents that the bruise on my face was because I got too drunk and hit my head on the side of the table. I made it into a funny story, roping Ginny into it without her knowledge.

I know they don't believe me, though.

Even worse, I know they think it's Vicente.

Despite how much concealer I piled on the bruise, you should have seen my father's face when he saw it the next morning. I swear he was going to start tearing the house apart. It was the same wild, nearly demonic look that Vicente had when I showed up at his hotel. I guess I should feel relieved that two of the most important men in my life feel that protective over me but relief is hard to come by these days.

I worry that I should have come clean with my parents. But they would have made me go to the police. And now that I know that Vicente has ties to a drug cartel, I can't risk it. I don't want to put him in any danger and there are a lot of cops and law enforcement out there that are just dying for this sort of thing. Any excuse to deport someone, regardless of what citizen they are.

I also know that if I had told my parents that I was attacked, they would never ever let me out of their sight again. Which would make leaving here a lot harder.

And they probably wouldn't let me see Vicente again.

Which, I know, is what this is eventually leading up to.

Every night that I come home from spending time with him, the questions come out. Both my mom and dad have started up some kind of patrol and I can never seem to get inside and to my room without being given the third degree.

Never mind the fact that I'm twenty and there is absolutely nothing they can do to stop me.

Two weeks. I've made it through one. I have two more to go.

They're going to be rough.

It's Thursday night and Ben is coming up tomorrow for the weekend.

He wasn't here the last couple of ones, I know now because he's been avoiding dealing with it and not because of exams. But he's finally decided to bite the bullet and face this all head on.

I'm ready for it. I've been ready for it since the moment he found out that our parents lied about his birth mother. We need to know why they lied. We need to know what happened to her. Where is Sophia now?

I try not to think the worst.

Then again, I've failed hard at that my whole life. Thinking the worst is what I do best.

Tonight I'm hiding out in my room until Vicente is supposed to swing by. I told him to give me some time to work on my project so I can at least get it out of the way before the weekend. I've got to come up with poetic captions to go along with the pictures I've been taking in the city. At least, I think they should be poetic. Part of the grade is on how well the viewer (the teacher) is supposed to interpret the subject and what I'm trying to say about it before he flips the image over and sees the intent. I'm hoping some flowery prose will win him over if the images don't.

Only now I wish I had saved the work for tomorrow. I can't concentrate at all and keep typing out the same thing over and over again, erasing the same damn sentence. It's the image of the bridge I took while on my first date with Vicente. Where I was supposed to teach him photography, which I now realize was a total crock of shit.

The picture of the bridge is nice though but I'm having trouble expressing what I told Vicente. If I talk too much about the beauty that no one else sees in the world, the more I resemble that creepy guy from the movie *American Beauty* who keeps filming plastic bags.

It doesn't help that the vibe in the house is unreal right now. Mom and Dad are on edge. I'm on edge. It feels like we're all seconds from imploding.

God, I really hope nothing happens before Ben gets here. If I had it out with them, I'm not sure I could keep what I know inside anymore. It's already eating me alive, every minute of every day.

Vicente is right. This is a house of lies.

I need to make some tea though, some sort of fuel to survive. I take a risk and leave my room, quickly and silently heading down the stairs to the kitchen.

The TV is playing in the living room and assume that's where my parents are but the moment I turn the corner of the stairs, I see my mom in the kitchen, sitting at the bar, a mug of tea in her hands.

She looks up slowly, eyes all wired and bloodshot.

It's like she expected me.

"Hey," I say, trying to make my voice sound as light as possible.

"Hey," she answers back, trying to match my tone.

"How's the work going?"

"Slow." I give a forced shrug. "But it's going."

"Mmmm," she says, tapping her nails along the side of the mug.

Something's coming.

The sound of her tapping speeds up, slows down.

"Are you going out tonight?" she asks. Too innocent. She's a great liar but innocence was never her strong suit.

"Yeah, I already told you," I remind her, trying to keep the impatience out of my voice.

"I don't know. You never said anything."

I grab the tea from the cupboard and whirl around to face her. "Are you kidding me?"

Tap, tap, tap.

"Mom," I repeat. "I told you this morning when you dropped me off. That I was finishing up my project then going over to Vicente's."

"About that," my dad says.

I nearly drop the box of tea. He's standing in the hall with his arms crossed, legs in a wide stance. How long has he been there for?

"Jesus, dad," I tell him. "What are you guys doing, ganging up on me now?"

"Violet," Mom warns. "We need to talk to you about something."

Funny. Very fucking funny, because I need to talk to you about something.

My jaw clenches as I look between the two of them.

"Okay, what?"

They exchange a loaded glance.

My father clears his throat. "Honey, we know you're

going through a difficult time right now and the last thing we want is to upset or overwhelm you. We need you to know how much we care about you and how much we worry."

"Difficult time?" I repeat. "What would you know about a difficult time?"

"You're acting strangely," my mother says. "Ever since you met Vicente."

I nearly choke on my laughter. "Acting strangely? Do you ever think it's because I finally have a boyfriend? Someone who I care about. Deeply." I shake my head in disbelief. "Have you never seen me happy before? Because that's what this is. I'm happy. I'm finally happy and you know why? Because I have someone who gets me. Fucking gets me. And accepts it. More than accepts it, Vicente *loves* it."

Okay, he's never told me he loves *me* but still…

"No," my mother says, staring down at her cup of tea with so much bitterness I think she might cry. "No, I looked into the eyes of that boy and he doesn't know what love is. That's not what he wants from you."

"Holy fuck," I mutter, pressing my hands into the sides of my temples. "You say I'm nuts, you're the fucking crazy one."

"Violet," my father says sharply. "Your mother is right."

"Oh sure, always taking her side Why don't you ever grow a fucking pair, dad, and stand up to her?"

That did it. That was the hit, right in the gut.

As usual though, it gets me in my gut too, to watch my father shatter in front of me like this.

Then it fades as a cold, cold look comes over his eyes,

something I've never seen before. It scares me. I immediately regret saying anything.

"I do stand up to your mother when I need to," he says. His voice is brimming with tension. "You have no idea, Violet, just what it takes to make a marriage work."

Oh god. I'm so close to saying something. So close. I literally have to bite my tongue until I feel the penny taste of blood.

"Violet," my mother says. "Just trust us on this. We know you think you're happy. But we also know that he's not good for you. And the longer you're with him, the further away you'll be. From us. From seeing the truth."

"And what's the truth?"

She looks at my father and back to me. "We know that bruise is from him."

"Aaargh!" I cry out, spinning around in frustration. I lean against the countertop over the stove, trying to get my composure back. "For the last time, Vicente did not give me this bruise! Do you really think I would stay with a guy who would do this to me?"

"Then tell us what really happened," my father says gently, coming forward until he's cornering me.

"That's the truth," I say, lying through my teeth. No way in hell am I mentioning the attack. "I was drunk. I hit the table."

"And we don't believe you," Mom says, getting to her feet and standing beside Dad. "You're not going to go see him tonight. You're not going to see him any night."

I blink at them in shock. "What? You can't be serious."

"We're very serious," my dad says. "And we don't care if you hate us forever. We don't care if you think we're treating you like a child. You're our daughter. We love you, we care about you, we worry about you. We've seen the world and it's not a nice place, Violet. And if you don't know that by now…"

"You're kidding me?" I whisper. "You really think I don't know how horrible the world is? You think because I'm quiet and sensitive that I must see things through rose-colored glasses? I don't. I see the world for what it is. Doesn't mean I don't find beauty in it, but I know how rotten it can be."

Don't do it, don't do it.

"Then you'll understand why we have to keep you safe," Mom says gently, reaching out for my hand.

"Keep me safe?" I repeat, yanking it away from her. "How is cutting Vicente out of my life keeping me safe? You're the ones I should be worried about."

"Us?" Dad asks.

I can't help myself.

"You think I don't know?" I ask. "You think Ben doesn't know? Did you ever wonder why he's been avoiding us these last few weeks, why he was so upset the last time he was here that he couldn't even look you in the eye?"

My father seems to age before me, like the color is draining from his blue eyes. He doesn't say anything. Neither does my mother.

They don't know what to say, I realize. They don't know what lies I've figured out. Holy fuck. How deep does this go?

I start with Ben.

And I go for the jugular.

I turn to mom and say, "We knows he's not your son."

She looks like she's been doused with ice water.

"We discovered the lie you've both tried to bury our whole lives. We found out many lies. That Ben's mother is a woman called Sophia Madano. That when he was three, just about the same time you went to Mexico, Sophia disappeared and suddenly he was your child, Mom. So when you say I'm safe with you, please, enlighten me as to how your lies are making my life safer."

I watch them carefully.

They're both reeling in different ways. Dad's more internal, just shock in his eyes, the crevice between his brow deepening even further. Mom is more visceral. Mouth open, skin paling, eyes filling with tears.

And just like that, all the anger I have starts to fade. The funny thing about hurting someone that's hurt you is that it never feels as good as you think it will. Because the only ones who can hurt you are those you love, and they in turn are the only ones you can hurt.

I don't regret it though. Despite the tightness in my chest, I had to say something. If it wasn't tonight, it was tomorrow with Ben. At least Ben doesn't have to witness me destroying them.

"So," I say, trying to clear my throat. "Explain. Please. And while you're at it, feel free to tell me why you lied about grandpa dying. Yeah, that's right. I found the envelope with the Palm Valley newspaper clipping inside. Who was he? Why did you guys lie about him too?"

But there are no easy answers, at least none that they want to give me. They both look so dumbstruck that they're frozen on the spot, unable to find a way out of it. If the lies are deep, I'm guessing they have to consult each other to get the truth straight.

Finally, Dad just shakes his head. "I'm going for a walk."

My mom's head jerks to him in surprise. "Camden!" she cries out as he turns and storms through the house, slamming the front door behind him.

Great. So he just bailed on all this.

My mother has one hand on the counter as if to keep her up, the other hand at her chest. She slowly turns her head to look at me.

We stare at each other for what seems like forever.

The fridge kicks on and hums.

A commercial blares from the living room.

She gnaws on her lip for a moment before saying, "I think you should go to your room."

I cock my head. Unbelievable.

"What? Am I grounded? You're the ones who have lied to me my whole life."

"With good reason," she says. "It's something that can't be simply explained."

"Well you could fucking try!"

She nods, looking away, cagey as fuck. "Tomorrow. Tomorrow when Ben is here we will all talk. Okay? You'll hear it all."

"Mom…"

"For now you need to go to your room and stay home. This doesn't change anything, especially not about Vicente."

"It doesn't change anything!?" I explode. I pick up the box of tea and throw it at her. She ducks, of course, because tea doesn't travel very fast. But she seems to have gotten my point.

"Violet!"

"Fuck you," I sneer at her, running past and up the stairs. Yes, going to my fucking room but it's different when it's your own choice.

I slam the door and lock it just as my phone beeps.

It's Vicente.

I'm on my way.

I'm so angry my hands are shaking, I can barely type back.

I want to leave tonight, I type and then toss the phone on my bed. I bring a duffel bag out of my closet and start throwing clothes in it. Just a few nights would be fine, the weekend. Ben can deal with this shit on his own. God knows I've tried.

I look back at the phone and Vicente's reply:

Ok. I'll text you when I'm there.

I text back: Park on Clayton. I'll have to sneak out my window.

Like Romeo and Juliet?

I actually laugh at that. God I hope not.

We all know how that turned out.

Vicente

I LIED TO VIOLET.

I'm not on the way to her house.

I'm already here.

I just drove past Camden who was walking down Haight, in only a T-shirt on this cold night, looking like he was ready to rip the head off something.

I have a feeling shit went down at their house tonight.

And I'm about to make it all worse.

I park on Clayton as she asked but instead of waiting in the car I get out and head down her street. With Camden out of the way, now is the perfect time to pay Ellie a visit.

Just the two of us.

I jog up the steps, my gun secure in the inside of my jacket.

I knock on the door.

No answer.

I have a feeling Violet is up in her room, waiting for the storm to blow over. But it's only getting started.

I open the front door and step inside.

It's dark except for the lights from the kitchen.

"Camden?" I hear Ellie's voice.

She appears in the hallway, a dark silhouette.

"Hello Ellie," I say to her, keeping my voice low.

Even in the shadows I can see the whites of her eyes flash as she storms over to me. I have to admire her lack of fear.

She stops a foot away, her finger jabbing at the air.

"You get the fuck out of this house," she growls like me.

I grab her finger and snap it downward. "Like a fucking mama bear, huh."

She yanks her finger back, cradling it with her hand. I guess I hurt her.

"You're the animal here," she says in a hiss. "What you did to her…"

I shake my head, giving her a wry smile. "That's what you think of me? You think I did that to her? I didn't. And I don't know who did but I can guarantee I want them dead as much as you do."

"I don't believe you."

"Why not? My father never hit you."

I watch her carefully. The realization as it slowly spreads through her.

"That was one of his personal oaths. Like a fucking

281

doctor, right? He could torture a man in the most gruesome ways but he would never ever strike a woman. I guess he thought it made him better than everyone else. Less of a savage. But we both know how savage he really is. Don't you, Ellie Watt?"

Her jaw clenches. Every muscle in her is primed, ready to fight or flee. And I don't think she'll be fleeing.

"Easy now," I murmur, raising my jacket enough for her to see the gun. "I didn't come here to start trouble. Well, I guess that's a lie. Sometimes I believe the lies myself."

"*You,*" she whispers. She shakes her head, her dark hair falling into her eyes. She's finally getting it, finally believing how right her instincts were. "You're Javier's son."

"Is it gratifying?" I ask. "To know you were right. Does it feel good, deep inside? Are you feeling vindicated right now?"

She swallows hard, eyes going to the gun and back.

"Careful," I tease her, reaching for her face, trying to brush her hair from her eyes.

She bats my arm away, stumbles backward. But doesn't run.

"What do you want?" she whispers.

"It's not you, if that makes you feel better," I tell her. "It's Violet."

"You can't have her." Her voice breaks with determination. I have to be careful. This is a mama bear that knows how to fight. I have no doubt that if I give her even the slightest advantage, she'll try and kill me with her claws. Her old habits have not died.

I sigh. "It's not a matter of being able to have her or not. I do have her. Go and ask her and she'll tell you. I'm guessing she already has told you."

"I'll call her down here right now and tell her the truth about you. All of it. Who you really are. You're not Vicente Cortez."

I laugh. "She already knows. And guess what? She doesn't care. Doesn't care that I belong to a cartel, doesn't care that I kill people. If anything, it made her fuck me even more." I pause, smirking. "Like mother like daughter, huh?"

Crack.

Ellie winds up and smacks me across the face.

I guess I should have seen that coming.

She packed quite the wallop too.

I rub my fingers along tender skin and give her an exaggerated wince.

"I suppose I deserve that one."

"Get out of here or I'll call the police." I watch her desperate fists clench and release at her sides. She's about to do something stupid. That's the last thing I want.

"I'll leave," I tell her. "But here's the thing. You have nothing on me. You call the police, I can bring up everything about Ellie Watt. Or Eden White. Or whatever names you used to call yourself. You think that just because you've spent the last twenty years trying to start over that you haven't left your mark on the world? Oh, Ellie. You've left it everywhere. All anyone has to do is lift up the floorboards and see." I bite my lip, my eyes searching her face. "You have nothing. Do you understand me?"

But she refuses to back down. She makes a move to turn and I'm quick.

I have her against the wall, my hand over her mouth, the gun under her chin. Such a similar position to the way

I was with Violet a week ago.

"How do I make myself more clear?" My lips are at her ear. She's breathing heavily against my mouth, her eyes wide. "You have nothing on me. I am Vicente Bernal, nothing but a ghost in your country. Before you can do anything about me, I'll be long gone. You, on the other hand, can easily be thrown away without a key. Is that what you want for your daughter? What about Ben, the son who isn't your son? Do you want them to live their lives knowing their mother was a criminal, a con artist, that their father was a money launderer who killed people? And whatever did happen to Sophia Madano? She's dead somewhere. I just can't figure out if it's your fault or my father's. It's hard to tell, you're both so similar."

Ellie whimpers, I press the gun harder into her chin, tipping her head back. "Shhh, shhh. Good girl. You be quiet now. Be the good mom you always wanted to be but never could. Now is your chance, you know. Just let your daughter go. Let her be with who she wants to be with. Let her live the life she wants and be the person she needs to." My lips raze the tip of her ear. "You know, she's a lot like you and you don't even know it. You hide it. She doesn't. She can't hide anything, that's what makes her so special. And in time, she'll know exactly what she's capable of. No more being weak. She's going to embrace every bad bone in her body and come out stronger. You'll see."

I pause, trailing the gun down her neck, to her chest. "Or maybe you won't see. Maybe she's never coming back. Maybe you'll never see her again because I can give her everything you couldn't." I feel it punch through me like a fist. "You won't believe this but I'm in love with her. So I guess you don't have to worry about that." I steal a glance at her face. She looks even more terrified than before. "Or maybe you should be more worried. I can see what my father's love did to you."

She tries to laugh.

I remove my hand, curious.

"Your father never knew what love was," she sneers, gulping in air. "And neither do you."

Then with sheer disgust she *spits*.

Right in my face.

I stare at her in shock before slowly wiping it from my cheek.

"I will never hurt your daughter, Ellie Watt," I tell her, fire rising from my chest. "But I don't feel the same way about you."

With one quick *thwack*, I bring the gun down on the side of her head, knocking her to the ground where she crumbles in a heap.

I glance up at the ceiling, listening, wondering if Violet heard anything. While a semi-conscious Ellie moans at my feet – clearly my pistol-whipping skills could use some work – I grab her by the arms and haul her into the kitchen and leave her on the floor. I quickly rifle through the drawers until I find the one with all the junk, then bring out the duct tape.

I tear off a few strips placing it across her mouth, then bring her over to the dining room chair which I sat in a few weeks ago. With her head slumped over, I make her sit up and place her hands around the back of the chair, tying them together with the tape before taping her across the chest to the actual chair itself.

It's not the best but it will buy us enough time.

I can only hope that Camden doesn't come back in the next few seconds – now that I know him better, I have a feeling that man fights dirty – and that Violet has already snuck out and is making her way to the car.

I shove the tape into my jacket along with the gun and then raise Ellie's chin to get a better look at her. She tries to open her eyes but can't, passing out. She'll be all right. Hopefully nothing more than a terrible headache when she wakes up.

"Sorry," I tell her, kissing the top of her head. "My father probably wouldn't have approved of that."

Luckily his approval doesn't mean anything to me anymore.

The only thing that does is hopefully waiting by my car.

I run out of the front door, gently closing it behind me, and head down the street like I was never in the McQueen's house at all.

Violet

WHERE THE FUCK IS HE? I'm standing by his Mustang, illegally parked on Clayton, mind you, but Vicente is nowhere in sight. It's freezing cold, my scarf and jacket doing little to warm me up and after everything I'm jumping at every shadow I see moving in the fog.

Am I doing the right thing?

I'm trying not to have doubts. We'll just go away for the weekend. When I come back, maybe everything will settle. Maybe when Ben gets here he can find a way to talk to them, to get the truth. I think with me it's that there's too much baggage, especially since they've somehow roped Vicente into all of this.

I wish they'd just give him a chance. Honestly, if they could see how he treats me, they'd know he's not capable of hurting me. I mean, outside of the bedroom of course. Plus, there's the fact that he really does seem to get me, know me inside and out, all my dark and ugly places, and he still wants to be with me. He celebrates it.

Of course they wouldn't give him much of a chance if they knew the whole truth, what with his father being head of a cartel and all but that's something they never need to know. They have their secrets, I can have mine.

"Violet," Vicente says, sounding out of breath. He's walking toward me fast, hands shoved in his pockets.

When he reaches me he pulls me into a long kiss that sends shivers on the inside of my skin. Fuck, this man leaves me breathless.

"Where did you go?" I ask softly once I have the strength to pull away from his warmth.

He unlocks my door and opens it for me. "I was early so I went to Haight to see if I could get a coffee. Everything was closed."

I throw my bag in the backseat and get in while he walks around the front.

"By the way, I saw your father," he says casually as he gets in the driver's seat.

"What?"

"On Haight." The car starts with a purr. "He looked pretty pissed. Something happen?"

My head leans against the window. "Oh god. What didn't happen?"

"I figured something was up since you said you wanted to leave tonight."

"Did he see you?"

"Your dad? No."

"Good." I exhale loudly. My breath fogs the glass.

Vicente pulls the car out onto the street and starts driving through the mist. The streets look extra dark tonight. An obscure song but one that I know well comes on the radio, Calexico's "Two Silver Trees." I lean over and turn it up, hoping to block out …well, everything.

Just everything.

Doesn't help that Calexico is my parent's music.

"Want to talk about it?" Vicente asks after a bit. "About why we're driving off late at night."

I shake my head. "Not right now. I just want to…go. Fly. Far away."

I can see him smile out of the corner of my eye.

"And where shall we fly to, *mirlo*?"

I want to say anywhere. But that's not true. I don't want to go just anywhere.

I still want the truth.

I want to understand where this all started.

"The desert," I tell him. "Palm Valley. To where it all began."

Vicente grabs my hand and tenderly kisses the back of it. "For you, I'll go anywhere."

I know he means it.

It's 6 a.m. when we pull into Palm Valley. We've been driving all night and I've been asleep for most of it.

Still, I'm beyond exhausted and can barely keep my head up while we cruise down the main street. The sun is rising from the east, casting a coral glow over the treeless mountains. This really is the desert, a land of shrub and cactus and date palms that hover over the sidewalks. It's dry, stark and beautiful.

I wish I could properly take it in but by the time we pull into our hotel, which I hastily booked on my phone during the drive, I just want to crawl into bed and fall asleep.

Vicente goes into the lobby while I wait in the car. I told him I'd let him do whatever he wanted to me as long as he was able to get us a room this early. I have a feeling I'll be doing something pretty fucking dirty later because that man is nothing if not persuasive.

He's been in the hotel for a while and I'm half asleep when I notice a man standing at the front of the car, just beyond the hood. Through my blurry eyes I can't quite make him out but I figure it must be Vicente, maybe getting the license plate number of the car for the hotel parking pass.

There's something a little off about the way he's not moving, though.

He's staring at the car for far too long.

Is he staring at…me?

My eyes close.

"Violet."

Vicente's voice shakes me awake. I open my eyes and look around. He's leaning in through his door, a wide grin on his beautiful golden face. The way his dark hair falls across his forehead makes him seem full of boyish charm.

"Let me guess," I say groggily, sitting up. "You were able to get us early check-in."

"What else did you expect from me?" he says, wagging his brows. "Remember, *mirlo*, you promised to do anything I want. I'll hold you to it. I'll hold you to a lot of things."

I roll my eyes, pretending that whatever dirty sexual thing he has planned will be a chore. The truth is I'm excited to see what limits he'll push with me, what path he'll bring me down.

He's already brought me down this one.

All the way to the desert.

To my parent's past.

To a glimpse at freedom.

I feel like I'm ready for whatever is next.

Javier

"JAVI," LUISA'S VOICE CALLS HIM FROM HIS SLEEP.

He rolls over, moaning bitterly, a sharp knife of anger striking through him. He hasn't been able to sleep for weeks, just bits and pieces here and there, and now that he has finally fallen asleep, his wife is fucking shit up. Sleep is a precious commodity in times like this.

"You better be waking me up to suck my dick or I swear to god, Luisa..."

"Javi, wake up," she says.

He blinks his eyes open and slowly props himself up on his elbows. His bones ache but he ignores it.

She's got the bedside light on and for a moment he thinks she looks like an angel in her white silk nightgown, the glow of the lamp radiating around her. For a moment he thinks he's still a very lucky man, no matter the insomnia and creaking bones.

And then she shoves his phone in his face.

"You were out cold," she says. "Your phone has been ringing like crazy. It's Parada."

He checks the time before he takes it. It's five in the morning. He could have slept for at least another hour.

"What is it?" he says, his voice husky with sleep. Luisa, such a good wife, props up the pillows behind him so he can sit up more comfortably.

"Javier," Parada says. "They made a run for it."

"Who?"

"Vicente and the McQueen girl."

"When?"

"They left the city last night around nine."

"And you're only telling me now?" Javier has to fight the urge to either chuck the phone across the room or smash it on the floor. Many phones have met their death this way.

"We wanted to be sure where they were going. We could hear them in the Mustang, through the wire. They said they were heading to Palm Valley so we got a man in Los Angeles to beat them to it. He's already there. They're just about to pull in. We're tailing them, a few minutes behind."

"Palm Valley," Javier says slowly. He smiles, amused. "Let me guess, Violet is the sentimental type."

Luisa looks at him sharply as she eases back into the bed. This is the first she's heard of anyone called Violet. Javier's been very good at keeping her in the dark.

"I guess," Parada says. "She told Vicente that she and

her parents had a fight over him. They forbid her to see him."

"Smart. Too bad that didn't work."

"Yes, well. The minute you tell your kid they can't do something, the minute they go out and do it."

"Spare me your anecdotes, Parada. Tell me the good news."

"The good news is that we have them. They'll stay at a hotel here for a few days. They already booked it through their phone. They'll settle in, look around. At some point, we'll grab them."

He eyes Luisa who is still watching him, perplexed. "You remember the rules, right?" he says to Parada. "Don't hurt him unless you have to."

"Javi!" Luisa exclaims but he raises his finger for her shut up.

Surprisingly, she does.

"We won't. Figure he'll be easier to take now that he has her. We just need to grab her first and he'll do what we say."

"Hopefully."

"He will, Javier. You haven't heard what we've heard, seen what we've seen. He's in love with her, no doubt about it."

"What about her, you know…*parents*?" Even the word is hard for him to say.

"They'll find out she's gone pretty soon. The funny thing is that Violet has said to Vicente that the trip is only for the weekend."

"Then you better grab them today."

"We'll do what we can. But we'll get them."

He's about to hang up the phone but pauses. "What

about the man who attacked her? Is she still being followed?"

"That we don't know. I thought I saw a man hanging around in front of their house the other day. He just stood there, watching. But didn't do anything. I couldn't get a good look without giving myself away."

"That's fine. Just keep your head up."

"Will do."

"Call me when you have them."

"*Si, patron.*"

Parada hangs up.

Javier puts the phone down and a smile slowly spreads across his face, making him look maniacal and distorted. He looks up at Luisa.

"Well I have good news and not as good news," he says brightly. "The good news is our son is coming home soon. Very soon."

"When?"

"Maybe tomorrow? Maybe the day after? But soon, my love."

She narrows her eyes suspiciously. "And the not as good news?"

Javier tilts his head, enjoying all of this a little too much.

"He won't be alone."

My dear Vicente, he thinks, nearly giddy.

Time to see what you're really made of.

Thank you for reading *Black Hearts*. The conclusion of this duet – *Dirty Souls* – will release on March 17th, so please look out for that. It's going be a very dark and wild ride!

In the meantime, if you haven't read the backstory of the Bernals and the McQueens, while you wait for Dirty Souls to release, it would be an excellent time to get acquainted with how it all began!

Start with The Artists Trilogy

Sins & Needles
On Every Street (just 99 cents!)
Shooting Scars
Bold Tricks

And then move on to the Dirty Angels Trilogy (please note that this series is set in Mexico and revolves around the Bernal family and the cartel lifestyle. Though a romance, it is very dark and disturbing and some books contain graphic scenes of rape and torture)

Dirty Angels
Dirty Deeds
Dirty Promises

Before you go…if you want future updates on my books and all the crazy and zany adventures I get up to, please:

- Join my exclusive readers group on Facebook where I have awesome giveaways, sneak peeks, fun trivia, great people and lot's more. Seriously. We're the best group of readers on the internet: Karina Halle's Anti-Heroes at www.facebook.com/groups/912577838806567

- Sign-up for my newsletter at authorkarinahalle.com/newsletter-sign-up to get alerts when new books come out, plus exclusives such as FREE books, excerpts and cover reveals!

- If you dare, follow me on Twitter (@metalblonde)

- Watch my daily adventures on Instagram at www.instagram.com/authorhalle (I practically live here)

Also, I have written over thirty novels in a range of different genres, from contemporary romance, to romantic comedy, to romantic suspense, to paranormal romance. Want a list of them all? Visit my Amazon author page and give me a "follow" while you're at it so you can stay up to date with new releases!

Read on for the acknowledgements (am I the only one who loves reading the acknowledgements section?)

ACKNOWLEDGEMENTS

I'm going to keep this short and sweet because I have a book full of mayhem to write and I just can't wait (hint, it's Dirty Souls).

The world is in some challenging times lately, so even while I live on a tiny hippie island on the west coast of Canada (it's called Salt Spring Island and yes you should come visit) it's not always easy to buckle down and write when things are turned upside down. But I'm grateful that I have such a large support network of people who are always rooting for me, because without them I'd still be curled up in the corner. Whether I know you from FB groups or Twitter, whether you're readers reaching out to me or my friends and fellow authors, know that I love and appreciate you!

Thank you to my Anti-Heroes for being so excited for this book and especially to my street team for going above and beyond when it comes to, well, everything, really.

Thank you to Hang Le for her amazing (as usual) cover design as we created the perfect Vicente and of course thanks to Wander Aguilar for having just the right model.

Thanks to Jovana Shirley and Stacey Blake for their ebook and paperback formatting skills.

Thanks to my agent Taylor Haggerty at Waxman Leavell,

editor extraordinaire Kara Malinczak, my publicist and fellow woman of awesomeness, Nina Bocci.

Thanks to my author friends who encourage me every step of the way (Jay Crownover, Kylie Scott, Pepper Winters, K.A. Tucker, I'm looking at you) and understand exactly how to handle my tender little heart.

Like Violet, I have hypersensitivity, which means a whole bunch of things but despite the "flaws" of this trait, it also lets me see the world in a different way and I hope that way comes across in my books. Also, if you feel like you relate to Violet in that way, I suggest you check out the book The Highly Sensitive Person by Dr. Elaine Aron. It's very eye-opening and comforting to know you're not alone.

However, if you relate to Violet because you're also running away from home with the man who may or may not be kidnapping you, I can't help you (and I suggest you call the police).

Last but never least – thanks to Scott and Bruce for putting up with it all.

And remember…keep fighting the good fight.

Persist.